# CARNIVAL *of* SOULS

## ALSO BY MELISSA MARR

*Wicked Lovely*

*Ink Exchange*

*Fragile Eternity*

*Radiant Shadows*

*Darkest Mercy*

Wicked Lovely: Desert Tales
(Art by Xian Nu Studio)

*Volume 1: Sanctuary*

*Volume 2: Challenge*

*Volume 3: Resolve*

*Faery Tales & Nightmares*

*Graveminder*

# melissa marr

# CARNIVAL
## of SOULS

**HARPER**

*An Imprint of HarperCollinsPublishers*

Library of Congress Cataloging-in-Publication Data

Marr, Melissa.

Carnival of Souls / Melissa Marr. — 1st ed.

p. cm.

Summary: A centuries-long war between daimons and witches sets the stage for three teens caught up in a deadly struggle for power and autonomy in the exotic and otherworldly Carnival of Souls, the mercantile center of the daimon dimension.

ISBN 978-0-06-165928-7 (trade bdg.) — ISBN 978-0-06-222335-7 (international edition)

[1. Fantasy.] I. Title.

PZ7.M34788Car 2012                                                      2012006566

[Fic]—dc23                                                                        CIP

                                                                                          AC

Typography by Joel Tippie

12 13 14 15 16  LP/RRDH  10 9 8 7 6 5 4 3 2 1

❖

First Edition

*To Loch,*
*this one wouldn't have happened if I hadn't married*
*a Marine/comic-book addict/film junkie.*

# PROLOGUE

THE MAN—*WITCH*—WHO'D summoned Selah was nothing like what she'd expected. In truth, he looked no different than many daimons she'd met: implacable expression and a musculature that would serve him well in one of Marchosias' fighting competitions. It was only his eerie blue-and-gold witch eyes that revealed his true nature—and those eyes were fixed on her.

Selah uncovered the face of the still-sleeping child in her arms. A tiny stone pendant was woven to the edge of the blanket that she'd wrapped around her baby when they'd fled. When she'd become pregnant, she'd sold most everything she had to procure the stone for her child. The rest of her coin she'd used for this audience.

She stared into the eyes of the witch who stood before her as she admitted, "Stoneleigh said you might help."

Sudden displeasure on his face made her pause, but she'd come too far to hesitate now. "I am not ruling class, but I'll find a way to pay. Information. Pleasure. Blood. I'll do whatever you want if you protect my daughter."

"Marchosias is her sire? You swear on it?"

"I do." Even if she wanted to lie, she couldn't: she was a daimon held in a witch's summoning circle. Adam was one of the oldest witches; he'd been one of the witch children who escaped several centuries ago when the wars ended. He could probably compel her without a circle, but he'd been given her name to summon her into his world and into a binding circle—at her request.

Adam continued to watch her with his unnatural witch's eyes, and Selah couldn't decide if bowing her head submissively or holding his gaze was wiser. Witches might look like daimons, but they were a different species, tolerated in *her* world only if they were weak or under Marchosias' control. Here in the human world they might hide from the other mortal creatures, but every daimon knew that they were terrifyingly powerful. She opted for kneeling *and* holding his gaze.

"What's her name?"

"Mallory," Selah whispered.

"Swear that Mallory is given freely into my care, that if I accept your offer you will obey me in all things." Adam paused and stepped as close to the circle as he could without breaking it. "Swear that you will accept death before endangering her or me."

Selah's arms tightened around her daughter. "Bound by this circle and my vow, I so swear."

He nodded. "Your bargain is accepted."

At his word of acceptance, the tension that had grown during pregnancy and intensified in the first few weeks of her daughter's life abated. Marchosias would have killed her when her daughter was born if he'd known she was seeking the aid of a witch, but the risk had been worth it. Now, at least, she could stay in Mallory's life—for as long as the witch allowed it.

Selah had traded one cage for another. The difference was that this cage would allow her daughter to survive. In the two centuries Selah had lived, every one of Marchosias' heirs had died before they reached adulthood. When he'd chosen her that unlucky day in the Carnival of Souls, she'd prayed that it was only for pleasure, not for breeding. Briefly, she glanced at her still-sleeping daughter. Now that she'd given birth, Selah could only pray that her child would live. That meant leaving The City; it meant leaving the only world she'd known and coming here—where witches and humans lived.

Adam spoke again, drawing her gaze to him. "I'm guessing Evelyn already expects us if she sent you to me."

"Expects us?"

"To arrive at her office. Even Marchosias can't send anyone to retrieve you or the child if we're wed. The Witches' Council won't allow it." He lifted one hand and swept it to the side, dropping the circle that had contained her. "Mallory is *mine* now. No one—not even you—will have authority over her before me. I can hide what she is, protect her here, until she is eighteen. You are welcome to stay if it's in her best interest, but if your presence ever threatens her safety, you will leave."

He reached out, and for a moment Selah thought he was going to help her to her feet. Instead, he took Mallory. With her daughter in his arms, he walked away, leaving her kneeling in the now-defunct daimon circle, hoping that she hadn't entered into a bargain worse than the one she was escaping.

# CHAPTER 1

*Almost seventeen years later*

MALLORY HAD AN HOUR to herself after school before she had to be at practice, so she'd ducked into the only independent coffee shop in Smithfield for some overpriced, oversweetened coffee. Admittedly, she'd spent more of the hour thinking about Kaleb than doing her homework, but AP Physics wasn't nearly as interesting as the first boy she'd felt at ease around. She'd even told him the names of a couple of the towns where she'd lived over the years—and talked about her family. And the moment she'd done *that*, she'd realized she needed to stay away from him. Anyone who made her let her guard down that much was dangerous.

As she returned her empty mug to the counter, she

looked out the large front window and saw Kaleb standing across the street from Java Junkies as if she'd conjured him with her thoughts. Admittedly, Smithfield was a tiny town, so she bumped into Kaleb every time he was home from school, which seemed to be a lot lately. Still, Mallory felt the same warm flush of excitement she did every time she saw him and then quashed it.

*Bad idea. Very, very bad.*

She lowered her gaze, suddenly finding the words painted on the door fascinating, and stepped onto the sidewalk with her eyes still downcast. She should be scanning the area for danger, but all she wanted to do was look at Kaleb. She stole a glance at him and debated going over to at least say hello. Nothing could come of it. She knew it—but she couldn't bring herself to tell *him* that. It was foolishness, but she wanted something to come of it. She'd never felt so instantly at ease or so embarrassingly attracted to anyone. Telling him to go away wasn't something she could bring herself to do—despite how inevitable it was. Instead, she walked away, forcing herself not to look at him. She let her gaze wander over the flowers in planters along the street, the man in the rumpled suit playing his cello for change, the debris that accumulated in gutters . . . anything but the boy who had occupied all of her free thoughts the past month.

She hadn't gone more than a few steps when Kaleb caught up with her. "Are you ignoring me?"

"No," she lied.

His voice always made her want to shiver. Kaleb's voice was like dark chocolate, so rich that she felt strangely sinful listening to him talk about the most mundane things. She resisted the temptation to close her eyes.

He stepped closer to her. "So you didn't just see me and walk away?"

"Maybe," Mallory half admitted.

If she needed to, she *could* put him on the ground, but Kaleb wasn't an enemy. He was just a guy. She stole another glance at him. *Just a guy?* He was six feet of lean muscle, perpetually unruly hair, and eyes that were too dark to be called brown. To add to his allure, he had a ferocity to him that slipped out when he looked around the street. He'd only ever been sweet to her, but he had an attitude that hinted at an ability to wade into trouble; it gave her a foolish hope that he could handle the world she knew, even as logic warned her that she was clinging to illusions.

Until she'd met Kaleb, she'd actually worried that something was wrong with her. Her classmates had started talking about boys—or girls—a few years ago, but she was almost seventeen and, until the past month, she'd never had the sort of reactions they all talked about. The forget-your-name nervousness, the racing heart, the why-did-I-say-*that*—it was as foreign to her as a life without witches . . . until Kaleb. He made her wish for things that were impossible, for a life that she could never have.

The sound of the cars on the street drew her attention, and

her gaze slipped away to check the shadows for threats.

"Mallory?"

"Yes?" Her hand went to the pendant she wore under her blouse. The reasons she shouldn't see him, the need to see him, the way she'd had to lie to him—thinking about all of that made her feel horrible inside.

"I'm glad I found you," he said.

He moved in so he stood just a shade closer than could be considered polite, and she wondered what he'd do if she thanked him for evoking the blushworthy thoughts she was having.

She realized that he was watching her expectantly, but she wasn't able to admit that she was happy to see him too. Instead, she said, "I didn't expect you."

"I just got into town," he said.

She started, "I need to go—"

"Do you want to go somewhere?" he asked at the same time.

They both stopped. She shifted the bag on her shoulder, surreptitiously adjusting the hilt of the knife she wore hidden under her arm. Her jacket concealed it, but sometimes the top of the hilt poked the underside of her bra. That was one of the many things she didn't want to discuss. *So, why are you wearing a knife?* She smiled at Kaleb, continuing the imaginary discussion in her mind. *In case I need to protect us from monsters . . . not that I've had to fight them yet, but, you know, just in case.*

"Mallory?" Kaleb stared at her in that too-intense-for-comfort way he had done since they'd first met a little over a month ago. Everything about him seemed intense though. When he listened to her talk, he acted like what she was saying was really important, even when it was just meaningless chatter about a show she'd watched on television or an article she'd read online. The thrill of being the center of his attention made her want to linger longer, even when she knew that she couldn't truly date him. Still, she suspected that even a small friendship with Kaleb would be better than dating any other boy.

He gestured away from the tiny downtown where the coffee shop was. "Do you want to walk or something? Even if you only have a few minutes, we could—"

"I can't," she interrupted and then silently added, *I need to go practice killing things.*

The temptation to skip practice crossed her mind, but that would lead to questions from her father, and those would lead to either admitting she'd met someone who interested her enough to skip practice *or* it would mean lying to her father. Neither of those seemed like very good ideas. But as Kaleb stared at her, frowning in frustration or maybe in confusion, she wished rather desperately that she could lie to her father— or tell Kaleb everything.

Instead, she admitted, "I have practice, and I'm already going to be late. Maybe next time we could do something. If you want to, I mean. I'm not sure if I can then either, but I want to."

"I'll ask again," he promised.

And then she turned and walked away from Kaleb as quickly as she could without seeming like she was running. She hadn't exactly mentioned that she couldn't date him, but that was just because there was no way to say it without sounding weird. It wasn't because she harbored a tiny hope of something more. *Really.* She smiled to herself. *Kaleb wants to see me again.*

A SHORT WHILE LATER, Mallory had temporarily forced away thoughts of the beautiful human boy she shouldn't date and concentrated on the task at hand: proving to her father that she was making progress with the semiautomatic.

"You need to get over it, Mals." Adam didn't scowl at her, but the censure was there all the same. "The revolver only has six rounds. Sometimes six won't be enough."

She accepted the gun, but it felt wrong in her hands. It *always* felt wrong. The weight of it didn't comfort her the way the heavier revolver did.

"They aren't like humans," Adam reminded her—unnecessarily. He'd spent most of her life teaching her how to defend herself against daimons. She knew that they were stronger and faster than any human could hope to be. Witches stood more than a fair chance against them, but Mallory wasn't a witch.

She sighted down on her target, inhaled, held her breath, and squeezed. "Just like taking a picture."

She'd learned the inverse though: she'd applied firearms

lessons to photography, not the other way around. Daimons weren't scared away by a 35mm camera. A steady aim with a 9mm pistol, on the other hand, could—hopefully—save her life someday. No matter how ready she felt, fear crept over her every time she thought about facing daimons.

"Again," Adam prompted. "You need to focus. By the time you realize what they are, you'll need to act fast. They look like us . . . and like you."

The pause was slight, but she heard it. *Us* and *you.* Her mother wasn't a witch, and Adam wasn't her bio-dad, so she wasn't an *us.* She also wasn't really able to be a *them.* She might be human, but Adam was a witch. That meant she was caught living among the witches, preparing to fight daimons with only a human's defenses. Sometimes, guiltily, she admitted to herself that *this* wasn't the life she wanted. A stray thought of Kaleb flitted through her mind, but she knew without asking her father that he'd never agree to her changing her training or workout schedules so she had time to date.

Steadily, she sighted, fired, and moved to the next target. Then once she reached the end of the row, she worked her way back. Mallory hated the ease with which the semiautomatic discharged bullets. It felt like everything went too quickly, but if the paper targets in front of her were daimons, she knew she'd appreciate that extra speed.

Adam began calling numbers. "Target three, eight, two, one, eight, six."

As he called them, she aimed and fired. It was an exercise

that required reaction and focus. Admittedly, it was easier with the 9mm in her hand, but she still felt tense.

She switched guns, sliding the 9mm into an under-the-arm holster and transitioning to the .357 that she wore in a thigh holster. The familiar weight of it was all she needed to summon that meditative space where the world was reduced to hand-gun-target. She had learned hand-to-hand skills, but her father insisted that most daimons had superior training and more physical strength than a human could counter. She had to be proficient with weapons too. Witches had magic; daimons had physicality; and humans had guns.

She emptied the last chamber in the revolver and glanced at her father. The furrow in his brow said what he didn't: he wasn't happy about her switching guns.

"I'm more comfortable with this." She lowered the barrel so it aimed at the ground.

Adam said nothing as she opened the cylinder and discharged the empty casings. He remained quiet as she pulled six bullets from her jeans pocket and reloaded. When Mallory closed the cylinder, he said, "I should never have bought you that gun. If I'd started you with the nine mil, you wouldn't use this as a crutch. The revolver was to be a starter, like training wheels."

She gestured at the targets. "I'm *capable* with both guns. I just like this one better."

When he didn't reply, she walked over to the targets. Using the barrel as a pointer, she tapped the first target. "Not one outside the 'preferred zone.' Tight." She went down the line, tapping each paper in the row. "I can use the nine; I just don't like it as well."

Adam sighed. "If you knew what they were like, Mals . . ." He shook his head. "I hope you never have to face them alone, but if you do, you'll be grateful for a clip, and hopefully you'll be packing an extended clip."

She softened at his worried look. "I know, and I *will* be prepared. Promise." For a brief moment she considered asking him questions she had never verbalized, but like every other time she'd considered it, the questions skittered away before she could speak them. She wanted to know why she'd never met daimons, why she couldn't go to his office, why they couldn't find a way to live a different life, but her tongue wouldn't form the words. A band seemed to tighten around her chest.

*Good daughters don't question. They obey.*

Her father held her gaze, and when she didn't speak, he nodded once. "I need you to be prepared."

Mallory straightened her shoulders and met her father's gaze. "I won't let you down."

He ejected the clip from the 9mm and replaced it with an extended clip. "Notice that it took a moment to reload this. Sometimes a single moment makes a difference. Daimons aren't like witches or humans, Mallory. You can't forget that."

"I won't," she promised. The pressure around her chest faded.

He held the 9mm pistol out to her.

Lips pursed, she accepted it. Daimons might be more capable at hand-to-hand, but she wasn't planning on allowing any of them close enough for that to matter.

"Empty it," he ordered.

Mallory aimed and emptied half the clip. After fifteen bullets tore through the existing holes in the target, daylight shone through the center of the paper as if it were an open window. She did the same thing to a second target, and then lowered the gun. Maybe if she was good enough, her father would let her take a little time to go out, to at least build a friendship with Kaleb instead of settling for a few moments when they crossed paths. She glanced at Adam.

He nodded. "Again."

SEVERAL HOURS AND SEVERAL clips later, Adam and Mallory returned to the three-bedroom house they rented in Smithfield, yet another of the interchangeable towns in the middle of the country. Like almost every other house the past few years, this one was nondescript. It was nice, clean, and in good order, but it was anonymous in a way she sometimes hated. The walls were white, and the carpets were beige. There were no houseplants or bric-a-brac that said "this is a home." Takeout menus were held to the front of the fridge by strips of tape, clips, and magnets. It added to the already generic feel of the house.

It had been five years since they'd had a real home.

*Since Mom left.*

That was the real difference: Selah had turned whatever rental they'd had into an actual home. She'd bought paint and rollers, and she'd spent days turning a plain house into a real home. Boring white walls became a different color in each house. "Make it an adventure," she'd said. One house had ceilings painted like a sky, blue with big, fluffy clouds. Another had a tree painted on Mallory's bedroom wall. Selah had added hooks for her robe and her coat at the ends of two big branches. Beige carpet was covered with rugs, the splashes of color Selah pulled from battered boxes to make boring space into flower-strewn fields or calm ponds. Claiming a house was a game, one they'd played over and over in new towns. Now that it was just Mallory and Adam, the walls of every house were white, and the only color on the carpet was from the stains left by the last residents.

Mallory walked into the dining room and sat down. Mutely, she put both guns on the weathered wooden table, and then she proceeded to wipe down first her .357 and then the 9mm. She'd been handling guns since she was seven, and the process—much like the routine of aiming and discharging her weapons—was reassuring. It was a cue that things were normal, that her life was unchanged even as the houses she slept in year after year changed.

"We have to move again," Adam said from the doorway to the dining room.

She paused. "When?"

"Now." His mouth was a grim line.

"Now," she repeated. "Like *tonight*, now?"

"No." He gave her a smile that did little to soften the tension in his expression before saying gently, "I called the company movers. They'll be here on the fifteenth."

Childish hurt warred with years of practicality. Adam wouldn't decide that they needed to go again, especially on such short notice, if he didn't think it was essential, but she felt betrayed. They'd spent hours together, and he hadn't mentioned it until now.

"That's my birthday," she said with as little inflection as she could manage. She didn't—*couldn't*—mention Kaleb, but the thought of never seeing him again tore at her. Her gaze was carefully fixed on the gun she wiped clean.

"I know." Adam walked into the room and hugged her. "I'm sorry."

She closed her eyes like the child she couldn't be. It was silly to make a big deal over a date on the calendar, but she still clung to the foolish dream that her mother would show up on her birthday. There was no reason to believe she would, but Mallory had held on to the hope that her mother would walk back through the door and into their lives some birthday with as little notice as her departure on Mallory's twelfth birthday.

Adam swore that Selah had ways to locate them. His employer always knew where they were, and Selah was the only person in the world who had been granted full clearance to be told how to find Adam and Mallory at any time. Mallory hated to doubt her father's judgment, but her mother had never been accepted by his colleagues. It wouldn't surprise anyone but Adam if they "forgot" or misled Selah.

"I'm going to be working at the Stoneleigh-Ross main office." Adam's expression was perfectly unreadable—which meant he was either hiding something or afraid.

*Or both.*

Mallory squared her shoulders and stared at him as he walked away. She never succeeded at questioning her father, but the thought of Kaleb made her feel strong. She knew she couldn't really date him, and she shouldn't get too close to a regular human. For his safety, she needed to keep a distance, but the possibility of continuing even the small conversations they now shared was a great temptation.

"I want to know why we have to go," she told her father. Her usually absent temper flared, and her voice rose. "I'm not a child anymore. I *deserve* to know."

Her father sat down on the sofa and waited as she reloaded the clips. After a couple of minutes, he said, "I love you more than I thought it possible to love anyone or anything. If I could put you away somewhere safe and take care of the threats on my own, I would."

"I don't *want* to be 'put away.'" Mallory laid the clip on the table. The soft clatter was in direct contrast to the turmoil she was trying to repress. She crossed the small distance to the living room, but didn't sit. "I want to know what's going on. I want to know why we have to move so suddenly. *Again.* I want to know why they're after you in the first place."

Her father gave her a curious look, and she wanted to apologize for raising her voice to him. She wasn't sorry though. He acted like she was too fragile to know anything, but he taught her how to kill. Maybe she needed to show him that she wasn't going to back down every time he skewered her with his gaze.

After a moment, Adam said, "A long time ago I took something very valuable." He leaned forward so that his hands were on either side of his knees, as if he had to hold on to the sofa cushion. "Maybe it was foolish. I knew it was dangerous, but I was angry. They killed my parents and my brother . . ." He paused, and she thought he'd stop as he always had on the rare occasions when he had mentioned The City, but this time, he continued. "If not for my sister, I'd be dead too. Evelyn saved me. I was so young, too young to fight, but after the wars, I waited. It took a couple of centuries, but then I saw my chance: I took what their ruler most valued, but I couldn't . . . I *can't* destroy it. Evelyn wants to use it as a weapon, but . . ." Adam bowed his head as his words dwindled.

This time, he didn't resume. He sat there with his head down.

Mallory shuddered at the thought of Evelyn Stoneleigh. She was supposed to be family, but family or not, the woman who ran the Witches' Council was the single most frightening person Mallory had ever met. She looked innocuous, like most witches, but she had stared at Mallory with flat, dark eyes reminiscent of sharks' eyes: all function, no emotion.

Mallory thought about the few possessions her father carried rather than allow the movers to pack and ship, and she could think of nothing valuable enough to kill for. "Could you give it back so we can stop running?"

Adam lifted his head. "I'd sooner die—and he'd kill me either way. They don't think like witches, Mals, and he's their ruler. It would be a sign of weakness to let me live."

"There has to be another option," she insisted. "Our choices are run or die? That's it? Maybe you can have someone else return it to them. Evelyn is strong and—"

"No!" he snapped. After a shuddering breath, he said evenly, "I'll come up with a plan. We'll be okay. You'll be careful, and we'll move as often as we have to. If I die, you go to Evelyn."

He held his hand out to her, and she went to his side.

Mallory blinked away tears as her father held her. This was her future for as long as she could imagine, running and hoping the monsters didn't find them.

*I hate daimons.*

# CHAPTER 2

MORNING HAD COME, BUT only just barely. The sky was still a mix of the gray and plum streaks that heralded a new day in The City, and as she had on so many other days the past year, Aya was readying herself for another fight. She wondered briefly what life would have been like by now if she hadn't entered the competition. She didn't like killing, but the thought of the life she was escaping reminded her that this was the right path. Every ruling-caste woman was required to reproduce. She'd avoided that for now by ending her engagement, but that only delayed the inevitable. Eventually, if she didn't choose a mate on her own, she would be given to someone by their ruler. Better to die in the fights than in captivity. At least within Marchosias' Competition, she had a chance of freedom. The rules didn't specify that the winner had to be male, only that the winner had to survive. If she survived, she'd be able to do what no other woman had—rule in The City's government. That chance was reason enough for what she'd do in a few short hours. It had to be.

A thrum in her skin let her know she had a visitor. It was light enough out that she was cautious as she went into the main room and opened the shades. A street scab stood on the fire ladder. After families were burned alive in the war with the witches long before her birth, the ruler of The City, Marchosias, had ordered ladders installed on the outside of every apartment building in the living sections of The City. Over time, the ladders had become the visiting routes for those not caste-equal. Security kept the windows impermeable, but the ladders enabled the lower castes a route through which to speak to the resident of a home.

The scab's black eyes darted left and right, assessing everything he could see inside her home. Scabs were the bottom of the lowest caste, daimons who lacked trade, pack, or family. They were also the ears and eyes on the streets within The City.

She slid open the glass pane. "No one else is here."

The scab nodded. "Verie's death is all they talk about in the Night Market."

"*All?*"

The scab shrugged. "All that's new."

Aya pulled a coin from the jar she kept by the window for just this sort of visit. She handed it out the window. "Anything else?"

"Word is that one of the fighters killed him." The scab leaned into the edge of Aya's house wards, stopping just before the wards would fling him into the street, unconscious. In The City, hers were the best wards that could be used without attracting unpleasant attention.

She turned her back as if she didn't notice the disrespect of testing her wards. Noticing meant she should rebuke him. It was a foolish game of trust the scabs often played: see if the high-caste girl is truer to her caste or to her fight reputation. Aya didn't like games.

"Which fighter?" she asked evenly.

"Depends on who's talking."

Aya glanced over her shoulder at him. "Including?"

The scab held out his hand.

Silently, she turned and gave him two more coins and repeated, *"Including?"*

The coins disappeared into one of the pouches that were sewn on the inside of the scab's shirt. "You, Sol, and Belias."

*The only three highborn fighters left in the competition.*

"Safe money's on you," he added, and then before she could reply, he kicked his feet backward, slid midway down the ladder, and dropped into the crowds on the street.

Aya leaned out the window for a moment and looked for him. She'd found increasingly reliable scabs over the past two years, but the last year—the fight year—had proven remarkable in that way. The longer she'd lasted in the fights, the more appealing working for her became. She'd proven herself to be ruthless and thorough, but she'd also been judicious. That sort of behavior earned her the grudging approval of a number of the trades-caste residents, as well as members of the lower castes.

Even before the competition, she'd never struck a scab. Sometimes, though, she wasn't sure if it would matter to the scabs themselves. Her willingness to pay for good information was all they heard, and her probable future was one of power and money—or death. After the competition, she'd either be in a position of use or in the ground. Either way, working for her now held no long-term risk for them.

She closed the window. Now was not the time to think about death. Today's bout was with Belias, and he wasn't a fighter to approach lightly. Her odds of winning against him were not high. The matchboard had him favored to win so strongly that the return on bets was fourteen to one.

As she padded into the front room of her apartment, her gaze fell to the knives that had been soaking overnight. She had already gathered her other weapons. The knives were the final items she needed for the fight, but taking them made her cringe. It wasn't a noble move by any stretch. Sol probably wouldn't do it; Belias wouldn't even think of it. The toxins on the blades would stop any daimon's heart. If Belias knew, he'd be disgusted with her, but she'd fought against him often enough in her life that she didn't see any other option. She didn't have the skill to beat him. He'd taught her a lot of the skills she did have, and he knew which tactics she favored. A fair fight wasn't possible between them.

*And the judges knew that when they matched us.*

Aya withdrew the knives and slid them into the sheaths that hung from her belt. She was so far from class-appropriate behavior by now that one more stain wasn't worth the guilt that threatened. It was bad enough that she lived alone, that she wore her hair in a short, nonornamented style more suitable for a soldier in Marchosias' army than for an eligible ruling-caste girl. Her behavior in the fights was an embarrassment to any ruling-caste family: noble women didn't engage in fights outside of sanctioned clubs, and they certainly didn't kill for sport or gain.

Resolutely, she pulled the door closed behind her and descended the stairs that led to the crush of people in the street. After almost a year of fights, of blood on her hands, of lives spilling into the dirt under her blades, she was one of the final standing contestants. The fights only happened once a generation, so the sheer number of entrants was daunting. Many fighters made a point of doing all they could to announce their participation in the competition, but the rarity of women entering meant that the female fighters garnered extra attention from the start. For her, that attention was multiplied: the unheard-of act of an upper-caste woman entering was more shocking than the violence of the matches themselves.

Women of every caste had a place in The City—but those of her caste were the only ones sheltered from the violence that was rife in their world. Her choice to enter the competition invited criticism from every corner. She'd moved into the trades-class section of The City, where upper-caste boys lived in their premarriage years and kept their favored mistresses after marriage. Leaving her family home and refusing her intended marriage added to the furor over her entering the competition, but she'd done it—and was succeeding better than even she had thought she would. Being pushed to the wall made a person do things that they'd not have believed themselves capable of, as the blades she carried proved. Winning the competition would mean changing the future for The City. That goal was worth any sacrifice—even Belias.

She took comfort in the excitement humming in the air. They were whispering about her past bouts, betting on her odds today, and telling tales of her supposed actions outside the fight grounds. She smiled at those willing to make eye contact. They were the people she'd protect and guide. They weren't the feral daimons who lived in the reaches outside The City. They were orderly even in their debauchery, and they'd be hers to rule.

As she reached the edge of the Carnival of Souls, she saw the black-masked assassins and red-masked pleasure vendors negotiating with daimons who were seeking the services of one of the trades. Many of the patrons hid their faces behind masks as well, but some bolder daimons carried on their negotiations without disguise. Those were more often the daimons of the highest stature; ruling-class daimons had less need to hide business dealings. Likewise, the best-paid assassins and pleasure dealers often signified their status by wearing only the barest of masks—or in rare cases, no mask at all.

Aya walked farther into the center of the carnival, where

the matchboard hung like a beacon, inviting people to place bets and buy tickets for the upcoming fights. Tall red letters spelled out the final ten fighters' names and ranks. Her name was after Sol, Flynn, Nic, Kaleb, and Belias, but before Dian, Tylo, Cree, and Jade. Finally being on the board was a victory, but it wasn't good enough.

The only matches left in this round were hers and the one between Nic and Kaleb. If she won, she'd move up to fourth position—unless she found a way to score sufficient points to take third from Nic or Kaleb. Unfortunately, she wasn't entirely sure she'd even survive fighting Belias, so taking bloodpoints wasn't likely. A fighter could score extra points by difficult strikes, maiming, or otherwise exceeding the necessary combat acts, but the assignation of points was entirely at the judges' discretion and thus unlikely to be of use to her in this fight.

Although all of the judges claimed that they were judicious in awarding points, only a fool would believe that there was no corruption in the process. Corruption was as common as violence in The City, and as a girl fighting against a ruling-class boy, especially one who outranked her in the fights, she wasn't going to get any help from the judges. Aya wasn't supposed to win. It wasn't a woman's place to be an equal.

Murmurs increased as she made her way through the carnival, and her mind went back to the rumors about Verie's death. No one approached her, but they watched her as openly now as they would when she was in the match. She was a spectacle, their entertainment as surely as the dancers or tale-tellers working in the stalls throughout the carnival. The fights were a chance to watch a display of the strengths that had protected The City, and Aya suspected that the fights were, in some way, Marchosias' method of encouraging his people to keep in top shape for any altercations that could come in the future. They stayed strong to enter the competition, but that also meant that he had ready fighters he could utilize if he needed to swell the ranks of his troops.

When Aya reached the entrance gates for the fight yard where she'd stand against Belias, she stopped to look at the line snaking past the pleasure stalls. It was probably meant to be an insult—or extra titillation—to set her fight here at the pleasure field, where coin typically only bought chemical or physical decadence, but perhaps it was a gift of sorts. She'd fought here once already, so she had field familiarity that Belias wouldn't have. She smiled at the customers lined up waiting to get into the pit seats, and she walked to the front of the line.

"I'm here to kill Belias," she told the gatekeeper.

Gasps and barks of laughter erupted down the line as her words were repeated and passed around.

"Smart money's on the boy," the gatekeeper said in a loud voice.

"Belias will lose—or if it's before fifth blood, he can forfeit." Aya turned to face the line. "Tell him for me: I'll accept his forfeit if it's before fifth blood."

Nervous laughter and bloodthirsty cheers mixed in the growing cacophony.

"Tell Belias," she repeated, louder this time, and then she turned away.

The gatekeeper lifted the bar for her to pass. "Someone ought to put you back in your place."

She stared only at him, ignoring the line now. No one would dare speak so to a proper upper-caste woman, but she didn't behave as women of her stature should. However, she couldn't pretend that she was anything other than upper caste, not if she intended to rule. "I know my place: I was born to the highest caste in The City. I was born to make The City safer and stronger."

"Women have no business ruling anything but the home," someone yelled from the line.

She looked steadfastly at the gatekeeper, but spoke loudly so as to be heard by those in line. "Unlike most every remaining contestant, I am *already* ruling class. They all fight for what Sol, Belias, and I were given by birth."

She knew the crowd watched her attentively now. She glanced at them and reminded them, "We fight to prove our worthiness to have what is our birthright already."

"Women don't rule. They are too soft," someone called.

"Tell that to the fighters I've defeated." Aya turned back to the gatekeeper who had started this argument. "I outrank you without winning, and even if Belias or someone else gets lucky and kills me, I will *still* outrank you."

The gatekeeper bowed his head.

Quietly, she suggested, "Take a piss."

He lifted his gaze to meet her eyes.

"Now." She pointed at the dirt.

Eyes downcast, he obeyed. The alternative was calling for judgment, but he had insulted a ruling-class woman in front of several hundred witnesses—many of whom had heard every word. Some of those witnesses would speak, and so any judge at the carnival would rule against him. The right of class allowed her to offer immediate punishment.

"Kneel," she ordered.

Just as the gatekeeper dropped to the ground, Aya saw Belias walking toward her. He raised his brows in silent question, but he knew not to vocalize that question in public—not that he had to ask. People in line were filling him in on the events that had just transpired.

Aya told the gatekeeper, "If I order you to drink from the ground, you will do so or face judgment. If I order you to ask for seconds, you will do so."

The gatekeeper looked up at her. "What do you want me to do?"

"Ask me for mercy." Aya glanced at Belias. "I have very few options, but if you ask me for mercy, this will go easier."

The smile on Belias' lips said that he understood that her words were for him too. He shook his head once; he would not ask for mercy. It wasn't as if he thought he needed it, but she'd thrown the offer to him so that he could speak the word midfight.

The gatekeeper, on the other hand, said, "Mercy."

"The difference isn't in how cruel women can be." Aya

spoke louder now so that the line of people could hear her again. "If by *action* you tried to 'remind me' of what place some think a woman deserves, I would break you, but I won't kill you for ignorant words. I can be a lady and still rule. One does not negate the other."

A few people in the crowd jeered. Others cheered.

"The ground seems wet," Aya said mildly, as if the urine-wet mud were a surprise. "I'd hate to soil my boots." She looked down at the kneeling gatekeeper. "Do you have something I could step on so I can cross?"

"I . . . I have no coat, but"—the guard started to pull his shirt off—"I can offer you this."

"That's not good enough," Belias said as he walked behind the gatekeeper, put a foot on the man's back, and pushed him flat to the ground. Then, he turned to Aya and bowed. "Please."

When she didn't reply, he held out a hand to help her over the fleshly bridge that now spanned the puddle of mud and urine. "Your servant," he murmured.

Aya ignored the proffered hand and stepped on the gatekeeper.

"I believe we need another gatekeeper," Belias called. "This one is otherwise occupied."

As Aya walked toward the ring, Belias assumed control of the crowd with practiced ease. She could hear him appointing a replacement and assisting girl after girl over the prone gatekeeper's body. He had co-opted her example and neatly established his own dominance. Worse yet, he had done so with the same charm that had once made her grateful that he'd been chosen as her betrothed when she was born, the charm that made her fall in love with him, the charm that made her heart break when she refused their wedding ceremony. Aya pressed her lips together tightly to keep words better not said from boiling over. She'd entered this competition to change her future, to attain the power she needed to improve The City, and she was going to do just that.

# CHAPTER 3

THE MEN NODDED AT Belias as he helped the girls and women over the back of the gatekeeper. They gave him the attention befitting his caste and his fight standing, and he accepted it without drawing attention to it. *Not everything has to be a show.* Belias couldn't get Aya to understand that. He could accept her need to make her way in the world, respected it even, but she seemed determined to choose the hardest possible path to do that. Highborn girls didn't brawl in the street, and they surely didn't enter death matches. If her father had survived a few years longer or if her brother were older, she wouldn't have been able to risk herself so foolishly, but the way things had unfurled, Aya had achieved her majority—eighteen—and with no one to stop her, she'd refused their wedding and entered the competition. Once entered, there was no way out save forfeiture or death.

"I hope you kill her," a girl murmured as she stepped gingerly on the gatekeeper's back.

Belias remained silent. He'd entered the competition to *prevent* Aya from dying. If she weren't so obstinate, he'd have teamed with her publicly. It wasn't the way the contest was structured, but he was ruling class, and with or without these wins, he'd be a general in Marchosias' government. It was what he had been raised to do. His father had died in the service of their ruler, killed by a supposedly tamed witch's treachery, and Belias had been raised to know that he had two functions in his life: to fight as bravely and ably as his father had and to have sons to carry on their family line. *Preferably with* Aya *by my side.* She'd been chosen for him, selected for her lineage, and she'd been trained to fight in order to be strong enough to help protect his future children.

Unfortunately, his chosen mate had decided she'd rather kill him and a slew of other people than be by his side. A growl of frustration slipped from between his lips and caused an older scab to tremble as he took her hand. Belias offered her his most comforting smile.

She squeezed his hand. "Don't go too hard on Aya. She's doing what many of us wish we could. Things need shaking up."

Belias nodded.

*Too hard?*

He wasn't sure he could strike her with intent to kill. Of course if he didn't, she'd be even more aggressive. There was no way to win this fight that wasn't also a loss—unless Aya forfeited.

Once the last of the females crossed the gatekeeper, Belias turned to face the remaining line, bowed once, and then walked into the fight zone. The space for their match was clearly marked by a fresh chalk-and-salt circle. The wooden seats that spanned the fight grounds were almost filled, and the stink of too many bodies in the heat mixed with other equally unpalatable stenches.

"Forfeit, please," Belias murmured as he came to stand beside Aya.

She ignored him as she slipped her arms out of her jacket, stretched, and checked her cache of weapons again. She removed a cloth-wrapped blade from her bag. Two knives were sheathed at her hips, and the hilts of two smaller knives protruded from her boots. Her left boot had a razor edge at the toe, and her left glove had jaw-busters built in.

He held her gaze as he peeled off his shirt.

Her right hand tightened on the hilt of the falchion she withdrew from its cloth, but she didn't look away. The daimons in the crowd were watching for her reaction, but Belias knew she wasn't going to give them—or him—that satisfaction.

"We can announce our reunion right now and walk out of the fight." Belias reached out to touch her cheek, but she raised the wicked curved sword as if she'd start the fight now. "We don't have to be here. We're already ruling class."

"I'm not meant for being a wife, Bel." Sorrow flashed in

her eyes, but it was gone just as quickly as it had appeared. "For what it's worth, I'm sorry for hurting you."

"If you don't marry me, you'll be given to someone else eventually. You can't avoid your duty." He looked up as the gate slammed shut with a thud. "Be with me, Aya. You know I love you."

"And you know I won't breed." As the last of the audience took their seats, Aya snapped a choke guard over her throat. "Tell me we can marry and never breed."

If he could agree to such an absurdity, he would, but they both knew that he couldn't. He needed to have an heir; it was his duty. It was *her* duty—that was why marriage and breeding ceremonies made female daimons fertile; it was why marriage entwined a couple's lives so that the death of one was the death of both *unless* the woman was pregnant. Children were essential to the survival of The City. He could wait for a while—*had* waited—but eventually, if she didn't marry him, she would be given to a daimon of Marchosias' choosing. Marrying her but never being with her wasn't really an option, either. If they were married but failed to produce a child, the marriage would be dissolved. He'd considered every possibility.

After a moment of staring blankly at her, he shook his head. "Don't be foolish, Aya."

"If I win the competition, I'll rule. Why would Marchosias force me to wed or breed then? *He* follows the laws too." She looked away from him to take in the crowd assembling to watch their match. "I have to win, Bel."

"You can't beat me, and I won't throw the fight."

"I know." She smiled sadly at him.

"At least leave the collar off," he pleaded.

"No."

Belias shook his head again. Aya hadn't ever made his life easy, but this was beyond unreasonable. He was fond of throttling his opponents. With his strength, it was a reliable way to incapacitate a fighter, maneuver them into an unforgiving position while they were unconscious, and then when they regained consciousness invite them to forfeit. It was legal, albeit not a crowd-pleaser. A lot of far less humane things were legal, too. *Those* were the crowd-pleasers. The fight rules were pretty basic: at least fifth blood had to be drawn before a kill, no outside aid, stay within the designated fight zone, and try not to die.

*Fifth blood will be harder tonight.*

Killing Aya wasn't going to happen, and he was certain she couldn't kill him, either. That meant that their fight would go until one of them had no choice but to forfeit. He felt a pang of regret for bribing the judges so that he could fight Aya, but better that than have someone else eliminate her by killing her. He'd had no doubt she'd make it to the final rounds, but now most of the remaining fighters were good enough to defeat her. She needed to forfeit before she faced a fighter like Kaleb or Flynn.

"It's time," Aya said as she laid her falchion just inside the edge of the ring.

With a lingering look at the girl he'd spent the last year fighting to reach, Belias walked to the center of the circle and called for her: "Aya."

She stepped over the sword and entered the circle.

As the lower-ranked of the fighters, she walked to him, clasped his hand, and bowed her head. While her head was bowed, she whispered, "I wish we hadn't been matched."

"You can forfeit at any time," he answered just as quietly.

She lifted her gaze to stare directly at him. "Likewise."

He released her hand reluctantly.

The witch waited just beyond them to raise the circle. Belias scowled at him. The presence of witches—even controlled witches—made him want to behave in very *un*gentlemanly ways. They should've been barred from The City centuries ago. It was one of the things he intended to put into motion once he took his place in the government.

The witch bowed his head, and Belias turned his back to him and to Aya in order to address the crowd. "Aya has stood against and defeated as many fighters as I have. She is an honor to the ruling class already."

Addressing the crowd was not typical, but he was ruling class. He turned to face Aya again and bowed deeply, as if they would dance.

She said nothing.

Together, they both reached into the bucket and took a handful of salt and chalk. Walking in opposite directions, they followed the perimeter of the already-drawn circle; when they met at the opening, they used the mixture in their hands to close the circle.

They stood face-to-face for a moment as the circle lifted around them. In a low voice only she could hear, he offered, "We can both win this. You can advise me, share my rule in secret, and we can . . . *abstain* until you're ready. All you have to do is say how long you need."

Aya slammed the flat of her palm into his face, breaking his nose, drawing first blood. "Forever. No children."

"When I win the match, I will offer again," he promised. "You've never beaten me before. You won't do so today, and I will *not* kill you."

She didn't answer, and Belias' crosscut slammed into her mouth, not with the force he could use, but still hard enough that he drew second blood as her teeth tore her lips.

Betting-house hawkers called out bloodpoints as Aya and Belias faced each other. Nothing mattered beyond this fight. The pleasure of standing against her filled him with the same thrill it had for years: she was unlike any other daimon he'd met.

He blocked a kick, and she dropped to her haunches to dodge a punch. They continued avoiding and blocking each other's blows for several minutes, and then Belias caught her in the stomach with a kick that knocked her to the ground. She rolled, and as she came to her feet, she ran to the edge of the ring and lifted the falchion she'd left there.

"Do you really want to do this, Aya?"

She charged him, shifting at the last possible moment and trying to catch his thigh with the edge of the blade. Belias knew her every cue, though, and easily dodged her. Twice more she approached and attempted to draw third blood, and twice more he avoided her.

Belias ducked her blows and watched her tire herself chasing after him. He was faster, better trained, and patient. If not for the angry looks she shot at him—and how furious she'd be when she had to forfeit to him—he'd be enjoying finally standing in a ring with her again. Unfortunately, defeating her was going to make her even less likely to forfeit graciously.

"Fight me, Bel," she demanded.

He dived out of the way as she slashed at him. "I don't want to hurt you."

"*Fight* me," she repeated. "You insult me by not even trying."

"Forfeit." As he said it, though, he withdrew a pair of throwing knives and launched them at her.

As she moved to avoid the first blade, the second sank deep into her thigh, as he'd known it would. Aya's cry of pain was hidden under the cheers of the crowd. Her gaze found him, and she looked happier now that he'd injured her. He knew, of course, that it wasn't the injury but the fact that he'd struck out at her as an equal that resulted in her smile.

"Third blood to Belias," the hawkers called.

"That's better." Aya shifted to put her weight on her

uninjured leg. "Only one out of two? You're not as good as I remember."

"Liar." Belias advanced on her. "Incapacitate your opponent. Go in for the close kill. You remember that lesson. You can't run now."

"Don't need to." She held up the falchion. "You're coming to me, aren't you?"

With a growl, he swept her feet out from under her. She landed hard, but he followed her to the ground. He had his not-insubstantial weight supported on his knees and one arm. With the other arm, he pinned her. His left hand flat on the middle of her chest, he demanded, *"Forfeit."*

"I can't." She withdrew one of the knives from her hip, but she paused before striking.

Belias yanked the throwing knife from her thigh as she stared up at him.

"You can't kill me with that," he said.

He stabbed the throwing knife into her arm, causing her to draw in a sharp breath.

"Fourth blood," the hawkers called.

The crowd cheered his name.

"I'm sorry," she whispered, and then he felt a blade sink into his stomach.

"That's not—" Belias gasped as cold rushed through him in a terrifying wave. His eyes widened as he stared down at her. "Poison? You'd *poison* me, little bird?"

Aya drove the second knife into his chest.

"I'm so sorry, Bel," she whispered as he fell atop her. "I didn't have any other choices."

He wanted to tell her that she was wrong, that there were choices she could've made, but his lips wouldn't move. All he could do was stare at her, looking for tears, remorse, something to prove he hadn't been so very wrong about her.

And then, even that was impossible. His eyes lost focus, and the world vanished.

# CHAPTER 4

EVENING WAS FALLING AS Kaleb walked toward the Carnival of Souls. After Mallory had fled, he'd returned home. There was no reason to be in the human world if not to see her, so he returned to The City to tend to business matters at the carnival. Hunting her was the only big contracted job he had currently, but until the contract was complete, he needed to supplement his meager funds when he could. That meant visiting the carnival.

Unfortunately, every time he saw Mallory, he was consumed by thoughts of her for hours afterward. Kaleb hadn't known much about Mallory when he was sent to find her, but in the past couple months, he'd studied how she moved, how she protected her home and her secrets. She was Marchosias' daughter whether or not she knew it, and whatever human had sheltered her had clearly taught her caution that she took to very naturally. Once he'd started approaching her, she responded with interest, but she'd never allowed Kaleb anywhere near her home, had pretended not to be seeking threats as they spoke, and in general demonstrated an innate sense of vigilance. She intrigued him.

Haage hadn't yet sent him to the human world to kill her, and the more time Kaleb spent with her, the more grateful he was for that. He *liked* her. It was foolishness, and he could work around it, but he found himself wishing Haage would change his mind. Stranger still, he had considered breaking his contract and bringing her to Marchosias. Both plans were risky; either option meant crossing one of the two most powerful daimons in The City. Soon, Kaleb would need to decide where his loyalties were—with Haage or with Marchosias.

His ultimate loyalty was to himself and his pack, regardless of whether he temporarily sided with Haage or with Marchosias. Right now, Kaleb's pack was only two—him and Zevi—but Kaleb would do whatever he must to make them safe. Neither Haage or Marchosias were pack. They were simply daimons with a lot of power.

Tonight, though, Kaleb would bide his time in the Carnival of Souls. It wasn't a hardship: everything of note started or ended here. Judgments were served here; negotiations of every sort took place in the shadows of vendors' stalls. Marchosias had decreed, long before Kaleb was born, that the carnival would serve as the mercantile and service center of The City.

It was the epicenter of The City itself. Spiraling out around the carnival were a tangle of narrow streets and old buildings that made up clearly stratified living sections. At the edges, the Untamed Lands encroached; nature tried to consume The City, and they tried to keep it at bay. Before the Witch Wars, The City was larger, but the witches had set nature against the daimons in their final departing blow. For several centuries now, daimons had worked regularly to cut back the growth and try to protect The City. Here at the center, though, was a place of business and pleasure. Music played constantly. Blind drummers played outside the tents where delicate deals were arranged; ensembles in the employ of the pleasure vendors enticed customers with their music as dancers demonstrated their flexibility; and others simply played for the coins that were tossed into their baskets. At times it was a glorious cacophony. Jugglers and fire twirlers showed their skills in time to the music. All the while, hawkers sold their wares to those ensnared by the music, sometimes literally.

For all the violence in the The City—much of it in the carnival—there was beauty, too, especially here. As he walked, Kaleb's steps caught the rhythm of a daimon who leaned against a vendor stall, tapping out patterns on a skin drum. The daimon had his eyes closed, and Kaleb smiled at the joy in the man's face.

Carefully, Kaleb swung up into the rafters that supported the vast ceiling covering the centermost stalls and worked his way farther into the heart of the carnival. He stopped when the matchboard was directly across from him. Aya's win over

Belias had been posted, so Kaleb's was the only match left undeclared. As with all matches, the public odds were listed for betting purposes. Kaleb wasn't favored to win, but he hadn't been discounted, either. It was a compliment to Nic's and his standings that this fight was the final match in this round—or perhaps it was a challenge. Either way, theirs was the only nonticketed fight of the round, so the crowd would be overwhelming and unruly. A few fights, those expected to be particularly exciting, were left unticketed so anyone and everyone could enjoy the spectacle. In such cases, the fight circle would be as much for keeping the bystanders out as for ensuring that the fighters stayed in play. Neither crowd nor fighters could cross the circle without debilitating pain.

Kaleb tucked himself behind one of the pennants that fluttered in the slight breeze. The vibrant swath of material hid him from the sight of almost all of the daimons below him, as he took a moment to study the betting that had begun on the ground.

"Ten to one Kaleb is maimed," one of the hawkers called.

"Bets on mercy deaths," another beckoned.

"Death by claws," suggested a cur. It was a popular bet for any of the cur fights; death by claws was a likely outcome, but the odds on claws were always better when Kaleb fought. He didn't like using teeth, but claws were comfortable—and a crowd-pleaser. Audiences liked to see the sort of fights that invited foot-stomping, guttural-growling bloodthirst. Kaleb's fights delivered what they wanted.

The cur met Kaleb's gaze, waiting for the cue. He was the one Kaleb had been seeking.

When Kaleb nodded, the cur sauntered over to stand underneath Kaleb's hiding place and leaned casually against a rough wooden post.

Kaleb crouched down and said in a low voice, "No claws before third blood. Cut me ten percent of the take, and I'll guarantee it."

The cur didn't look up at him, but he flashed a toothy smile and nodded. He didn't call out yet, but he'd only be able to wait for a few moments before attracting attention.

Side business complete, Kaleb hopped up and walked along the crossbeam. Once he was far enough from the betting house he'd tipped, he swung to the ground. Getting caught adjusting odds wasn't likely since he didn't tip any betting house regularly, and none of the houses were likely to submit him for judgment for adding to their profits. If the other fighters had any sense, they'd do the same, but too many of them were from castes that didn't think creatively. That, as much as their skills in the matches, would keep them from changing their futures. Kaleb was a cur though—a daimon species that was near the bottom of the caste order. As a child he'd been even lower: he'd had no pack. His parents had abandoned him, so he survived as a street scab, too low to even *have* caste. Most such daimons died; Kaleb hadn't. He'd fought, killed, and endured until he had the strength and power to earn respect on the streets. The competition could enable him to achieve far more than that.

Because most daimons couldn't achieve caste mobility the way Marchosias had—through military actions—once every twenty years, Marchosias opened the caste lines to allow one daimon to win the right to join the ruling caste. It was a fierce fight, one with few survivors, and anyone of age to enter was forever disqualified from future competitions. To Kaleb's mind, though, it was no less brutal than the future he'd face if he remained in the lowest caste. As a cur, odds were that he'd die by violence, better to try to change his status while he was at the top of his game than to grow complacent and be caught in the streets by a fighter intent on establishing status by eliminating an older cur. The only other fate he could have if he survived long enough was to find a protector who would use him for pleasure or violence. *Or both.* That was the lot in life for those in his caste. Those in the middle castes were educated or trained as tradesmen. The ruling caste made the decisions. In The City, one's lot in life was determined by birth. Kaleb wasn't content with that lot—but he wasn't going to overlook the assets it offered either.

During the fight year, he had wandered the Carnival of Souls regularly. Being seen made him available for tips; it made him accessible to those seeking mask-work. He hadn't accepted many jobs this year, but it kept him plugged into the underground where he'd grown up. The carnival was a thriving network of favors traded and impossibilities procured. It was as much a part of his success to date as his fighting skills.

This time, information was what he needed. Nic wasn't the

same caliber of fighter as Sol or Flynn, but he was the best that Kaleb had faced in a while. Skill wasn't everything though. If it were the only determining factor, Kaleb would be dead by now. Information on the opposition had been essential. Spies reported on injuries, fighting weaknesses, and any number of little details that could change a bout. Equally game changing was the willingness to do things that would disgust one of the upper classes. Those of better breeding castes didn't use claws or teeth; those of the highest breeding castes didn't fight dirty against women.

Curs, on the other hand, didn't fight by caste rules. Such luxuries were reserved for those who had learned their skills in fight clubs where they sparred for bets or trophies. Kaleb—and his opponent in this match—had learned to fight in order to survive, to eat, and to avoid being meat to every predator in the shadows. It made for a different degree of ruthlessness.

The sounds of the carnival were raucous this late. The evening hours between the carnival and the Night Market were often the quietest part of the day, but the hum of energy hadn't yet died down from the day vendors. Instead, it was almost as busy as it was midday. Several of the other fighters were out still. Aya, the only highborn female to ever fight, stood in the shadowed enclosure of a weapons vendor. Sol was leaving with a pair of trades-class girls. As Kaleb passed the stalls, curs, midclasses, and a few of the ruling-class girls stared boldly at him, but he wasn't so naive as to believe it was about him personally. They were intrigued by his brutality, or they were forward planning. He'd have power if he won the competition. Few people in The City would outrank him after that.

He wandered farther into the carnival. Across from the stalls that sold clothing for pleasure vendors, a crowd had gathered. Crowds weren't unusual here; they were, however, a good sign of what to notice. He wound his way between the bodies, snarling a few times at foolish pickpockets and people taking advantage of the crowd to sneak a grope.

"For the crime of unauthorized witchery—" The remaining words were lost under the yelling of the spectators.

A guillotine blade lowered on a woman's neck, and Kaleb realized with a start that it was a Judgment Day. The most important laws in The City were enforced by witch magic so that punishment was instantaneous if the law was broken. Only lesser or unexpected crimes were subject to judgment. Many laws were absolute, and for matters open to debate, judgment for transgressions was rendered quickly.

Before the corpse was done twitching, the next case was being called, and the volume of the crowd increased—which meant that there was an interesting case. Kaleb had no idea what it could be. He'd been so focused on the fight tomorrow and on having seen Mallory that he'd missed any news.

As he pushed to the front, the crowds parted more easily for him than for any save the ruling caste and the other fighters. It was a strange feeling after years of being shoved aside like refuse. When Kaleb reached the front of the crowd, he saw that Aya now stood near the platform.

"I bring charge for the unsanctioned death of Verie," the accuser said. He didn't look like the sort who'd be friends with a cur, but the actual accusers were rarely the ones to bring charges. The risk was too great. Retribution against accusers fell swiftly. Paying or blackmailing a daimon to level the charge provided anonymity for the higher-caste accusers and offered easy income to those willing to risk the retribution—or willing to sell out the accuser.

It was a gamble either way. If the accuser didn't kill you to protect his anonymity, the accused—or their loved ones— might kill you. On the other hand, it was an easy way to profit both from the accuser and from selling out the accuser. The trick was in knowing how far to push and when to let go.

"Aya, you are charged with nonsanctioned death," the judge announced.

The ripples of excitement in the crowd made more sense now. The fighters were increasingly newsworthy at this stage. It had been almost a year of fights, and the remaining contestants were all known by sight—none more so than Aya.

By now, many of The City's inhabitants had come to believe that Aya walked the edge of civility. She was at the carnival, seeming completely at ease despite having eliminated her former betrothed, Belias, only hours prior and currently facing judgment for an unsanctioned kill. At this point, Kaleb wouldn't be surprised if he heard that she stayed for the Night Market after judgment was passed. Aya seemed determined to prove that she was utterly undaunted by every part of their world that highborn women were taught to avoid—and curs wished they could avoid. She made no sense to him. She had been born to privilege, yet she risked everything to gain the right to *work*.

Kaleb decided to walk away. He had a fight in the morning, and watching judgment always made him feel ill. He would hear the ruling tomorrow just as easily. He left the crush of bodies, and in the shadow of an unoccupied stall, he slipped on an unornamented black mask. His current mask didn't cover his whole face, but it hid enough of his features that between the mask and his plain clothes, he could disappear into the crowd. *Just another killer.* He walked farther from the seething press of bodies, as eager to get away from them now as he had been to be among them earlier, but before he got very far, a ripple of excited words stopped him.

"Marchosias."

"Marchosias is *here*."

"To deliver punishment?"

"To deliver absolution!"

"Who cares? He's *here*."

The words were uttered with reverence as the ruler of The City strode across the wooden stage with the same casual ease he'd use walking into a shopping stall. As he removed his jacket, he made his stance on the proceedings known: Marchosias had donned a sleeveless tunic that revealed a number of scars from long-ago fights. Without a word, he made clear that he stood with the accused fighter.

As Marchosias turned to face the crowd, he glanced at Aya and smiled, and Kaleb felt a burn of envy. Not only had Aya defeated an opponent largely expected to force her to forfeit, but now she'd secured the backing of the head of the ruling class. Being lower in the ranking didn't matter nearly as much if she had already gained Marchosias' support. The judges would bow to Marchosias' will, and Aya's ability to score bloodpoints would increase immediately.

"Call witnesses," Marchosias directed.

Aya's stand-in accuser blanched, but he held his voice steady as he called forth a number of witnesses. Each and all offered very precise details citing Aya as the deliverer of Verie's death.

Finally, Aya herself stepped forward.

The judge was now barely restraining himself from looking at Marchosias. He looked directly at Aya, who stood as if she were without any care. Like Marchosias, she had decided to make a wordless statement: her kill trophies hung over a shirt that was one of the finest weaves and cuts available. At first glance, it appeared to have a floral pattern, but a second glance made clear that the pattern was bloodstains. In her simple choice of clothing, she reminded everyone there of her bravado, her caste, and her kills.

The judge motioned her closer, and as she stepped onto the platform, he looked at her bloody kill trophies. Aya touched her fingertips to the claws, talons, and teeth she wore like pearls.

The judge opened his mouth briefly and then closed it as Marchosias laughed.

"Do you offer answer?" the judge asked. "You are charged with—"

"She heard the charge," Marchosias interrupted. "Aya?"

She shrugged. "Verie offered unlawful aid to one of my competitors. He tipped Reni about the fight site, providing information that resulted in unfair opportunities to hide weapons there." She reached up and tapped a claw that hung in the center of her necklace. "I still won, but his interference was a violation of competition rules."

The crowd took a collective breath.

Marchosias growled before asking the accuser, "Do you have evidence that Verie was *not* aiding one of the contenders unfairly and undercutting the rules of my competition?"

"No."

"Do any of your witnesses?" the judge added with a brief glance at Marchosias, who now stood with his arms folded over his chest.

"My witnesses . . ." The accuser looked around him; all of the witnesses were gone. "No."

"Do you have evidence that this cur's death was unjust and by a ruling-caste woman?" the judge prompted. He paused only briefly before pronouncing, "Aya, the judgment on your action finds you unaccountable and—"

"I ask to be held accountable." Aya lifted her gaze to Marchosias. "If judgment finds that Verie was interfering with the competition, his death is eligible to be counted as a competition kill. I request judgment that Verie was interfering."

"Do you have evidence?" the judge asked.

Aya's attention shifted to the judge. "If you doubt my word on this, shouldn't I be held accountable? Either he was interfering or he wasn't. If he wasn't, his death is unjust. If he was interfering, I should get credit for his removal. There is precedent."

The smile that Marchosias had barely been restraining became a wide grin. He stepped in front of the judge and walked to the edge of the platform. "It would seem that, as arbiter of the competition, that would be *my* ruling." He looked at the crowd, who fell completely silent as he let his gaze slide over them. "If I award this kill to Aya, she will move from fourth- to third-ranked position on the matchboard. It could upset a lot of bets . . . at least for those souls who weren't attentive enough to stay at the carnival to attend judgment."

The crowd strained as the urge to rush to the betting houses conflicted with the danger of walking away from Marchosias. He knew it, let the tension build, and then held his hands up as if he hadn't made a decision already. "What say you?"

Cries of "Aya!" mingled with "Yes!" and "Her kill!"

Marchosias lowered his hands as he turned to Aya. "The people have rendered judgment. The kill is counted as justifiably yours."

The chaos of the crowd running and trampling one another drew Kaleb's attention so much that he almost missed the desperate look that came over Aya's face when Marchosias leaned forward and kissed her forehead. *Why?* It didn't matter:

what mattered was that Aya's power play had changed *his* game. He had just lost his third-place position, and he was now in danger of dropping further unless his points for his match tomorrow were significant.

*No mercy.*

He didn't like to inflict injury for point count before killing his opponent. He was decisive, but not cruel. If a fight started, it ended with a kill, but he didn't torture. Until a match began, a forfeit was a solid win: it meant that he'd succeeded in winning without needing to take the field. Midmatch, accepting a forfeit was a sign of weak nerves, of an inability to do the job thoroughly. Kaleb kept to those rules, but he didn't enjoy engaging in blood sport for the purposes of getting a kill-plus.

Now, as a result of Aya's play, he would have no choice but to do so tomorrow.

# CHAPTER 5

MALLORY PREFERRED TO DO her morning run in the quiet hours just before sunrise. Once people were headed to work or school, she felt self-conscious. They rarely commented on her odd attire, but they looked. Attracting attention wasn't on her father's list of good ideas. The goal was to blend in, to be unobtrusive so that if anyone came around asking questions, there were no details strangers could share. A teenage girl running in jeans, boots, and a jacket instead of the more standard workout attire attracted attention. Running shorts had nowhere to hide her revolver, and training in her everyday clothes was more practical. Boots were heavier than tennis shoes; jeans didn't have as much give as bare legs (but were far better than long skirts); and the awkwardness of running with weapons was a lot different from running while wearing an MP3 player. She trained for reality—not that she could say that to the people who looked askance at her.

She pulled the door shut behind her, slipping away from the safety of her warded house and watchful father and into the soft violet of the last moments of night. Something about the peculiar purple-gray skies made her relax. It felt right in a way that the harsh midday light never did. This was the time when her body felt intensely alive, as if her very skin were too tight to contain her and the only way to relieve that pressure was to be outside. The only other times she felt that pressure were when it had been too long since she'd seen Kaleb. In that case, too, she knew how to cure the tension—she simply needed to be nearer to him.

The feel of the ground under her feet was a comforting rhythm as she set out on today's path. She had a series of routes, and before each run, she drew a letter from an envelope she kept in her dresser. That kept her routes random, which made her harder to follow or stalk; unpredictability was a priority when hiding from daimons. Today's path took her toward the community college, along the river, and around the shopping mall. One of the things she looked forward to each time they moved to a new town was charting her run routes. *Make the moves fun,* her mother had often said. Mallory still tried.

Not quite a mile from the house, two men ran up on either side of her like they'd been waiting for her. A quick glance verified that they didn't have witch eyes, but they didn't look like they were in shape to be running easily beside her. They were bulkier than most runners, but even if they were fit, she'd never met a human who could keep up with her. It was one of the few quirks of genetics that she figured she'd inherited from the stranger who had been her biological father.

"I'm not looking for company," she said as she picked up her pace. They weren't the first men to try to hit on her or intimidate her, but she ran a little faster, pretending they were threats and letting herself run as if they were.

Both men sped up so they were alongside her again, and her pretend fear became actual fear.

"Back off," she said.

The one to her left grinned at her as he increased his pace and stepped in front of her. "There's a lot of interest in you at home."

Mallory put out her hand to keep from running into his now outstretched arms. Her hand slammed into the middle of his chest. He took one step backward, but he didn't move farther away.

The trickle of fear became a rush of adrenaline. Flight wasn't going to work; the only option left was a fight. Mallory turned her head, tracking the location of the second man, who now stood several steps behind her, and tried to reason with them. "You don't want to do this. Go back to wherever you're from and—"

The man in front of her flashed his teeth in the sort of smile that made her think of angry dogs. "I don't want to hurt you. You're more use as a pretty, living bargaining chip, so just come along peaceful-like. We'll take you to The City, and you'll be treated like you deserve."

"The City?" she echoed.

His words clicked into place for her, and the extent of the danger became clearer. *Daimons? Here?* Mallory stepped to the side, trying to evade him. Her hand was already reaching for her gun as she moved. If they were really daimons, the idea of facing two of them made her mind slip into that eerily calm place she found during training.

But it felt like the world hit fast-forward as the man lunged at her. He had appeared human, but in a split moment, he was something else. She wouldn't call him a dog, although he looked more canine than anything else. Claws too long for any dog extended from long digits on hands that appeared human. The body had a dog's fur, but the limbs were more muscular. The tatters of his clothes clung to an animal shape.

In that same moment when he lunged, Mallory drew the revolver from the holster hidden under her jacket. Suddenly her father's fixation on a gun's firing speed made good sense.

The daimon stopped just short of touching her. The other one was off to her side, but he wasn't moving either.

"We don't want to hurt you," the human-shaped one said.

Mallory had her feet planted and arms straightened; her hands were steady and the short barrel of the revolver was aimed at the doglike daimon. She took several steps backward, wishing she had a gun for her other hand.

"We *can* hurt you," he said, "but we only want to take you home."

The doglike one stared at her with eyes that looked as human as her own, and she paused.

She didn't move, couldn't move.

*It's a daimon. Pull the trigger.*

The shape of it was unsettling, not quite canine but not quite monstrous.

"We need you to come with us," the other one said. He was still in the shape of a man, but his voice sounded rougher now, like the sound had to roll over heavy rocks before words were fully formed.

Mallory shook her head. "I'll shoot."

The daimon in front of her made a sound like a laugh or a cough.

"You won't get both of us," the other one said.

He grabbed her arm and tugged her off-balance.

She let the momentum of his action spin her to face him— and then she shot him. She only got off one shot, but it was a good shot. The bullet pierced his chest, and at such close range, the spatter was enough to make her feel sick.

It did not, however, stop him. He grabbed her gun and yanked it out of her hand. He moved so quickly that the clatter of the revolver hitting the asphalt was simultaneous with a cuff to her head.

Mallory tried to evade both daimons, but they moved quicker than she could have imagined. Her father had told her that they were crazy fast, but seeing it was still shocking.

The doglike one had her wrist in his jaws now, holding her in place. The other one had sunk to his knees. He was motionless on the asphalt, but he still stared at them.

"You ought to help him," she said to the daimon in doglike shape. She wasn't sure he understood her, but she knew she wasn't going to fight her way out of this. Maybe logic could buy her time for . . . something.

She swiped at the blood on her face, and when she pulled her hand away, her fingers tingled. As she glanced at them, weird claws seemed to extend from her fingertips. *It's contagious?* Her gaze darted to the daimon in front of her. The claws growing on her hand were the same as his.

She swiped her claws at the head of the daimon restraining her, and he released her with a yelp.

Mallory held up her claw-tipped hand like a weapon and darted away.

The daimon that was crouched in front of her grabbed at her, but this time she moved almost quickly enough to avoid him. She felt the edges of his claws graze her arm.

None of this made sense. Adam had never said that their blood would change her. The horror of seeing the change to her hands mixed with the pain in her arm, and she stumbled backward.

The bleeding daimon caught her again, but she tore away from him and ran toward the gun.

She only made it a few steps before the daimon on all fours

landed in front of her in a leap that should've been impossible. She swerved too suddenly, twisting her ankle and falling in the process.

"Stop."

The voice cut through the haze of pain and confusion. The only person who could fix things was there. "Daddy?"

Adam stepped in front of her. The daimon's claws scored his side, but that was all that the daimon had time to do. In mere moments, her father had spoken a spell that left the doglike daimon immobilized on the ground. It looked at her from eyes too like her own, but didn't move. Its chest rose and fell in silent breaths.

The second daimon wasn't so lucky. When it had started changing, Adam spoke another spell—this one fatal. It dropped to the ground dead in a form that was neither man nor animal, but a sick mix of the two.

Her father drooped.

"Daddy!"

"I'm fine." He pulled her to her feet. "Everything's fine."

"It's not!" She tugged him away from the blood on the ground with her malformed hands.

"I'm here now." Adam put an arm around her, steadying her. "Everything is fine."

"It's *not*." She held her hands out. "Look at me!"

"Shhhh," he murmured.

"Hush, Mallory." He grabbed her face, and she noticed that there was blood on his hands too. They weren't changing, but before she could ask why, he told her, "We were running together today, and you fell. The bruises are from a fall."

"But . . ." She nodded even as her mind fought to hold on to the truth of what had happened. The daimons, the blood, her hands—all of it was replaced with a hazy memory of a twisted ankle and bruised arm from tripping over something. *A dog. One of those tiny little ones had darted into my path.*

Mallory leaned on her father. "Why can't people keep their dogs on leashes?"

Other people had arrived, and they were talking to her father. She tried to look at them, but she couldn't focus. *Witches.* They were pulling a man and an animal into the back of a black van. She didn't know why there were witches with her on her morning run. "Daddy?"

"Just a minute, Mallory." He held her to his side.

"We have this, sir," a woman said. Mallory blinked, but the witch was out of focus.

Her father pointed at her ankle. "Someone fix that. She can't walk home like this."

"Yes, sir," another voice said.

Mallory's eyes drifted shut, and when she opened them, her father was helping her into the house.

"Stay here." Adam left her standing just inside the door and went into the kitchen.

She knew there was something she wanted to ask, but she couldn't remember what it was. Mostly, she wanted to take a nap until her headache went away. The walk home from her run was hazy. All she knew for sure was that if she'd gone running alone like she did most days, she'd be hobbling home because of that yappy little dog that had darted into her path.

When her father returned, he had a trash bag in his hand.

"Thanks for coming with me today," she said.

"Of course." He walked her to the bathroom. At the door, he stopped. "I need the clothes you have on. Put them in the bag. Then take a good soak, and stay home today. Make sure to use the bath oils I made for you, Mals. That will make your head feel better too."

Mallory did as she was told.

*Good daughters always obey.*

# CHAPTER 6

As KALEB DRESSED FOR the fight the next morning, Zevi paced around their cave so rapidly that Kaleb had to say his name several times before the manic cur heard him. Even then, Zevi's only response was a curled lip. The mornings of a fight were harder every time, but today Zevi was in rare form. He'd obviously been awake for hours, trying to be silent, because from the moment Kaleb opened his eyes, Zevi was in motion. The pent-up energy that he'd been containing all but erupted.

"Zevi!"

All Kaleb saw in the blur was a flash of red eyes and exposed teeth, but in the instant before Zevi actually tackled Kaleb, he stopped and dropped to the floor in a heap of too-thin limbs. "I don't like this."

"I know." Kaleb stroked his hand over Zevi's hair.

"We could leave The City." Zevi pushed against Kaleb's hand and tilted his head. Despite years in The City, Zevi often seemed more animal than anything else. His childhood among quadrupedal creatures in the Untamed Lands outside The City showed even more when they were home—and when Zevi was anxious.

"Have I lost yet?" Kaleb asked.

Zevi snorted. "'Lost' is dead."

"Or forfeit."

With another headbutt, Zevi muttered, "Curs don't forfeit. I know, Kaleb. I *know*. You wouldn't forfeit. You need to win. It's the only way for us to jump castes, but"—Zevi took a whimpering breath—"I'd rather stay cur than you be dead."

Kaleb petted him for a few moments. "I'd rather die. This is not enough."

The answering sigh was expected, as was Zevi's resolute attitude shift. He stood, walked to the fire, and dropped several rolls of wraps into a large metal pot that simmered over the coals. He said nothing as he did so. When he was done, he collected his bag and went to stand at the mouth of the cave. "I'm ready."

They walked in silence to the carnival. When it was first begun, the Carnival of Souls was where the witches had worked their arts and sold talismans to protect daimons from summoners' circles. Of course, now, everyone knew that not many human-born witches could draw a daimon to the other world. It was The City's witches who had been behind the summonings; they'd roamed *both* worlds then. Daimons who troubled them were summoned to the human world, where they were entrapped. Until Marchosias had stopped them, the witches were the daimons' greatest source of death or imprisonment. Marchosias had been the lion at the front of the fight, slaughtering the oldest witches and their children to prevent another generation of their kind until they accepted the treaty that gave them the human world and left The City to daimons.

Centuries later, Marchosias was still pushing back the unending growth of the Untamed Lands, cutting away at the wild plants that the witches had set to flourish. He had changed things and continued working for the good of The City, and they all knew it. In return, they followed him absolutely—and fought for a worthy role in the world he'd carved out for them.

Some fighters, ones who forfeited after a good fight, would be chosen to serve in his militia. Others might be found deserving of trades training. The competition was as much a fight arena as it was a showplace where daimons could try to improve their lot in life, even if they had no actual expectation of winning. Kaleb, however, had a real chance at winning.

With no more acknowledgment than terse nods at those he knew, Kaleb made his way to the fight grounds for his match.

The wood shavings and sand under his feet were still wet from the judgments that had required punishments. Often, fresh shavings were brought in after Judgment Day, but the crowds were hungry for the sort of violence they'd been denied by Aya's match. The still-bloody ground where the fight would happen today was testament to the expectation and hope that there would be ample blood spilled.

"Tell me again that you won't die," Zevi demanded as they stood at the edge of the circle.

"I won't die here." Kaleb pulled his boots off and handed each to Zevi. "Tell me *you* won't forget the rules."

"I promise." Zevi ducked his head sheepishly. Neither mentioned the time that Zevi had launched himself at a fight circle and been summarily knocked backward like a bit of flotsam, but Kaleb knew that they both thought of it every fight. Seeing Zevi unconscious made Kaleb lose focus that day. It had nearly killed them both: Zevi from the force of the shock and the impact of the fall and Kaleb from a set of claws that ripped furrows down his chest and then tore clear through his stomach muscles.

Zevi shoved Kaleb's boots into his bag. "Nic will draw claws fast."

"I know." Kaleb peeled off his shirt, but kept on the loose trousers he was wearing. He hated ruining another set of clothes, but he wasn't going to strip bare in front of the audience.

Absently, Zevi accepted the shirt with one hand, and with the other he dug around in his bag. In short order he retrieved Kaleb's mouth guard from the depths of the bag and held it out. "He'll aim for a straight kill with you."

"I know, Z." Kaleb took the mouth guard, looked at it warily, and then handed it back. "I can't use this for more than a minute today. I need my teeth."

Zevi's eyes widened as he realized what Kaleb was planning. "You don't need to do that. You're good enough to—"

"Bet security," Kaleb interrupted. "No claws before third blood."

The mingled anger and fear in Zevi's eyes made Kaleb regret telling him. They stood silent, neither giving voice to the inevitable truth that Kaleb's teeth would mean the fight would be bloodier faster.

"We need the money," Kaleb said mildly.

"I could earn it." Zevi held his bag open so that a tattered red mask was visible.

"No." Kaleb smacked Zevi's hand away from the bag. "I will take care of us, Z."

Kaleb would do a lot of things that he found abhorrent before he'd ask Zevi to whore himself. Life as a cur in The City meant that the choice between whoring or killing was inevitable, but when he'd brought Zevi out of the Untamed Lands and into his home, he'd tried to make sure Zevi didn't have to do either of those things. Zevi was his pack, his family, and Kaleb would do anything to protect him.

The crowd parted to allow Nic and Kaleb to reach the ring. As they were equals, they took the ring simultaneously. Neither one bowed.

Kaleb had removed his shirt only. Nic, however, had stripped completely; he had no compunction about baring himself to the crowd. However, he also made no secret of his willingness to wear the red mask as well as the black one.

The crowd on the ground around the ring was packed so tightly that several hawkers had to prod them backward in order to raise the ring. One enterprising hawker had brought a white-masked witch with him for crowd control. The status and wealth implied by having his own witch made the citizens all notice the hawker. The witch's clothes were stained with dirt, and as he lifted his arms, his sleeves fell back, exposing the ownership brands on his wrists.

The hawker preened under the crowd's nervous attention as his witch muttered whatever words he needed and gestured with his outstretched hands. As the spellwork became manifest, the blue-and-gold eyes of the witch gleamed, their eeriness highlighted by the starkness of his mask. It was part showmanship, but it was still effective: in moments, the perimeter of the circle was free of obstructions.

The witch and the hawker both bowed to Kaleb and Nic. Then the hawker held out his card to Zevi. "At your service, sirs, if you should need us."

With a low chuff of warning at the witch, Zevi took the card. No one liked having any witches in The City, but laws and contracts were enforced by magic, so witches were a necessary evil. Kaleb nodded once at Zevi, who shoved the card into the morass of things in his ever-present bag.

"Are we going to do this or are you going to stand around making eyes at your bi—" Nic's words were cut off when Kaleb slammed his fist into Nic's mouth.

Kaleb said, "Show respect."

"No bloodpoints!" The hawkers scurried and waved their hands. "Circle first."

"Right," Kaleb said mildly. He bent to the bucket and withdrew a handful of the salt-and-chalk mixture. The salt stung the scrapes on his knuckles where Nic's teeth had torn the skin.

Nic moved to stand back-to-back with Kaleb. "You'd better hope your bitch has a protector lined up for after today."

After a lifetime in the streets, Kaleb wasn't going to be truly angry about Nic's barbs. They necessitated a statement— which Kaleb had made with his fist—but they didn't upset him in any way that would benefit Nic. As they finished drawing the circle, the barrier snapped into place.

"To a better future," Kaleb said as he extended his hand to Nic.

For a moment, Nic's facade of callousness wavered. He nodded once. "To not being the bottom of the order."

They exchanged a smile.

Kaleb hadn't released Nic's hand more than a moment before they both struck. Nic hit Kaleb with a combination; both punches drew blood.

Instead of wasting time with fists, Kaleb had slashed Nic's arm with a pair of knives he'd withdrawn from his pockets the instant Nic punched. Only one of the knives actually cut Nic, but between that cut and the two punches Nic had landed— and Kaleb intentionally hadn't dodged—they were already at third blood.

The judges only counted it as second blood though.

"Foul," Zevi snarled at the hawkers.

To win his cut of the bet pools, Kaleb had to deliver third blood before either of them drew claws. Nic flexed his hands, starting the transformation that would result in Kaleb losing his share of the betting pool. In that brief moment while Nic was distracted by transforming, Kaleb surged forward and bit off the bottom of his earlobe.

"Third blood!" the hawkers yelled over the shrieking crowd.

That was all the time Kaleb had though. Nic's hands no longer had fingers, but extended digits with claws. Unlike Kaleb, Nic preferred to fight in full animal form. As Nic's transformation continued, Kaleb grimaced and accepted the inevitable. He shed his own bipedal form. His teeth lengthened, and his jaw reshaped itself. Hands and arms were replaced by grotesque limbs with thick claws.

Nic transformed completely in every fight, so he was animal before Kaleb. He lunged for Kaleb's throat, but the brutality of such a move was easy to predict. They'd both fought in the street since not long after their infancies. Every cur who'd fought to survive knew that a quick kill was better if the other fighter was of equal tenacity.

Kaleb angled his body so that Nic couldn't bite his throat. Immediately, though, Nic took hold of Kaleb's right foreleg. Teeth tore flesh and muscle.

Vaguely, Kaleb understood that the hawkers were saying, "Fifth blood," but he wasn't sure what the *fourth* had been.

Since he didn't feel it, he assumed that he had drawn blood without noticing.

The warm taste on his tongue seemed to support that theory as well.

He felt Nic's muzzle too close to his stomach and kicked him. The force of the kick sent Nic into the circle, and the jolt of that contact sent a surge through Kaleb too. The protective setting kept opponents from using the circle as a weapon, so both Nic and Kaleb yelped as the current singed their hides.

But it didn't stop them or slow them for long.

Neither cur would forfeit. No one outside the circle would expect it of them, and both fighters knew well that a forfeit in the competition was the same as marking oneself as meat. With stakes this high, curs ended fights in death. The alternative was worse than death. Going from being deadly to being meat wasn't an option. It would mean fighting every day.

*No forfeits.*

Nic was sailing through the air, midjump.

Kaleb kept all four feet spread on the ground and waited. Just as Nic was about to land on him, Kaleb moved. At the same time he snapped at Nic's throat.

Nic dropped to his belly, and all Kaleb got was a mouthful of fur.

As Kaleb turned and lunged to get another bite, Nic's claws ripped into Kaleb's hind leg. Blood poured so freely that Kaleb looked back. Something important had been pierced.

Rather than let the blood leak out, Kaleb stretched his

neck, angled, and bit on the foreleg that was gouging into him. He clamped down over and over and ground his teeth, ripping through the flesh and muscle of Nic's leg until the long, clawed digits were severed.

Nic's growls were thunderous, but he was losing blood fast.

With every bit of strength Kaleb had left, he rolled, pinned Nic, and clamped his jaws on Nic's throat. For a moment, Kaleb hesitated, but it wouldn't do any good for them both to die, and Kaleb was feeling so dizzy that he suspected he'd be out soon if he didn't get aid. He bit down and yanked his teeth away, tearing a hole in Nic's throat and ending the fight.

Then he rolled off of the shuddering, dying body and began to transform again. He was too exhausted and savaged to move very far from the blood-wet ground. His gaze was locked with Nic's as the light went out of the dying cur's still-animal eyes.

When Nic died, Kaleb felt the circle drop. He heard the roar of the audience, but closer, he heard Zevi's voice. "You survived, Kaleb."

*I'm not sure*, he tried, but failed, to say.

Then Zevi hoisted him into the air and carried him away from the carnival.

# CHAPTER 7

THAT EVENING, MALLORY SCANNED through the television channels, realizing as she did so that she'd spent more than half an hour watching a minute of this and a few seconds of that. Her ankle and wrist still ached, and the cuts on her biceps made it look like she'd been attacked by the shrub that had broken her fall when she was out running that morning. She knew from experience that taking a tumble in front of her father always meant that he'd get more overprotective; she couldn't imagine how crazed he'd be if she ever had to face a daimon—not that she felt very confident in her ability to do so when she couldn't avoid a silly little dog.

Her life was lame, truly and completely lame. Because of the way they moved, too many nights were like this. Unlike at the last four schools in the last four towns, she hadn't even made casual friends here.

*Maybe it's just harder in high school.*

She was used to moving, used to picking up midway through classes, and by now, she even relished those first few weeks. Then, people talked to her. They answered questions about homework, maybe even decided she was worth getting to know. That was the routine.

This year, though, she'd gone from new to sick to catching up to getting ready to move again. The bouts of sickness were unpredictable, and her father made her feel better every time it happened. Still, being sick meant big gaps from school sometimes, which added to her inability to make friends. Aside from a few parties she was halfheartedly invited to and her unpredictable encounters with Kaleb, she'd had exactly zero social life.

The time with Kaleb the past month was her greatest joy. Even though going against her father's wishes was high on her list of "things to avoid if at all possible," it was hard to follow good sense where Kaleb was concerned. He made her feel all of those things that she'd thought were missing in her. He was different, and he made her feel different—not that she was about to try to have *that* conversation with her father.

For several years now, Adam had been her only parent, and all things considered, he did a great job at even the things that were supposedly "mothers' tasks": he'd taken her to salons, spent hours shoe shopping, brought her chocolate when she needed it. Admittedly, she'd seen his stash of "being a single dad" books, and she'd had to literally bite her cheek a few times to keep from laughing when his books led to ludicrous parenting moments. His "birds and bees" talk, in particular, made her giggle just thinking about it, and his "chick flick" movie nights when she was due for her period were endearing but absurd. He'd actually gone so far as to try to discuss the comparative hotness of actors he'd apparently researched in entertainment magazines. He was committed to giving her the most normal upbringing he could. Aside from the hours of firearms training and the nonstop lectures on the threats all around them, she could almost believe things were just fine. *Almost.* The disparity between the illusion she wanted and the reality she lived was vast. *Daimons want to kill my father.* That detail was never far from her mind. Unfortunately, lately, neither were thoughts of Kaleb.

She flicked the television off and hobbled to her bedroom to work on packing. Every time she started to get settled, they seemed to be leaving again. She'd been the new girl in class every year. The school where she started the year and the school where she finished the year were rarely ever the same.

While she packed, she whispered a quiet prayer that she'd make friends in Franklin—or maybe even that Kaleb's school was near her new town. That was all sorts of unlikely; she knew it, but she clung to the tendril of hope. She'd wanted some normalcy for years, but Kaleb was the first person she'd liked enough to want to try to find a way to really have in her life.

Sometimes she thought her father saw threats where there

weren't any. She'd never even seen a daimon, but the house was warded, and she was covered in protection spells. Life was a series of flights and thwarted attempts at a real life.

She walked to her father's bedroom and considered searching for the item he'd taken from the daimons. If they gave it back, maybe they could stop running—and she could stay here and go on actual dates with Kaleb. Life would be so much easier . . . except finding it was only part of the problem. If she *could* find the missing item, she wasn't sure what she'd do with it anyhow.

*Where does one find daimons?*

The daimons that kept them ever in flight hadn't appeared in her daily life. No creature with shifting forms had approached her. No doorways to another world had opened in her path. Sometimes, she found it hard to believe that daimons were real, but she'd seen irrefutable proof of witches, and they *all* believed in daimons. More so, they talked about how, for over a century, daimons had massacred witches and their families at any opportunity. No, Adam wasn't delusional. If anything, all evidence indicated that he was in very real danger—and her with him.

She opened the door and glanced inside his room. His bed, dresser, and footlocker were all utilitarian, battered and familiar. A heavy quilt covered his bed, and the footlocker had a bulky padlock on it. She assumed that whatever he had stolen would be in there. *Unless keeping it in a locked box is too obvious.* Her father was practical, and he'd been running from the daimons all her life. He wouldn't hide it in an obvious place. *Would he?*

Despite the temptation to explore, Mallory didn't go into his room, knowing it was as likely to be spelled as not. He wouldn't put a restriction on the room, but he very well might have an alarm on the threshold—or the trunk or the dresser. She shook her head: it was impossible to keep secrets from Adam. If she went rifling through his things, he'd know and be upset.

She closed his door, returned to her room, and resumed packing.

An hour or so later, she heard the front door close.

"Mals?"

She tossed the jeans she'd been folding onto her bed and walked out to greet her father. As always, his attention swept her from head to toe. As a little girl, she'd thought he had special superhero radar vision. Now, she realized he was simply very, very attentive to details. She knew that he didn't miss anything as he examined her: freshly painted bright-red toenails; blue-and-green gecko pajamas that were too loose lately; faded tee stolen from his wash-the-car clothes; earbuds dangling around her neck; and mousy brown hair caught up in a ponytail on top of her head.

"Are you feeling any better?" He studied her. "The ankle? The scratches?"

"All fine." She offered him a reassuring smile. "Mostly just embarrassed."

"Everyone has accidents." He gave her a one-armed hug.

"Sure," she said.

She wanted to reassure him, to promise she could handle any real threats they encountered, but she knew that if he had his way, she'd never encounter any dangers.

"Maybe at the next school you can meet someone to watch shows with or do whatever girl things with." Adam stepped past her and dropped his briefcase on the kitchen table. "There are more witches there, and you'll be safer."

"It's fine." She walked over to the stove, checked that the teakettle still had water, and then turned on the burner.

"It's not fine. I should be home more. We should do more together."

"I'm almost seventeen, not seven." She measured tea into the teapot and resolutely didn't look at him. "Plus, we train. It's not like I don't see you."

Behind her, she heard him rummaging in the fridge. "Once we get settled, maybe we ought to take another father-daughter class."

She turned to face him. Once he had pulled a container of leftover Chinese out of the fridge, she told him, "Maybe what we ought to do is both of us find some people our own age to socialize with. I was thinking that this move might be a good time to start a few new things . . . like dating."

"Like *dating*?" he repeated. Her usually unflappable father stared at her with a look of horror on his face.

"I'll be seventeen tomorrow," she reminded him as she pulled out dishes.

He opened the top of the container and spooned some sesame chicken onto a plate she handed him. "How about this: you can date if you meet someone we both think is worthy of you. You don't want me to be stuck at home all by myself, do you?"

Mallory turned as the teakettle whistled. She'd been his whole life since her mother had left, and she *did* feel guilty at the thought of abandoning him. "Mom's not coming back, is she?"

Her father sighed, but instead of ignoring the question like he typically had when she'd tried to ask about her mother, he said, "She loves you, Mallory, and we both want what's best for you." He paused. "But she doesn't love *me*, and we agreed that it was best for her to leave."

"Best for whom?" Mallory asked.

"You."

Mallory felt tears trickle down her cheeks. It wasn't that her father was saying anything she hadn't suspected, but it hurt to hear him finally admit aloud that her mother was truly gone and that he didn't think she'd come home.

"She could visit me," Mallory suggested softly. "I could visit her. If you knew where she was—"

"No." Adam turned his back. "No more talk of Selah. She's gone, and she has no business in your life."

"She's my mother," Mallory said.

"Which is why she was in your life as long as she was." Adam kept his back to her, so she couldn't see his face. It didn't sound like hurt in his voice. There was a lack of emotion that sounded far too like his sister, Evelyn, like the callousness of most of the witches Mallory had met. Hearing it in her father's voice, especially about her mother, unsettled Mallory.

The silence that filled the kitchen was weighty with things that she didn't quite understand. Had her mother done something awful? He didn't date, so Mallory had thought for years that he must still love her mother, but now, she wasn't sure.

He *could* date. Maybe that would help—and make him more likely to let her date. He was attractive in that old-guy way. He had hair that was dark enough still that she teased him that he secretly got it dyed, no wrinkles that she could see, blue eyes with the sort of thick lashes only seen on cartoon characters and baby dolls, and, despite only minimal exercise and an atrocious diet, a physique that would shame most guys her age. If not for the way he dressed, she suspected that he could pass for an older brother rather than her father. It was the benefit of being a witch: he was almost creepily attractive to human women despite being hundreds of years old.

She, unfortunately, had none of his genes. Her hair was a nonremarkable brown; her eyes were a normal brown; and her calories added up. She wasn't unattractive; she was simply closer to average than to inhumanly striking, smart, and healthy like Adam. If she were more like Adam, she'd have had no trouble getting boys to actually ask her out. If she were a witch, she'd be able to learn spells to protect herself. If she were a witch, so much would be easier. Regrettably, she was just a human.

She sighed as she poured the tea.

"Mals? Is something else wrong?"

"I was just thinking that it's not really fair that I *want* to date, but I look like me when you look like"—she motioned at him—"*that* and don't date. I wish I had your genes . . . well, for a lot of reasons, but sometimes, for utterly shallow reasons too."

He ignored the reference to dating and said only, "I wish you had my genes too." Then he glanced at the clock. "I have an hour free. Cards? Television? Chess?"

Mallory picked up both cups of tea, feeling guilty for hoping that the rest of her life wasn't like this. She loved her father, and she understood that there were dangers in the world, but sometimes she felt like she was smothering under his protections—and every time she tried to argue with him, the will to do so vanished before she could speak more than a word. It sounded ludicrous, but she'd wondered if his being a witch made it impossible to argue with him. Humans found witches attractive. Maybe it made it hard to argue with them too.

Adam walked over to the door, took a handful of the powder he kept there, and spilled it in a line over the doorway as he did every night. Then, he grabbed his plate. "Come on, Mals. I think we have a few episodes of that police show recorded."

# CHAPTER 8

BELIAS CAME INTO CONSCIOUSNESS with a yell that rolled into a name: "Aya!"

"Keep it down," someone muttered.

The unfamiliar voice brought Belias to his feet. Several frightening moments wherein he couldn't see passed, but as he blinked and stayed still, his vision returned. However, what he saw wasn't particularly comforting: a strange woman in a gray suit sat on a chair in front of a table.

Belias felt his flesh where he'd been stabbed with Aya's toxin-laden knives: no injury remained. *Am I dead?* If he was, he had been thoroughly wrong about the afterlife. If not, he wasn't sure where he was. The woman, her clothes, and the room were unlike anything he'd seen in his life.

He stepped toward the woman—and hit an unseen wall.

*Witch.* He looked again at her. *Unmasked witch.* That clearly couldn't be good. No witch walked around unmasked in The City.

She looked only a few years older than him, but witches—like daimons—lived for centuries, so he had no idea how old she truly was. Few witches older than three hundred existed. Most of the older ones had been killed in the wars, but this witch seemed more poised than even the elder ruling-class daimons were.

He watched her as he put both hands up and pushed, but unlike the fight circles, this barrier didn't shock him. It simply wasn't permeable. He paced the perimeter of the circle, running his hands over it, nudging the base of it, and confirming that he was held as securely within it as he was within fight circles.

All the while, the witch continued to work on whatever the papers on her table were. She paid him so little attention that if not for her initial words, he'd wonder if she knew he was there. He felt for the weapons he'd had in the fight, but only found one knife. After ascertaining that he was still armed, he decided to speak. "Witch!"

She glanced up, spearing him with a cold gaze from her blue-and-gold witch's eyes. "Daimon."

Then her gaze returned to the paper in front of her.

Belias had never been ignored. He was a favored son in a ruling-class family, a well-regarded fighter, an experienced bedmate, and, of late, a finalist in Marchosias' Competition.

He frowned, and then said, "I demand my freedom, witch."

"No."

"You cannot—" His words died on his lips as she lifted one hand and waved it in the air.

"I can do whatever I want, Belias." She didn't look up even as she silenced his voice. Her pen continued scratching across the paper for several more moments.

He tried to speak, tried to clear his throat, and finding no sound possible, began running his hands over the barrier again. She had *silenced* him. It was more effective than anything he'd ever encountered in The City, but he didn't need to speak, especially if she wasn't going to listen. He'd tried conversation, but she resorted to her spells rather than act honorably.

It wasn't surprising: witches were lesser beings, capable only of treachery unless they were kept in check. They'd murdered his father and countless other daimons. This one had imprisoned him. If witches tried to live openly in The City, they would be murdered in their sleep—as they should be. It had been that way for centuries. They'd traded in the flesh and blood of daimons to work their spells, had set nature against The City, and until they were all but purged from his world, they'd been a constant threat to order.

After the war, the witches had been given the human world; the daimons kept The City—what little of it they could save from the uncontrollable growth of the Untamed Lands. It was a fair treaty, far more so than the witches deserved. There were little conflicts after the treaty. A few daimons had exposed some witches somewhere called Salem, but daimons had become too complacent. Rumors of daimons summoned and bound as witches' familiars circulated from time to time, and there was talk that other, stronger witches lived in the Untamed Lands, but there was no proof.

*Except here I am, caged and silenced by a witch.*

He'd been taught to always win, to never give in no matter the odds, so he wasn't going to let some witch kill him. He was going to escape, and once he was home, he would use this experience to gain support for his plan to eradicate the remaining witches from The City.

Methodically, he began at the ground and slid his fingers around the edge, seeking a flaw or opening he could use to tear a hole in the circle. As he did so, he let his fingertips become talons. Animal wasn't a form he preferred, but his talons were sharper and more sensitive than fingertips.

He heard a book close with a soft thump, and the witch's footsteps clacked over the stone floor.

At her approach, he stood again. Even if he couldn't get out of the circle, he wasn't going to stay on the floor as if he was her subordinate. When he stood, he saw how very tiny she was: frail bones and no musculature to speak of, yet she had boldness unlike any witch he'd seen in The City.

"I dislike being interrupted when I am working, Belias." She walked around the circle, and he turned as she did so, continuing to face her rather than let her stand behind him. "You're different from the ones I've summoned before."

He opened his mouth to speak, but no sound came out.

She murmured something in the language of witches and motioned to him.

The temptation not to speak at her command vied with the need to know. The desire for knowledge won over pride. "Summoned where?" he asked.

She studied him as objects were studied in the Carnival of Souls, and Belias felt an unfamiliar prickle of fear spread over his skin. His hand went again to the hilt of the knife strapped to his thigh—and he realized that it was Aya's knife, one he'd bought for her.

*Why do I have Aya's knife?*

Nothing made sense.

"Where am I?" he asked.

"You are at the offices of Stoneleigh-Ross, Belias. Specifically, you are in my office, in my summoning circle." The witch looked bemused. "You are also completely and utterly unable to be anywhere else unless I allow it."

Belias hadn't ever heard of Stoneleigh-Ross, but he had heard of summoning circles. Daimons were only able to be summoned if the witch had their full name. "How? Who are you? Why? I don't know what's going on, but I'm not going to stay here as your prisoner. Witches aren't free from judgment. If Marchosias—"

"You aren't within *his* domain," the witch interrupted. "This is *my* domain."

Belias narrowed his gaze. "Who are you? *Where* are we?"

"I'm Evelyn Stoneleigh, and we are in North Carolina."

"Where?"

"The human world, Belias."

Horror filled him. The human world was terrible. Every treatise his father had given him on the place highlighted the perversions and barbaric nature of humanity. The City wasn't perfect, but it had a functional caste system, breeding control, and healthy commerce. Marchosias kept order, and judgments were swift.

The witch walked past him then, leaving him alone in the room, trapped in her summoning circle.

*How did I end up here, in a world where witches hold dangerous amounts of power?*

The last thing he remembered was his former betrothed stabbing him. He'd expected to die, been certain of it, in fact— and he wasn't sure that waking up imprisoned by a witch in the human world was a much better fate.

# CHAPTER 9

KALEB WATCHED THROUGH HOODED eyes as Zevi heated the needle in the candle flame. The amount of blood he'd lost this time was alarming enough that he wasn't sure if this was going to be the end of his fighting or not. A tiny but very real part of him hoped it was. He wanted to rest, even if resting meant slipping into unconsciousness. The other, more insistent part of him could only focus on how few competitors were left. To be so close and *lose* seemed wrong.

"Stay awake." Zevi didn't bother to clean the knife blade—or heat it—before he cut away the remains of Kaleb's torn trousers. He wasn't rough, but he wasn't wasting time on unnecessary steps either.

"Am." Kaleb's eyes fluttered shut again—until Zevi poured a bucket of saltwater over the bloodied gashes in his thigh. The water was clean; Zevi was always prepared with clean water when Kaleb fought. It wasn't freezing, but it stung.

"He tried for an artery. Smart move." The hands on Kaleb's leg were as gentle as possible, but that didn't make them painless. "Keeping the claws in here was wise." Zevi poked around the wound, digging out the claws that had been left behind.

Kaleb blacked out again, but he came to a few moments later when Zevi stabbed the needle into his leg. Thankfully, he'd missed the second dousing with saltwater. Zevi was thorough, and finding foreign objects in the wound always meant saltwater washes. It was wise, but it still hurt like hell.

*Not that stitches are fun.*

The hot metal jabbing into his skin burned, and the feel of thread being forced through the tiny hole in his leg felt alien, but Zevi was good at stitching evenly and quickly. It was a rhythmic pain—piercing, tugging, piercing, tugging, pushing flesh together, piercing, tugging—as the stitches closed the gash.

"He missed the artery."

"Good." Kaleb looked up.

Zevi knelt over Kaleb's bloody, wet leg. He had one knee on either side of Kaleb's leg, and he squeezed tightly. "Not enough," Zevi muttered. "Can you push here?"

"Where?"

Zevi positioned Kaleb's hands on his torn leg. "Like this. Just hold the skin together."

Mutely, Kaleb did as he was told.

"Better." Zevi stabbed the needle into the flesh again and again. He finished sewing the tear closed without another word. When he was done, he left the needle and remaining thread lying on Kaleb's bruised leg.

"Hate this part."

"I know." Zevi's voice held no sympathy, though. Sympathy was reserved for the truly dreadful in his world. This wasn't the worst injury Zevi had tended. It wasn't the worst either of them had recovered from either.

The cave was silent for a moment as Zevi walked to the bucket that hung over the fire. Kaleb turned his head to watch. He'd experimented with the idea that not seeing it coming was better, but for him, at least, the shock was worse.

Methodically Zevi wrapped his hand in a faded but clean cloth; he reached out and gripped one of the handles that stuck out of the bucket and withdrew a knife that had been heating in the saltwater over the fire.

The instinct to run wasn't as easy to ignore as it had been the first time. Then, Kaleb hadn't known how much this part would hurt. Now, he'd had plenty of experience with it; he knew cauterization was worse than stabbing. That first injury happened quickly, and for the first few moments, the shock kept the pain at bay. Sometimes, if Kaleb was fight high, the pain didn't hit him for a few minutes. This pain, however, was on top of the injury; this pain was without the rush of a fight.

Kaleb swallowed. Every muscle tightened in anticipation. Then, Zevi pressed the blade to the skin he'd just stitched.

The sizzle and the stench of burning skin added to the already awful feeling, and Kaleb turned his head to the side and vomited.

HE WASN'T SURE HOW long he'd lain on the floor after Zevi had cauterized the incision. Heat and salt worked on most of the toxins that could be left behind in a fight. The few extra-magical ones that made their way into The City were countered by steel or silver. Kaleb and Zevi had bought or acquired enough blades that had both metals in them that Zevi usually had a reasonably sized blade for most injuries. Occasionally, he'd had to resort to multiple cauterizing blades, but thankfully that was not the norm.

"Drink." Zevi handed him a mug of something.

Kaleb sniffed it.

Zevi snorted. "I'm not going to drug you after I just sewed you up. If I wanted to knock you out, I'd have let you bleed out or skipped burning you."

"Sorry. Reflex." Kaleb propped himself up, lifted the mug to his lips, and drank the contents. It was far from tasty, but whatever noxious plants Zevi had brewed were mixed with halfway-decent whiskey instead of the home brew he usually used. From the taste of it, these were plants not found for sale at the Carnival of Souls—at least not without far more coin than they had. Kaleb had been nursed back to health often enough in his seventeen years that he'd learned which medicines were rarer than others.

Kaleb looked at Zevi as he handed the mug back. "I'd have been dead years ago without you, but that doesn't mean that I want you going into the Untamed Lands without me."

"I thought the whiskey might cover the taste." Zevi shrugged unapologetically.

"It didn't."

Neither of them liked to mention the years Zevi had spent in the Untamed Lands outside The City. Out there, witch magic had made nature grow so rapidly that the pockets of daimons who lived beyond the safety of the overcrowded city were not so far removed from animals. The City might seem barbaric, but there were entertainments, pleasures to be bought and sold, and reasonably safe streets. Admittedly, *safe* was a relative concept, but on the occasions when Kaleb had needed to leave The City briefly with Zevi, he had been disturbed by how primitive life was in the wilds.

"I needed things. You were busy," Zevi pointed out in that absurdly factual way of his.

Kaleb debated starting the old argument about Zevi traveling outside The City, but knew the other part that they didn't discuss: Zevi had lived there for years. *He* was more comfortable there than Kaleb ever could be. He was quick enough to avoid predators, and out there, he could let himself be that quick without attracting attention. The problem was Kaleb's, not Zevi's. His instinct to keep Zevi safe at any cost was the inevitable result of being in charge of their little pack of two. Zevi was his packmate, his responsibility, his only family. That's what pack was, and losing Zevi would destroy Kaleb. None of that was stuff he knew how to say—or even needed to. All he said was, "You could've told me."

"Could've. Didn't. We're both fine, so what's it matter?" Kaleb growled.

"I won't let you down, Kaleb. Not ever." Zevi stood there for an awkward moment. Then he said, "It's not all selfless, you know. I'd be dead if I wasn't under your protection. The City still confuses me sometimes."

Kaleb sighed as he lay back on the floor. "And you'd be less of a target without my being in this competition."

"True." Zevi frowned. "The prize is worth it. You said so. You'll win. Then everything will be better . . . unless you die. Flynn and Aya are both good enough to kill you at your best. Maybe Sol. And right now, even bad fighters could kill you."

The beauty of Zevi's honesty was that there was never any guessing as to his thoughts on anything, but there were times that his bluntness was less than encouraging. His doubts were as freely verbalized as his hopes. Sol was likely to kill Kaleb, especially in the shape Kaleb was in now. Flynn was the fighter likely to win the entire competition. Aya wasn't as good a fighter as Sol or Flynn, but she'd had the strength to stand against the untrained, the strategy to defeat the cagiest of the contestants, and the ruthlessness to resort to means that were as unsportsmanlike as a daimon could get. She had more total kills than anyone left in the running.

*Except me.*

His, however, were mostly from years of fighting and from wearing the black mask. Very few of *those* kills were ones that anyone knew about. There were rumors, murmurs crediting a few particular kills to him. Rumors were useful tools in establishing a reputation. Most of the stories were the ones he'd allowed to leak. His true kill count was known only to him.

Kaleb forced himself to sit upright and offered the only reassurance he could speak with reasonable honesty. "I'm not going to lose to Aya."

"Maybe not in a ring," Zevi muttered as he walked away. He said nothing more as he gathered his needles and knife and dropped them into his postsurgery water basin. He remained silent as he collected the remains of Kaleb's ruined trousers and several bits of cloth that were on the floor beside Kaleb. He dropped them into another, much larger bucket.

Kaleb waited as Zevi paced and put away everything that he could possibly put away. Zevi always liked to keep things orderly, but when he was stressed he was obsessive about tidying up. Right now, he was about as stressed as he got.

"She's not like us," Zevi blurted. His hands moved like a conjurer creating a storm as he ranted. "You only fight or kill for a reason. She doesn't need to, but she does. If you're going to have to fight and kill without contract or competition, we should just go home."

The younger cur ducked his head when he realized what he'd said. It had been seven years since Kaleb had found Zevi in the Untamed Lands and brought him to The City, but that place was still "home" to Zevi. It wasn't, had never been, Kaleb's home. Sometimes, Kaleb thought that what he feared most about the Untamed Lands was that it would take Zevi from him. Before Zevi, he hadn't been afraid of the overgrown wilderness that encroached on The City, but being a cur meant needing to find and form a pack. Kaleb had only ever found one cur who felt like home to him—and in that way that he now knew as uniquely Zevi's, the cur in question understood their bond long before he did. Zevi didn't question what was obvious to him. When Zevi found and tended to the then-wounded Kaleb, he knew that they were to be connected. Kaleb had taken longer to figure it out, but now that he had a pack, the terror of losing Zevi was what woke him at night. Winning the competition meant Kaleb could protect Zevi— and find other curs who fit with their small family.

"It's okay," Kaleb reassured him. "Everything will be okay."

He was too injured to get up and follow Zevi. He waited for several minutes until Zevi paused, and then he said, "Zevi? Be still. Z?"

Zevi looked at him, and Kaleb asked, "What's really wrong?"

"Aside from you're hurt again?"

"Yes," Kaleb said as patiently as he was able.

Zevi came and sat on the ground beside him. "I don't understand her. I don't trust Aya. What if she just kills us?"

Calmly, Kaleb told him, "There's no *reason* for her to kill you."

"There was no reason for her to kill Verie either," Zevi muttered.

And there it was: Verie had been one of Zevi's friends. The truth was that Kaleb wasn't convinced Aya had made the kill. He'd listened to what she had and very carefully had *not* said on Judgment Day. Of course, he also understood that Aya *did* have a reason to attack Zevi. His packmate's injury or death would affect his ability to fight, and Aya was devious enough to know that. She took advantage of opportunities. It was why she was a likely candidate to win—and why he was all but certain that she hadn't actually killed Verie *and* that Verie hadn't illegally aided anyone. Aya was merely taking advantage of the situation. He'd watched her throughout the whole competition. She was practical, but not unnecessarily violent.

She looked like she was everything that Marchosias respected. If she weren't female, Marchosias would have offered her a choice position in the government, but no female had held such positions during Marchosias' reign. Aya would be the first, but only if she won. If she lost, she'd still have a cossetted place in the palace. Marchosias had very clear taste in breeding: admirable traits or good alliances. Aya's family was among the highest in the ruling caste, and she had demonstrated superior skill as a fighter.

Kaleb put a hand on Zevi's forearm. "I have no intention of letting Aya or anyone else stand between me and the future we deserve. I'll take care of us, Z. I promise."

# CHAPTER 10

KALEB HAD WAITED UNTIL Zevi was asleep before leaving their home. He wasn't ready to talk about Mallory. The options weren't vast: either he chose to stand by the contract—accept the payment and kill Mallory when Haage determined it most advantageous—or he violated his contract and went to Marchosias. He wasn't sure if admitting to finding the missing daughter would overcome the fact that he'd *hidden* that information. Marchosias could reward him as easily as condemn him. The dilemma was the one he'd been wrestling with more and more as he got to know Mallory.

He crept through The City, only upright due to willpower and the medicinal skills of his packmate, and went to the gate that he'd paid for not long after the competition began. Before this contract, he'd been to the human world periodically.

Something about them fascinated him. As a child, he'd followed a mark over there, and when the situation got out of hand, he'd been taken into custody and placed with what they called a foster family. Years later, he'd honed the skills he'd learned in those weeks and felt relatively able to blend into the human world. That didn't mean, however, that the twinge of sheer panic ever faded when he crossed through the gate.

A flicker of fear of being trapped again, away from his Zevi, assailed him as he stepped into the other world. If not for the desire to protect his packmate, he would bring Zevi here, but the younger cur already had trouble coping with The City. Kaleb wasn't sure how he'd deal with a third set of rules, so unless it was essential, Kaleb's trips would be solo excursions.

He took a moment to calm his nerves, and then he made his way to Mallory. He'd never been to her home with her knowledge; like any daimon on the run, she hid her den. Still, he knew where it was, had known before he'd ever spoken to her, and it was to that home that he now went. For the first time, he stood on her porch and knocked on a side door to her house. It was shadowed, unlike the front door, which would leave him exposed and standing with his back to the street.

Moments passed before she opened it. He could smell the sharp tang of metal, of *gun*, that he now associated with her. It wasn't a scent that existed in The City; it was of the human world, the world Mallory thought of as hers. In The City, guns were forbidden. Death was to be an act of closeness. That was the law: "If you cannot touch the person you are ending, you can't kill them." Guns made death impersonal.

She opened the door only partway. At first, she simply stared at him, a pistol clutched in the hand she kept out of sight. "*Kaleb?*"

"Hello."

"What are you . . . ? I mean . . . *Hi.*" She paused almost imperceptibly before asking, "How did you know where I live?"

"I was passing by one day, and I saw you going inside, so I took a chance." Kaleb did his best to look harmless. "Are you busy?"

"No, not right now." Mallory ducked her head briefly and whispered something he couldn't hear.

He suspected that she was allowing him entry into her home and wondered briefly if humans had become more aware of magic or if some meddling witch had warded her house. *How much does she know?* He couldn't think of any way to ask her that without alarming her, and he didn't think that tipping her to what he knew was in his best interest. Whether he killed her or delivered her to The City, he'd need to gain her full trust to do it. Asking if her house was warded wouldn't do that.

"Do you want to come in?" she asked aloud.

"I do," Kaleb said.

"We're moving, so there's no furniture, but if you want . . . unless you weren't really staying. I mean . . ." Her words trailed off and her hand went to the stone that hung on a cord around her neck.

He'd seen such amulets in the possession of Watchers.

The stones helped keep a daimon healthier, giving them strength that was stored in the stones. The Watchers' tolerance of witches made them more trusting of stronger spells. The combination of her amulet and the wards made sense; a Watcher must have hidden Mallory and paid for the wardings on her and on the house.

"I'd like to stay." He smiled, but the expression was ruined by a wince of pain as he stepped into the house. He grabbed the kitchen counter. "Sorry."

"Are you okay?" She whispered something hurriedly again and then put her hand on his biceps. "Kaleb?"

They both froze for a moment when she touched him. It wasn't until she retracted her hand that he could say, "I'm fine."

He focused his attention on her, and she looked away—not fast enough that he missed the interest in her eyes. She was so different from the daimons he'd met in The City. They'd made no secret of their interest, but tried to hide fear or worry. Mallory tried to hide her interest, but had no qualms showing that she worried.

A small sound of pain escaped, but he tried to turn it into a laugh before he said, "Just a minor injury. One of my matches went a little wild."

She'd been clear on what she thought when he'd told her previously that he was a fighter, so he wasn't surprised when she said, "Boxing is barbaric."

"I know. Today, I *really* know." He winced at both the pain and the extent of what he'd hidden, what she'd eventually *know* he'd hidden if she was brought to The City instead of killed. It was peculiar to care what she thought, but he did. He didn't want her to know that when he said he boxed, he really meant he fought to the death; or that when he said he was away at school, he meant away in another world. He'd tried to find close approximations of the truth when he told her about himself, but some things had no human equivalent.

"I don't have anywhere for you to sit." She looked around her barren house. "Everything was sent out already. The movers left a few hours ago."

He smiled at the thought of not only bringing her to The City, but of seeing her in *his* home, of having a new home— one furnished to him as winner of Marchosias' Competition.

"What?" She couldn't look away from him, and he heard the flicker of fear in her voice.

"Do you know what would make me feel better, Mallory?" He stepped close enough to her that the edge of his shirt brushed against hers.

Mutely, she shook her head, but she didn't flee.

He leaned down until their lips were nearly touching.

She parted her lips to say something, but he kissed her before she could utter a word. He'd never kissed anyone for reasons other than base need or being hired. None of that prepared him for the way Mallory responded to him—or how he responded to her. His body burned like something had pierced his veins, and it took more effort than he'd ever known not to let their first kiss become the first night with their bodies entangled.

After several wonderful moments, Kaleb pulled back abruptly. They were both breathing heavily, and her eyes were wide with a mix of longing and shock.

She looked as startled as he felt. The difference between them was that he knew what that sensation meant. Mallory was pack, his in a way that only Zevi had ever been. She belonged in his life, in his home, but how could he say that to a daimon who thought she was human? Marchosias was a cur, but a lot of daimons were curs. Kaleb had bedded some, killed others, but he'd only ever felt the fierce need to protect one other cur.

"You're . . . not what I was expecting," he said. Nothing he'd ever experienced came near the wash of heat that felt like it would burn them both alive.

She started trembling.

He stared at her, trying to find words to explain, to help them both understand, but there were none that he could share without telling her what he was and what she was. He wasn't sure either of them was ready for that. He slid his hands up and down her arms to quell her chills and to have an excuse to keep touching her. "I'm sorry."

"For kissing me?" she asked.

"No," Kaleb said quietly. "I'm sorry I didn't do that the moment I met you."

Mallory took several steps backward, out of his reach. "I don't understand, but I think that maybe you should . . ."

"Kiss you again?" Kaleb walked toward her, and she

continued to back up so that she stayed just out of reach.

She trembled violently, and he wondered if the spells that were wrapped on her were being loosened by their kisses. He wasn't having *that* reaction. He wanted to pull her to him and calm her, but she was wide-eyed with fear. That he did recognize. The first time he'd felt the pack connection, he rebelled. Then, he'd been unprepared for the urgent need to be near anyone, to protect them at any cost.

He watched Mallory force herself to try to be calm. Tentatively, she laughed and said, "That seemed w—"

"Perfect," he interrupted.

She smiled. "I was going to say weird."

"*Perfect*," he repeated.

He reached out toward her, and this time, she stepped closer again. He knew how she was feeling, and even if he couldn't explain it all, he did know how to help. He remembered it, that feeling like discovering a wound inside that he hadn't even known existed. The only way to ease the pain inside was to be closer to pack.

"I should have kissed you sooner, Mallory." Kaleb put his hands on her shoulders, slid them down her arms, and then settled them on her hips. "So many answers are clear now."

"Answers to what?" She breathed more than spoke the question.

"I'll go wherever you go," he promised.

"Because of one kiss?" she asked.

"Yes," he said. "And because of what that kiss means. We

belong together. You know it. Somewhere inside, you know it. Even though the words sound crazy, you know they're true."

She didn't reply, but she melted into his embrace. It was an answer without words, but he needed the words. They were *pack*. She was meant to be in his life, and now that he knew it, there was nothing he wouldn't do for her. It was different, not more, but unique from the bond he shared with Zevi, and he wondered briefly if every packmate would feel different to him.

"MALLORY?" KALEB PROMPTED.

She looked into his eyes, wishing she could tell him something, anything, that would make this be something more than one fabulous—but fleeting—surprise. She couldn't. Any words she had were ones she couldn't speak. *My father is a witch. Daimons are real. I can't be with a normal boy because it's too dangerous for both of us.* She couldn't admit those sorts of secrets—even to someone who made her feel like her blood had just become liquid fire. All she knew was that the thought of him leaving her life made her feel panic. *It was just a kiss,* she told herself. But the way he looked at her made her believe that it was more than that—for both of them.

"Kiss me again," she said.

He didn't build from tentative to feverish; he started with the sort of kiss that asked questions she didn't know how to answer, the sort of kiss that reminded her how little she knew about him and quickly made her forget everything she knew about caution. If the boys she'd kissed before had been like him, she wouldn't still be a virgin, but no one else had made her feel like she could be happy spending the rest of eternity kissing. It was perfect.

It was also exceedingly stupid. They barely knew each other, and no amount of physical connection would bridge the gulf of secrets that she had to keep between them.

She pulled away and put a hand on his chest to keep him at a distance. *What do I really know about him?* They'd run into each other a number of times over the past month, when he'd said he was home from school, but a few casual conversations and a soul-searing kiss or two weren't reason enough to ignore all common sense. Hours of defense training had made her feel confident that she could handle anything boys tried, but in all of what she'd learned, there weren't any lessons on how to avoid feeling like a skeeze because you reacted to a boy's kisses like a cat discovering catnip.

"I think you need to go," she said as steadily as she was able.

"I will go wherever you tell me. I want to see you again. I *need* to see you." There was something desperate in his eyes and in his voice, and she wondered if it was the same urgency she felt.

Kaleb lifted his hand and caressed her cheek. "Please?"

"I'm moving *tonight*," she said.

"I'll come to you anywhere," he promised.

"You hardly even know me."

"I *want* to know you though. Are you going to punish me

for just now finding you?" he asked.

"No, but . . ." She vacillated between wanting to believe him and doubting every word.

"Do you kiss everyone that way? Or did that feel like . . . magic? Like something unusual? If it didn't, tell me to go, but if it did"—he shook his head and stared straight into her eyes—"admit that. I swear to you, Mallory, I've *never* felt like that because of a kiss."

She looked directly at him, refusing to be embarrassed. "It was perfect, but one kiss doesn't mean—"

"It could." His hand slid up her back, and she closed her eyes as he whispered, "Tell me I can visit you. Please?"

"I'm not sure that's a good idea," she hedged. She couldn't think of anyone she'd ever felt so at ease around, anyone she instinctively wanted to trust, and she certainly hadn't ever wanted anyone as much.

"Why?" He watched her, waiting for her answer, and she had to restrain herself from kissing him again.

She couldn't answer.

He didn't move. He simply asked, "Tell me where you're going. Please?"

"What if it's too far?"

Kaleb laughed softly. "Nowhere is too far."

She clenched her hands, trying not to touch him. Now that they'd kissed, it seemed so easy, so natural, to pull him back to her.

*He wouldn't object.*

Her mouth felt dry, and she took another steadying breath. She reached up to touch the skin where her pendant rested under her shirt. It was a silly habit from childhood that she'd never quite surrendered. The stone pendant was from her mother's family, and her mother had made her promise repeatedly to never let it out of her reach. Mallory wrapped her hand around it for comfort.

All the while, Kaleb stayed completely still, watching her, waiting for her.

Mallory felt half dazed as she walked away to grab a piece of paper and a pen. She wrote down her new address and then, while she was at it, she added her cell number. "You can call me too," she said in an almost-calm voice. "If you want to talk or whatever."

"I do." He took the paper, read it, and then tucked it into his pocket. "I'll call you as soon as I'm able. I can't call when I'm away, but when I get back here . . . I'll call."

"You aren't allowed to make calls from school? I get not being able to make calls in class, but you should be able to call in the dorms or the grounds or whatever." She looked at him with renewed suspicion. "What do they do? Take your cell phones?"

"I don't have a cell phone, but I can get one if you want me to." He took her back into his arms. "I'm yours to command, Mallory."

She started to laugh, but stopped when she saw that he wasn't smiling. He stared at her with the sort of intensity that briefly made her want to flee, and then made her want to grab hold of him and never let go.

He stared into her eyes and promised, "I'm *yours*, Mallory."

He didn't add that she was *his*, but she heard it all the same—and believed it.

# CHAPTER 11

WHEN AYA ARRIVED AT the carnival, she took a moment's pleasure in the crush of bodies and chaos of sound. Ruling-caste girls weren't to be at the Carnival of Souls unaccompanied, but because of Marchosias' Competition, no one tried to enforce that rule with her. Belias would've, but he was gone. A wave of grief swept through her at that thought. *It's for the best.* She hadn't asked to be in this situation, but she was determined enough that she would force herself to do what she must.

"Witch teeth!" a hawker called out as she passed.

"Grave dirt," another beckoned.

"I know what you are," a crow-eyed Watcher murmured into her ear, only to vanish before Aya could catch her.

A prickle of fear made Aya scan the crowd. *She doesn't mean* that. *I have been careful.* No doubt the woman was accusing Aya of caste failure, abhorrent behavior, or any number of missteps. Still, Aya's gaze darted over the masked and unmasked, seeking but not finding the Watcher. All that she found was the normal carnival fare.

Vendors were selling the absurd, the unbelievable, and the mundane. A buyer could purchase vats of herbs, freshly butchered animals, and delicate shrouds within a few steps. Children of the established families were kept in sight by their minders. Pickpockets twisted through the crowds, risking broken hands or worse if they were caught. Scarlet-masked escorts lounged in opulent stalls catering to any and all tastes, and mind-altering medicinals were hawked by loud voices. A Spousal Emancipation, Exchange, and Dissolution Agency was advertised only by the suit-clad greeter in front of the shuttered booth. All around the carnival, transactions of varying degrees of legality and ethical questionability were happening. The City wasn't a world that seemed beautiful to everyone, and Aya was able to admit to herself that it had flaws. It was *her* world though. She felt the peculiar hum of it inside her skin. She wanted to rule in it, to make it better, and then to keep it flourishing.

Without the land the witches had destroyed by creating the feral fecundity of the Untamed Lands, the castes struggled to coexist in an ever-shrinking city. The middle and lowest castes grew resentful of the same restrictions and sharp caste lines the ruling caste embraced. Consequently, Marchosias' Competition was all the more important to them. For many daimons, it was the one chance to change the future, to survive when logic made clear they should've died by now—just as it was for her.

With that morose thought, Aya found a bench at the edge of the carnival and pretended to wait calmly for reports of Nic and Kaleb's fight. Neither cur was the high-money bet to win, but curs were so unpredictable that she wasn't looking forward to facing either of them. The upside was that they had both thinned the field considerably.

*As Bel had.*

No amount of training would replace the discipline of growing up as a cur. Kaleb and Nic had both had to fight to preserve whatever dignity they could.

"Nic is dead," one of her informers said as he plopped down on the bench.

She looked at the boy. Like Kaleb had once been, he was a street scab. His hair was matted, and old scars ran down his neck and arm from what appeared to have been boiling liquid thrown on him at some point. The rough, scar-thick skin made him stand out, but for jobs that weren't secret, he was still of use.

"And Kaleb?" She held a coin in her still-closed hand.

"Ripped open high enough up that he won't be using his assets anytime soon." The boy shuddered, but even as he did so, he was on to the practical matters: he stretched out his open hand. "Might be fatal. Might not. I can find out for extra."

"Not *much* more, but a little extra something if you find

out first." Aya released the coin, and before it hit the scab's open palm, he'd plucked it out of the air and secreted it away.

"Don't cross his threshold," she warned before the scab left.

Kaleb's sole packmate, Zevi, wasn't vicious as a rule, but she'd seen him leap to Kaleb's defense against attackers far too big to cross overtly. If Kaleb was seriously injured, Zevi would be even more rabid in his already heightened protectiveness.

A moment after the scab nodded and vanished into the throng, Marchosias swept through the market with the grace of a wolf prowling his territory. The thrill of seeing him out in public rippled over the crowd—at least those parts of the crowd who weren't slipping away to avoid his notice. Marchosias didn't have to offer coin for what he wanted. He was their lord and master, their judge and jury, their terror or bliss, their savior or destroyer. Whatever he wanted was his.

Aya slipped to the side, watching him. It wasn't a matter of avoiding his attention: she'd killed so many fighters that he'd known who she was for months. That didn't mean that she wanted him looking at her as if she wore a red mask.

Another of the street scabs appeared at her side. "Kaleb's not dead, probably won't die from this, but he's not going to be in any shape to fight next week."

A scuffle across the street heralded the beginning of one of Marchosias' announcements. He stood atop a small riser and surveyed the crowd growing around him. He saw her, and he beckoned her to him.

Silently, Aya handed the necessary coin to the scab,

and with her head held high, she strolled toward the crowd watching Marchosias.

"We are nearing the end of the contest," Marchosias began. "I am honored by the ferocity of my people." The crowd cheered. "This competition has been a beautiful, bloody addition to the Carnival of Souls." The din of cheering rose higher. Even those who didn't enjoy the savagery of the competition knew to cheer whatever Marchosias declared to be good.

"Upon meditation, I have decided to add an incentive to the final rounds." Marchosias' gaze fastened on Aya.

He was a good ruler, a daimon worthy of her loyalty, but she felt a creeping sense of dread as he watched her approach.

"The winner of the competition will be awarded the right to join my family's line to theirs," he announced. "My daughter is alive, and she will be returned to The City by her eighteenth birthday."

The cheers grew near deafening.

Marchosias let them continue as Aya waded through the crowd. When she was standing in front of him, he held up a hand for silence.

Dread evolved into terror when he announced, "Not all of the contestants are male, though, so to keep it fair, I have decided that if Aya wins, she will bear my next child."

The crowd cheered again, and she wasn't sure if it was because Marchosias was putting her back into what many considered a woman's rightful place or because he was looking out at them expecting them to cheer. Perhaps, it was both.

Aya, however, could not have been more devastated. The very thing she'd fought to avoid was suddenly the *prize*. She tried to keep her emotions from her expression, but apparently failed—or perhaps it was simply her silence that revealed her lack of enthusiasm.

"Are you not honored, girl?" Marchosias prompted.

She ignored the crowd behind her. "I am honored by your notice, Marchosias, but if I win, I won't have time to bear a child."

As he stepped down from the riser, Marchosias smiled like the wolf he resembled in his other form. "Do you expect to win?"

"Every fighter does," she hedged.

The assessing glint in his eyes didn't dim. "The prize for winning is to join lines with mine. As with any of those I've taken to mate, if you bear my son, you will be my next wife."

Aya ignored the question of marriage, and instead focused on the larger issue. "If any of the other fighters win, they will have your missing daughter. *She* will raise the child, so they do not have to stay in chambers with a child. For them, it is doubly a prize."

He smiled again, and it took more effort not to flinch than it ever did in fights. "Be careful, Aya. It sounds as if I am not a prize."

She bowed. "For a daimon who wants to bear a child, you are the best of rewards, but I do not intend to bear a child, my lord. I would rather die in the fights."

He put his hand flat on her abdomen. "We all have a duty to The City."

When he turned away, Aya fled. There were fates worse than being a breeder, but she wasn't sure there were any fates that would be worse for *her*. Witches' magic, spells she couldn't overcome, meant that marriage or a breeding ceremony would make any female fertile. She would be unable to stay childless if she went through the ceremony, and a child would reveal the secret that would result in her inevitable death or enslavement.

# CHAPTER 12

AFTER KALEB HAD DISCOVERED that Mallory felt like pack, that she felt like she was *his*, he knew he had to try to talk to Haage. Crossing Haage was the sort of action that ended a black-mask's career. Most often, the only reason to cancel a contract was the assassin's death. To add pressure to an already explosive problem, Kaleb wasn't at the carnival for but a few minutes before he heard about Marchosias' pronouncement. If Mallory had been found by someone who reported to their ruler, Kaleb's time was even more limited. Unless he could get to Mallory before she was brought to The City, he risked crossing *both* Haage and Marchosias. Even if he could reach her first, he'd have to confess what he was. Every direction he could turn felt deadly.

He mulled solutions as he walked from assassin stall to

assassin stall. There were kinder words etched on the stalls, but they were what they were. Calling them "conflict resolution consultants" didn't change the nature of the service they provided. Murder for hire was a thriving business—one that had provided steady work for him for several years.

At the third stall, Kaleb found Haage. The older daimon was easier to locate than most assassins: he never wore a mask. With Haage, his career was a sign of pride. His ability to do his work without needing a mask spoke of skill and brutality, both prized traits in The City.

The two daimons with him, however, were masked from brow to chin. Vibrant blue masks protected the customers' identities as they solicited murder; despite that, they still stepped farther into the shadows when Kaleb approached.

Haage turned his back on them with the confidence of someone who knew he was terrifying. His meaty arms and bare chest were covered with so many scars that the flesh was raised in intricate textures in more than a few places. He wore those scars with the pride that came from killing nearly every daimon he'd fought. The one notable exception was Marchosias. Years ago, long before Kaleb had been born, there was even less chance of caste movement. Marchosias and Haage had led the daimons who'd routed the witches from The City, and then Marchosias had led his troops to the palace and made himself ruler. Haage had thought his brother would reward him— and he had, making Haage head of the militia, a role Haage had subsequently lost by trying to repeat his brother's action and declare *himself* ruler. It had been treason, selfish power-grubbing of the sort that should have resulted in Haage's death. Instead, Marchosias had laughed and offered forgiveness.

"I wondered where you'd been," Haage said by way of greeting.

"Around."

"You're a credit to our kind in the matches," Haage allowed. "The last cur to nearly win was corrupted by my brother."

The compliment would've thrilled him a month ago. Today, it meant nothing. Mallory was the future.

"I can't kill her," Kaleb began. He didn't get any further before Haage's fist smashed into his mouth.

Haage grabbed Kaleb's shirt, holding him upright and shaking him. "You seem to forget what you were sent to do."

"I didn't forget." Kaleb spat the blood from his mouth. "You said find her. I did. You said watch her. I am."

Haage dropped Kaleb. "And when I say kill her, you will."

"Marchosias has found her though." Kaleb stayed on the ground. "And I'm not exactly anonymous these days."

"She's old enough to breed. That means he'll have two possibilities for an heir." Haage scowled.

A witch-wrought spell meant that some ruling-caste daimons were able to have only one living child every eighteen years, so unless the child died, no more children could be born until that child reached majority. This meant that some children were left to die—or were simply killed—to allow for a new child to be born. For years, the common knowledge in

The City was that Marchosias' daughter had died. When no new heir was born, Haage had begun to suspect that the child, a daughter, lived, but he had wanted her to live so that no new heir would be born. "Better a girl child than a useful heir," Haage had pointed out. Unfortunately for Mallory, she would reach majority in the next year. That would mean that not only could Marchosias father a new child, but he could also allow his daughter to be bred by a daimon he found worthy.

Kaleb didn't bother getting up. "She doesn't know what she is, and none of your other black-masks know where she is."

Haage said nothing for several minutes. His gaze traveled slowly across the stall. The few remaining occupants walked toward the exits. In moments, the slap of one of the heavy cloth doors signaled the departure of the last of the customers and killers. Daimons who dealt in the business of death were more discreet than a lot of The City's residents, but they were also cautious. Discretion and caution helped increase survival odds.

Haage stared down at Kaleb. A grimace came over his jowly face, and he made a noise that sounded like a cross between a grunt and a snort. "You accepted the job. Word everywhere is that you're too proud to take easy jobs, but you're a good spy and a better killer. I picked you. Are you breaking the contract?"

"I *did* the job. I found her." Kaleb came to his feet slowly. The injuries from his fight were aggravated by Haage's rough treatment, and the pain in Kaleb's leg throbbed like an extra heartbeat. Even at his best, he didn't know if he could take Haage, and he was definitely not at his best.

Haage folded his massive arms over his heavily scarred chest. "And you knew that the contract would include eliminating her when she reached her majority or if he got close to retrieving her. The rules of the competition changed. That means he knows where she is and that she needs to die. It's not complicated; now, is it?"

Kaleb bowed his head briefly, offering the submission that Haage sought. "I suppose not. You'll need to pay more if I'm to be killing her. . . . Unless you have someone else who can find and kill her?"

Haage shook his head, but he was grinning. "Now, *that's* the cur I hired."

# CHAPTER 13

ADAM TRAVERSED THE TOWN of Franklin with the same caution he'd once learned as a child in The City. The human world was a lot different from the world where he'd been born and spent his formative years. The primary similarity was that both when they lived there and when they'd fled here, he'd known to obey his sister if he wanted to survive. She was a stickler about caution.

That obsession with caution was nowhere as obvious as it was at the main office. If Mallory were a witch, these were the places that would be safest for her. Since she was a daimon, taking her there was dangerous. The tears in her wards from encounters with daimons he could repair—and he had, every time she'd fought daimons—but if she entered any of the offices, the tears would be too extreme to patch. All of the spells he'd woven onto her aura would be stripped away and the daimon nature he'd worked so hard to hide all of these years would become manifest. At best, Mallory would discover what she was *and* be exposed to the daimons tracking her. At worst, she'd be dead from the witches' protection spells and wards.

To him, however, the barriers outside the building were not prohibitive. The air felt weighty as he walked, as if he were wading through water, but it didn't stop him. If Evelyn wanted to stop him, she could. That thick air could become solid, if necessary, but he was there with her permission, so the barrier was nothing more than a reminder that he was entering one of the most protected areas in this world.

Adam opened the door, registering the gentle shock as the spell identified him. Once inside, there were witches aplenty who could deal with any intruder, but it was unlikely that a daimon would be able to get this far, and any human carrying weapons would be detected and stopped at the door.

The pretty young witch at the reception desk smiled at him as he handed over his company ID card. She scanned it, nodded, and handed it back. "She's in her workroom, ninth floor, third door on the left. Let me know if you need anyone to show you around the offices *or* the town."

"No, but thank you." He smiled politely. He'd been flattered by the openly inviting offers of witches when he was younger, but he was a father and by law still married to Selah. He hadn't violated that vow ever. To do so would put the validity of his marriage in question—which would then put his paternal claims to Mallory in question. If Mallory's biological father, or even Selah's sisters, thought they had grounds to contest his paternal rights, they'd do so in an instant. They didn't, but there were still daimons who tried to snatch her away, either to curry favor with their ruler or for whatever other political reasons they had. Those threats he handled. Mallory's birth family was another matter. Marchosias was inflexible in his adherence to the law, so much so that he still used magic in The City to bind contracts. So, unless she was married, Mallory was Adam's daughter until she was eighteen. That would change if Adam broke his vows to Selah. No witch, or human, was worth endangering Mallory.

Adam walked up the staircase, nodding at those who greeted him. The precautions employed inside were less obvious than those he'd had to get through to enter the building, but he knew that there were spells that could be triggered by the receptionist or by whatever security guard watched from the observation room hidden somewhere in every Stoneleigh-Ross building. The biggest threat in the building, however, was the witch whose attention he now sought.

He made his way to the ninth floor. Only one witch had offices there. Her work space, office, summoning room, and conference rooms were all on this floor. In his prior visits to Franklin, he'd seen a variety of rooms on her floor, but he still had no idea what all secrets she kept hidden here. He was, however, more than a little certain that there was a gateway to The City. He would call her foolish for having such a door on the one level where no one else could go without her explicit consent, but he'd learned decades ago that calling Evelyn foolish was dangerous.

He knocked at the thick steel door at the top of the stairs and waited for her to lower the barrier. She knew he was there, had known when he crossed the first line of defense at Stoneleigh-Ross, but Evelyn demanded adherence to protocol. She considered it another sort of ritual, and even though they had a unique relationship, it didn't exempt him from the rules.

After a few moments, the steel door swung open, and he walked down the wood-and-stone hall. He stopped outside the third door and asked, "May I enter?"

"You may." Her voice was as crisp as everything about her. No one had ever accused Evelyn Stoneleigh of being particularly approachable. Like most witches, she looked significantly younger than she was; she also looked far less deadly. Of the hundreds of witches in Stoneleigh-Ross' divisions, Evelyn had become the second most powerful— and the most feared. When they first fled to this world, the company had been Ross' creation. He was the only of the truly old witches to have survived the war, and upon their exile to the human world, he'd immediately begun consolidating their power base under his guidance. Evelyn had stayed loyal and steadily climbed the ranks. Her success in the hybridization program not quite two decades ago had been the final step in ascending to a position of power equal only to that of Ross himself. She wasn't exactly heartless, but she was practical enough, cruel enough, and thorough enough that she did a great mimicry of it. Adam knew better than most how far she'd gone to achieve the status she held and how it had hurt her.

She stood now within a salt-and-blood circle that enclosed a worktable with herbs steeping in vessels on three separate burners. She held a carved bowl in which she was grinding a fourth substance.

"I assume you're settled," she said without looking away from the bowl in her hand.

"I am."

"You know the truth will be better coming from you than him," she reminded him. "Tell her what she is. Tell her what she is meant to do. Stop patching her memory."

Adam ignored her comment.

She took two small vials of blood and tapped them into the ground powder in the bowl. Her attention was on the contents of her potion, but Adam knew that she was still acutely aware of where he was, as well as any number of other details that were fed to her silently from various sources in the building.

The blood circle shimmered as she spoke over the contents in her bowl. The salt crystals absorbed the blood even as the three simmering liquids all began steaming simultaneously. Evelyn didn't glance his way as she reached into two of the jars. Flames licked up her wrists, and pain flashed on her face.

Silently she drew her hands out and added the contents to the bowl where she'd already added the blood. The fire peeled from her flesh, leaving her skin unmarked. Then, with both hands, she lifted the bowl and poured the entire mixture into the third, still-steaming, vessel. As she did so, the fire retracted into the mixture, held there by her will and magic.

"Sacrificial magic, Evelyn?"

She smiled tightly as she lifted her gaze from the now-mixed potion. "A necessary evil sometimes, Adam, or have you stopped using it?"

"No, but I didn't think you were still practicing it. Don't your lackeys work the spells that require pain?" Adam wouldn't accuse her of weakness, but he wouldn't expect her to take pain if she didn't need to do so. That was the privilege of leadership: there were others who could do the unpleasant things.

"Some things are too important to trust to anyone else," she murmured. Absently she tucked her hair behind her ears, even though it was already tightly tied back in a twist. As a boy, he'd fallen asleep clutching that hair like it was a security blanket. Then, he'd been a child plagued by nightmares of the deaths he'd seen, and she'd been the one who sat beside him in the dark while he wept. Until Mallory, Evelyn had been his entire family; until Mallory, he'd loved Evelyn with a devotion that bordered on zealotry. Now that he had a daughter who could be hurt by Evelyn's desire for vengeance, he and Evelyn had a distance between them that often felt insurmountable. That didn't mean that he missed her any less.

As Evelyn crossed the circle, another wash of pain made her hesitate. The salt flashed crimson as new blood was added to it. No mark was visible on her skin, but both the pain and the blood had been drawn from her flesh.

Adam stepped up to the edge of the circle and wrapped an arm around her waist. Before she could object to his support, he told her, "No one will see."

"You forget yourself, little brother," she chided, but she leaned on him all the same.

"I do," he agreed. "I'm sure you can lecture me on it later. It wouldn't do to admit to needing help for even a moment, not the indefatigable Evelyn Stoneleigh, conqueror of worlds and executive extraordinaire."

"You're a nuisance."

Adam laughed, and then he led her to the door. "Shall we catch up a little while that cooks?" he suggested.

"I already know everything you'll tell me," she reminded him, not unkindly.

"Let's pretend you don't spy on me." Adam reached out to open the door, but she had already opened it with a quietly whispered word. He frowned at her stubbornness, but didn't bother commenting.

"She's seventeen," Evelyn said, beginning the discussion they both knew he'd come here to have. "It's time for her to be put to use."

"I can't send her back. I know we agreed, but . . . she's my daughter now. That world isn't any place for her." Adam accompanied Evelyn down the hall and stopped at the double doors that had swung open as they'd approached.

"Do you think they won't come in force next year?"

"I *know* they will." Adam had spent the last several years trying to think of a way to keep Mallory safe. Until she was eighteen, she was his child by law, but too soon she'd be an adult by both daimon and witches' law. He'd been preparing her as best he could, teaching her how to fight and use weapons, knowing that if he found no other solution, those skills would become essential. He hoped that she'd stay with him, continue to run, but once she discovered that he'd adjusted her memory, spelled her to hide her nature, and prevented her from disobeying or questioning him, he suspected she wouldn't want anything to do with him until her temper cooled.

And even if she did keep running, she wouldn't be able to escape the throngs of daimons who would come for her once she was of age. Their greatest defense to date had been that no one had the right to take her from him. If Marchosias stole Mallory away before she was an adult, it would give Evelyn justification to attack him. Unfortunately, dangling Mallory as bait to get that justification was not outside the realm of possibility with Evelyn.

"So you're desperate enough now to bring her near me?" Evelyn asked as they settled on the stiff chairs in her meeting room.

"It's a calculated risk—she will be vulnerable in a year unless you help me. I have to believe that you won't alienate me to gain one year's time."

Evelyn smiled, neither confirming nor denying his theory, and Adam wasn't sure if he was relieved or disappointed that there were no illusions between them. He liked to believe that he could ask her directly if she meant to cause harm to them, but he knew her well enough to know that her answer would be fluid. There was no person or ideal that she'd put before her vendetta.

"If you want my help, you have only to ask," Evelyn said.

"What I want is for my daughter never to know Marchosias exists, never to know what she is, never to go to The City. . . ."

Evelyn laughed. "I work spells, Adam, not miracles."

"I want her to access her daimon side completely without her realizing what she is," he said. "Let her think it's witch heritage that she's just developing. We can pretend her mother was one of us . . . or even that her unknown father is."

"That's not easy," Evelyn began.

"I don't have any other ideas left. She has strengths she can't use without tearing away the spells that hide her nature, and I know there was a daimon who crossed the barrier of the last house—one she didn't fight." He hadn't mentioned it to Mallory since they were leaving anyhow, but the terror he'd felt that night reaffirmed his belief that going to Evelyn was the right choice—the *only* choice, really.

Evelyn Stoneleigh might claim she was unable to work miracles, but aside from Ross himself, Evelyn was the closest thing there was to a miracle worker in the two worlds. Unfortunately, she was also aware of her worth, and his being family didn't negate that knowledge.

"I could give her what she needs to face him," she admitted, "if you meet my terms."

"Name your price."

"Vow that you'll obey when I demand it of you," she said.

Adam paused. "On the condition that it doesn't injure, entrap, or kill Mallory, I will."

Evelyn withdrew a short silver knife and held it out. He knew his sister loved him, but she'd loved their parents and brother too. She was old enough that she remembered them in a way he couldn't. Their deaths fueled a hatred of daimons that he'd surrendered years ago.

*Because of Mallory.*

As he accepted the blade, he looked at the only person he loved aside from his daughter. He cut his palm crosswise, and then he held both the blade and his bleeding hand out to her and promised, "You have my vow."

# CHAPTER 14

WHEN KALEB SHOWED UP outside the coffee shop in the late afternoon two days after Mallory had arrived in Franklin, she wasn't sure what to think. He hadn't called; instead, he was just suddenly there beside her. *Just like every other time we ran into each other.* He knew her weakness for overpriced, oversweetened coffees, though, so it was a logical place to look for her—which made her realize that all of their other surprise encounters might not have been as much of a surprise to him as they had been to her. But then he kissed her, and she couldn't think about anything.

When he pulled away, he whispered, "I thought about this, about you."

She couldn't stop the smile that she was pretty sure made her look like a complete fool.

"I thought about you too," she admitted. She didn't, however, tell him exactly how much she'd thought about him—or that she'd had a dream about him that was, by far, the most detailed dream she'd ever had about a boy. She wasn't embarrassed by it, but that didn't mean he needed to know how much he was in her thoughts.

He put his arm around her shoulders, holding her closely to his side. "I could only get away for a couple hours, but I needed to see you."

All she could do was nod. When she'd thought about him, *need* was a pretty accurate term. It was strange to have an almost physical ache to see someone, but she didn't feel ready to divulge that detail. She wasn't sure she was ready to admit anything. For now, she simply enjoyed the feel of his arm around her.

"If you're free, we could eat." Kaleb pointed at a café across the street. "What do you think?"

Like innumerable little restaurants in the countless towns where she'd lived, it was a perfectly serviceable place. Tables and chairs were crammed into a space slightly smaller than they needed. People were laughing and talking; waitresses slipped through narrow spaces carrying overflowing trays. The tables were taken up by couples and groups of people her age— none of whom she knew—but she was there with Kaleb, and that changed everything for her. Maybe it was silly, but having him by her side made her feel braver.

Over the next couple hours, he asked her about everything

from her ideal home to her favorite memories. She told a mix of truth and omissions as he watched her like she was far prettier than she was.

Eventually he pulled some cash out of his pocket, counted it painstakingly, and left it and the bill on the table. "I'm glad you weren't dating someone already."

"My father hasn't been very in favor of my dating. He's . . . protective."

"He should be," Kaleb said.

Mallory smiled at him, but didn't reply. She wasn't entirely sure how to tell her father about Kaleb, but she knew she had to introduce them. She couldn't keep secrets from Adam. *Could I, if it meant seeing Kaleb?* She pushed that thought away. Adam was a perfect father; he'd understand once he met Kaleb. *He has to.* She was suddenly sure she shouldn't keep Kaleb a secret a day longer—so much so that she almost called her father.

Kaleb stood and pulled out her chair. "Are you still with me?"

"Just thinking." She smiled at him, and he put his arm around her.

She was grateful that he didn't press the matter. He never did when she dodged questions—which meant that she didn't feel as on edge with him as she did with a lot of people. It wasn't that she lived some great big exciting life; she was simply aware that there were daimons and witches in the world and that there was another world filled with daimons. Those weren't exactly truths she could share openly.

They left the din of the restaurant, and Kaleb directed her toward the side of the building where the shadows were thicker. It was as close to an alley as one could find in Franklin, dark but relatively clean. Kaleb kissed her with the same intensity as he had in her kitchen. For a few minutes, Mallory let herself enjoy it, but when his fingers skimmed her waistband, she forced herself to pull back. Considering the way he was acting, she wasn't entirely convinced that Kaleb had limits on what was acceptable in public. There weren't any people around just then, but anyone could step into the alley. More importantly, if his hands wandered much farther, he would discover the guns she wore secreted on her body.

She put her hand on his chest and pushed gently. "We're in the middle of the street."

"Not really." He leaned in again.

"No," she said firmly. She would've said more, but her attention was caught by a woman who stood deeper in the shadows, staring intently at them. At first, Mallory thought she was just nosy, but then the woman opened her mouth, stretching pink-pale lips to reveal something feathered. It leaped from her tongue and took flight, expanding in size as it went.

*She just exhaled a bird.*

The sight of it tickled some niggling memory Mallory couldn't reach, but the more immediate issue was Kaleb's safety. Mallory tried to shove him behind her. Simultaneously, she reached for the tiny derringer in her coat pocket.

Three times the woman opened her mouth as if words were imminent. Three times a raven flew from between her lips.

Mallory looked away from the woman for a moment and realized that Kaleb was about to see a part of her life that she'd really rather he didn't.

"Go on," she said. With one hand, Mallory shoved him toward the street. Then, she walked into the alley. *A derringer isn't much of a defense.* Her other hand went to the holstered gun she had only moments before been hoping to hide from him.

Kaleb grabbed her shoulder. Mallory froze, her .357 half drawn.

"I'll handle this. Go," he ordered.

But the bird-breathing woman was in front of them now. She was familiar in a way that made Mallory struggle to identify, like a word on the tip of her tongue, an answer just out of reach. Her eyes were ringed with blue and red lines, and the shape of her pupils wasn't quite right. But aside from the whole birds-flying-from-her-mouth thing, she was beautiful.

The woman touched Mallory's arm, and without planning to do so, Mallory slid the .357 back into its holster.

With her odd eyes and impossible mouth, this woman looked inhuman, but at her touch Mallory felt peaceful.

Then Kaleb stepped forward, using his body like a shield in front of her, and told her, "Run, *now.*"

Mallory frowned. She didn't know why she felt like she

could trust the strange woman, but she did. She also wanted rather desperately to protect Kaleb. The two instincts were both unexpected—and at odds.

She wasn't sure what to do until, with a flick of her fingers, the woman flung Kaleb with such force that he landed several storefronts away. He wasn't moving.

"Distraction," the woman said, the word pushed from behind her teeth with deliberation and struggle.

She stepped closer to Mallory.

The peaceful feeling evaporated, and Mallory backed away from her. Kaleb was injured; the woman had hurt him. That clarified everything.

"I *will* shoot you," Mallory threatened. She reached for her gun again.

Simultaneously, the woman reached out and snapped the cord that held Mallory's pendant. She cupped the stone in her palm and curled her fingers around it. All the while, she stared at Mallory as if a question had been left unanswered in the air between them.

"That's mine." Mallory grabbed the woman's wrist with her free hand.

Across the street, the three black birds stood in a row on one of the cables that stretched between poles.

*Waiting for me.*

"I really don't want to hurt you, but . . ." She resisted the urge to look at Kaleb. "You hurt him. If he's not okay, I'll kill you."

The woman looked heartbroken for a fluttering moment.

She took Mallory's hand and put the stone in it.

Mallory backed farther away, not running—*not yet*—for fear of leaving Kaleb at the woman's mercy. She eased toward him, hoping that she could reach him but unsure if it would do any good.

The woman didn't speak. Two of the three birds looked in opposite directions so that one was peering up the street and the other down the street. The third bird swooped toward Mallory.

The woman lifted her hand. She stood with arm outstretched and palm open. The black bird touched down in her hand. As it did so, it disintegrated into ash and smoke. The woman lifted her cupped palm filled with silty dark ash while tendrils of smoke twisted above it. "Remember."

"What?" Mallory lifted her gaze, and as she did so, she realized too late that the bird-breathing woman had opened her mouth again.

She blew the ashes into Mallory's face. "To free your voice and your mind."

Mallory coughed as the dark cloud of ash hit her face with far more force than was possible from an exhalation—not that disintegrating birds or women breathing birds into being was possible either.

*Daimon. Daimons don't do magic . . . but witches don't exhale birds.*

"What are you?" she asked.

The woman exhaled again then, and feathers cradled

Mallory's fall as she dropped to the ground unable to breathe or see—or stay awake to hear the answer to her question.

WHEN SHE OPENED HER eyes again, Kaleb was crouched on the sidewalk beside her. He had one arm around her shoulders and was holding her chin with the other hand. He tilted her head, peering into her eyes as he did so. "Do you feel able to stand?"

"I think." She accepted his help and came unsteadily to her feet. She didn't know what to say. Anything she could say would seem crazy.

She looked around, confused. They were standing just outside the restaurant. No bird-breathing, weird-eyed woman stood anywhere in sight. Kaleb wasn't tossed down the street. Everything was perfectly normal.

"You hit your head pretty hard when you fell." Kaleb slid his fingers through her hair. "I don't feel any blood. I'm so sorry I couldn't catch you."

"It's fine. *I'm* fine." Mallory was mortified; she tried to step backward but swayed a little as she did so.

"The ground is uneven." He lifted her into his arms and started walking toward her house. "Your father will kill me if you're injured. Do you need a healer or—"

"*Healer?*" she interrupted as she tried to get free. "Kaleb, I'm fine. You can put me down. Seriously, I hit my head, but my legs work fine."

"No." His grip tightened as he held her closer to his chest. "I *can't* let anything happen to you before we even . . .

I need you to . . . We'll go to your father, and tell him what happened, and—"

"No, we won't," she interrupted. Then she softened a little. He sounded so frightened that she kissed his cheek. "I'm *fine*. Are you . . . did you . . . ? Are you injured?"

He frowned and paused for a moment, but then resumed walking. "You hit your head, Mallory, and you're unsteady. I can carry you."

Mallory smiled at him and then tentatively said, "Before I hit my head, there was a woman. . . ."

"She startled you." He stared in front of him as he walked, but he held her even closer. "I should've seen her. I didn't expect . . ."

"Expect what?" Mallory prompted.

"Her." Kaleb carried her down the street at a rapid pace. "If anything at all feels . . . damaged, you'll tell your father?"

"Sure." Mallory closed her eyes. Her head really did hurt, and she felt like a complete fool. He could've been injured— was thrown down the street—because of her. She couldn't date a human boy, not while daimons were pursuing her father and thus her. Unfortunately, she also couldn't tell Kaleb any of that. If Kaleb knew about the daimons or witches, he'd run the other way. He *should* run. Even for her, what had just happened was unprecedented.

*Witches don't exhale birds; daimons don't work magic. And what was she talking about? What do I tell Dad? What do I say to Kaleb?*

When they reached the house, Kaleb gently lowered Mallory to the ground. Her father's car was in the driveway. Kaleb looked at it, but he made no move to walk toward the door with her. "I need to go take care of some things. You'll stay awake to make sure you don't have a bleeding brain, right?"

Mallory stared at him for a minute, and then said lightly, "I don't think anyone has ever said that to me before."

"I just want to know you'll be okay," he said. "I'm not actually sure when I'll see you again, so I—"

"I'll stay awake," she promised.

The moment stretched awkwardly, and then Kaleb leaned in and kissed her cheek. "I'm sorry I didn't catch you."

*He won't be back. He shouldn't be back.*

She, at least, already knew they weren't alone in the world. Kaleb was doing that thing most humans did: coming up with ways to explain the unusual. She still fought against that instinct, and she'd grown up surrounded by magic. *He's probably better off without me anyhow.* Even as she thought it, though, she wanted to clutch him to her. Instead she stepped away and opened the door. She looked over her shoulder and said, "Good-bye, Kaleb."

"Good night."

The look of pain in his eyes made her feel like crying. Her bizarre and exciting date had turned into something awful, but she wasn't sure what to do other than watch him as he limped away.

She wondered if whatever had prompted Adam's sudden

desire to move had followed them here. Mallory went into the house and closed the door behind her. She was glad to be in her safely warded home.

"Daddy?"

No one answered.

She walked through her empty house, checked her phone to make sure she hadn't missed a call. He didn't date at all, and he rarely rode with anyone.

Mallory worried that they'd found him too. "Come home safe, please," she whispered.

# CHAPTER 15

KALEB DIDN'T KNOW HOW the Watcher had found Mallory—or if the Watchers had always known where she was. Selah had been a Watcher, and the Watchers were peculiar in their trust of the witches. Even so, few daimons moved between worlds. To do so required both access to a gate and the knowledge to open it. He had a gate, acquired at great expense, and he'd been careful to avoid witnesses when he'd gone over to Mallory's world. The only other way was to be summoned into a circle, and even Watchers weren't likely to trust a witch enough to risk being trapped in a summoning circle.

Up until now, Mallory had acted like she was utterly unaware of daimons, of witches, of anything other than the ordinary human world. Whatever bargain Selah had made when she'd hidden Mallory in the human world seemed to have kept Mallory herself unaware of what she was—or so he'd thought. This evening, though, she had faced one of the Watchers with no discernible shock. She was obviously more aware than he'd thought, but what that meant for him was unclear. Maybe after he was home safely, he could start to try to make sense of it.

He slid through the gate and found himself in the tiny room where his doorway was hidden. He unbolted the door and stepped outside. The dim purple sky overhead made The City appear to be nothing more than pools of shadows divided by the flickering lights that were mounted on poles or walls. This particular corridor had no such lights.

In the center of The City, the Night Market glowed with pulsing lights, a beacon to anyone in city limits. The carnival evolved into an even deadlier version of itself in the wee hours, so much so that the denizens of The City had assigned it a separate identity. While even the ruling class might visit the Carnival of Souls, the Night Market was the domain of those who were without constraint or inhibition. Women of the highest caste and many of the women of the middle castes avoided the Night Market; those few who dared wander the Night Market were without recourse if they had unwanted encounters. Dallying in the shadows was always dangerous, but doing so in the Night Market was especially deadly. Several years ago, Marchosias had declared that what happened at the market was "unable to be held for judgment." That ruling meant that neither murder nor kidnapping was forbidden after hours.

If an elimination job was low paying, the market was the place to do it—or at the least where the body was dumped. Kaleb refused to accept any job that meant using the market's lawlessness as an assist. It made him more expensive to hire, but it also told the buyer that he was good enough to finish a job without crutches.

The dream was that he'd be able to stop taking black-mask jobs. He'd had enough of blood. What he wanted tonight was to lose himself in numbness for a few hours. Unfortunately, Kaleb was far from fit to venture into the Night Market in search of indulgences. The thought of something narcotic didn't even lure him in. Being challenged was ever a danger, and tonight, he wasn't sure he could handle a fight. At best, he'd survive but reveal how injured he was. Tonight, Kaleb felt like he'd been beaten, stabbed, and thrown down the street. Of course, between the fights and this evening's encounter with the Watcher, he *had* been, but the combined effect of the abuse had hit him with what had to be more than the weight of all of the individual pains.

By the time he reached the mouth of his cave, he had all but breathed a sigh of relief, so seeing Aya standing in the dark waiting for him made him wonder which god he'd pissed off. He was certainly in no shape to fight *her*—not tonight, possibly not for at least a week. He knew that tomorrow he'd feel even worse, although he wasn't quite sure what worse could entail just then.

"Do we have to do this tonight?" He couldn't muster

intimidating, but he tried for at least sardonic. "How about I give you a few free hits before I retaliate *if* we can postpone this?"

"What were you doing out when you are in this shape?" She came over and half supported his weight with one of her shoulders under his arm and her arm around his waist. "If one of the others saw you, you'd be dead."

He snorted. "The only one who's ballsy enough to come here is you, and unless this is an elaborate ruse of some sort that I'm too tired to follow, you"—he turned his head to look at her as they paused at his threshold—"seem to be *helping* me."

"I am," she said. "My word: I mean you no harm this night."

"Then come into my home for this night, Aya."

At the words that allowed her entry, they stepped into the cave, and less than a heartbeat later, Zevi launched himself across the room.

"Stop! I invited her in by choice, not under duress." Kaleb took a faltering step away from Aya and was promptly lifted into the air by his now-growling friend.

With a snarl that made Kaleb both proud and nervous, Zevi carried him toward the bed he should've been in hours ago. It was embarrassing to let one of his opponents see him in this state, but there was no help for it. After Zevi lowered Kaleb to the bed, he paused, sniffed, and looked at Kaleb with confusion clear in his expression.

Kaleb held up a hand. "I'll explain once Aya goes." He pulled his arm out of Zevi's reach. "Can you add something to the fire? I'm getting feverish."

Anger vied with worry in Zevi's expression. Muttering to himself, he went over and stoked the fire, and then returned with one of the blankets from his bed. He sniffed Kaleb again as he spread the blanket over him. "Someone was against your skin, but you didn't have sex."

"I didn't."

"Were you rejected?" Zevi's gaze narrowed, and he ran over to Aya.

Before Kaleb could speak, Zevi had bent down and pressed his nose to her crotch.

"No!" Kaleb yelled. His exclamation was simultaneous with Zevi's yip of pain and the sound of crashing.

"I'm not up on cur customs, but I'm pretty sure that putting your nose there is not something you do with outsiders." Aya had her foot on Zevi's chest. "Don't do that again."

Instead of replying to her words, Zevi stared up at her and asked, "Did you kill Verie?"

Aya pressed her lips together and looked from one cur to the other.

"Zevi, I told you I'd explain everything later," Kaleb called. "Aya is our guest. No more. When I came home, she was outside, and instead of killing me, she helped me inside. She wasn't with me when I was out."

Aya stared down at Zevi, who was looking at her like she was his new favorite snack.

"Kaleb was right," Zevi said. "You didn't kill him, did you?"

"I'd rather not break your ribs right now" was all she said.

Zevi turned his head and looked at Kaleb. "She smells nervous, not guilty." Then he put his hand on Aya's foot as if to keep it there and stared up at her again. "I'm glad you didn't kill Verie."

"I never said that," she muttered as she looked across the room at Kaleb. "Is he safe to release?"

"He is." Kaleb sighed and then winced at the sharp pain in his chest. "Zev, if you can stop provoking her, I need willow bark and some of those bandages you boiled earlier."

At that, Zevi rolled out from under Aya's foot and was at the fire in almost the same instant. Aya stared at him with her mouth agape. "He's *incredibly* fast. If he wanted to get away, he could've avoided me."

"Yeah." Kaleb watched the realization settle on Aya. She studied Zevi as he moved from his medicinal boxes to the fire and back to the bed with the speed that made it seem that he was in several places at once. Kaleb still marveled at him sometimes, but seeing that dawning clarity on Aya's face made him remember his first few years around Zevi. Quietly, Kaleb said, "I used to get dizzy watching him."

When Aya looked at him, he continued, "I've never seen anyone who can move like that."

"If he wanted to fight—"

"Kaleb says no," Zevi interrupted as he passed her. He went from blurringly fast to slower than even humans moved as he pulled the covers back and removed Kaleb's shirt. "I attract too much attention when I forget to stay slow."

Silently, Aya walked over to the bed. She couldn't seem to decide whether to look at Zevi or Kaleb. The bruises on his chest *were* remarkable in their colors and shapes, and Kaleb could see as well as feel the proof of his very obviously broken rib. On the journey home, a fragment of bone had pierced his skin.

"Do you need help?" Aya asked.

Zevi looked at Kaleb, who nodded. Then Zevi held out a metal box.

"We need to adjust the bones first," Zevi told her. He didn't look at Kaleb. "Do you want to press or assist?"

She looked at Kaleb in confusion.

He said mildly, "She'll want to assist. I'm guessing she's never adjusted a cur."

Zevi frowned, then he shrugged, opened the box, and pulled out a handful of heated, oiled bandages. "Hold these while I—" Then he slammed the box down on Kaleb's ribs.

Kaleb screamed, swallowed, and tried to sound unaffected as he asked, "How about a little warning?"

Aya looked like she might fall over.

But Zevi was as calm as he always was when he was working. "You tense up if I warn you."

Kaleb winced as Zevi took one of the bandages and smoothed it across his rib cage. "Then why do you warn me sometimes?"

"So you don't know *when* to tense." Zevi took another bandage and methodically layered it over the first one. "Open the bin and grab me two more."

Without a word, Aya did as Zevi directed.

"You, sit up."

Kaleb smothered a curse as he obeyed—and another one when Zevi grabbed his legs and dropped them over the edge of the bed. Humming now, Zevi wrapped bandages all the way around Kaleb.

In a few short minutes, Kaleb's chest was wrapped, and the pain-relief concoction in the bandages was seeping into his body. Zevi helped him to lie back. "I need to check the other wounds before morning. I'll wake you."

As the blissful numbness hit him, Kaleb told Zevi, "Thank you."

Zevi nodded, brought over a mug with willow bark, poppy extract, and who knew what else, and then he walked to a pile of blankets in front of the fire. Without any seeming discomfort at resting in front of an outsider, he stretched and settled himself on the blankets. He was snoring before Aya could close her mouth.

AYA HAD NEVER SPENT much time around the curs. They were, by nature, not very embracing of outsiders. These two acted like she wasn't there, or maybe this was restrained for them. If so, she wasn't sure she wanted to see them relaxed.

She wasn't sure what to do. Kaleb was a ferocious fighter, but he wasn't cold or cruel here in his home. It was like he was a completely separate person from the cur she'd seen fight.

*Because he's at home or because of Zevi?*

"Should I go?" Aya asked in a low voice.

"You don't need to whisper." Kaleb's gaze fell on the snoring cur. "Zevi will sleep unless the threshold is violated or I call for him. He'd sleep through the excesses of the Night Market right now."

"Is that . . . normal?"

"For Zevi or for a cur?" Kaleb started to reach for the mug Zevi had left beside the bed, pursed his lips, and lowered his arm. "Or do you mean is the way he shoved my bones back normal?"

"Any of it?" Aya walked over and picked up the mug. "Actually, *all* of it." She handed him the mug.

"Hard to say. The bones, yes. They need rebroken so they set right. He broke them, and now I will stay still and drink the nasty concoction he has for aiding in mending them." He drained the mug. "And, yes, the sleep thing is normal for Zevi. He feels safe when I'm home."

She waited, not quite sure what to say or do.

After a few moments, Kaleb looked up at her. "Not that I'm complaining about this new side of you—I appreciate the help tonight—but I'm pretty sure you didn't show up to learn how to nurse a battered cur."

Unlike Kaleb, Aya didn't have a warmer side she wanted to share. In an expressionless voice, she asked, "You've heard about the new competition terms?"

"The winner gets to mate with his daughter or with him," Kaleb said flatly. "Why are you telling *me*?"

"I don't want to breed with Marchosias or with anyone.

If I had, I would've wed Belias. I refused. I want to rule." Aya sat tentatively on the edge of Kaleb's bed. "When I realized the competition didn't specify gender, I thought I'd found the answer: a woman can rule in The City by winning Marchosias' Competition, but now, winning would force me to do the very thing I am trying to avoid."

Kaleb's gaze swept her from head to toe, and even injured, he was clearheaded enough to assess her like she was wearing a red mask. "Do you oppose the act too?"

"No." She tilted her chin up. "But you know that already. You've had your scabs bring you what they know of me and the other contenders—as I have of all of you."

Kaleb laughed. "Right now, I'm not feeling as confident that I'm still a contender."

"You won't be without help," Aya said.

To his credit, Kaleb didn't deny the truth. "I can't forfeit, and I'm not looking for a protector, especially one who killed the last daimon she took to bed."

Aya barely resisted flinching at his mention of Belias. "I've sufficient wealth to take care of you both. Neither of you would need to do mask-work again."

"I'm a *cur*. Curs don't forfeit. I'll win or die fighting. If I die, Zevi will need—"

She interrupted, "If you die, you're no use to me. I need you alive."

"Do you?" Kaleb gestured at his bandages. "Then we both have a problem."

"If I'm going to avoid breeding with Marchosias, I need a protector. You're my best option."

When he didn't reply, she added, "I have a plan. I know protector arrangements are usually about money, but I have that. I need your ferocity."

Kaleb glanced back at Zevi, and she saw the struggle he faced. As a cur, he had two competing interests: to protect his pack and to counter any challenge.

Finally he looked at her and said, "How can you help me?"

"I can weaken your opponent, so you'll win." She folded her hands in her lap. "Then, I'll forfeit and offer a blood oath as your chattel in public. For one year, you'd be *my* protector. If I'm your property, no one—even Marchosias—can claim me. If you take me as a bloodmate, only you could impregnate me, and we can agree privately not to do *that*. I'll buy time, and you'll survive the fight. I can help you win. You'll get the prize and the girl. All I need is someone strong enough that my being . . . property is believable."

Kaleb shook his head. "If I accept you as mine after he made this announcement, I look like I'm rejecting Mal—Marchosias' daughter. No deal."

"Then I'll move in as *Zevi's* bloodmate for one year. You can announce that as your price: you accept my forfeit in exchange for the right to gift me to your packmate." Aya's temperature dropped as her mind filled with fear that she couldn't entirely quell. "You'd still own me."

"Why would you do this?" he asked, not unkindly.

"I can't breed." She shuddered. "It's the one thing I can't do. All I want is to rule, to make The City be the place it could be. If Marchosias is already noticing me, do you think he'll lose interest? If I win, I'm his. If I forfeit a fight and am an unclaimed breedable woman, the odds of him not claiming me are so slim as to be laughable. And if I have a child . . . I'll lose everything. You understand"—she glanced at the sleeping cur—"what it means to risk it all for something or someone. I want to serve The City, and if I have a child, I won't be able to."

Kaleb's attention was fixed on her now, and as he watched her, Aya knew that he also had secrets that would cause her problems she couldn't see yet. She hadn't survived this long in The City without learning to read the clues people didn't think they revealed.

*Does he suspect me as well?* He'd be a fool not to.

Finally, he said, "I'll only accept your offer *if* you can guarantee my win."

"I can do it." She held his gaze. "My kill count will be yours, too, if I'm your chattel."

Kaleb paused as that detail settled on him: with her kills added to his, he'd be ranked first by a huge margin. He could win the whole competition without killing anyone else in the fights. "And all you want . . ."

"I won't breed under any circumstances. That term must be inviolate," she stressed. "If we do this, if I'm bound to you or to Zevi, I'll not bed down with whoever I'm bound to."

"Agreed, but if I win and breed Marchosias' daughter, I

will live in the palace. That will mean that *you* will live within Marchosias' reach too." Kaleb spoke very clearly. "I cannot tell him you are for Zevi's uses exclusively. He'd kill Z, and anything that results in injury to Zevi is a no-starter."

"If you gift me to Zevi as a bloodmate, only he can get me with child," she murmured. "If I have to be lent to Marchosias or anyone else, I'll do it. All I ask is that you help me avoid one thing. Everything else is negotiable."

After an indeterminate number of moments during which Kaleb stared silently at her, he nodded. "There are knives on the fire. The short one is silver. If you grab it, we can do this once it cools."

Aya walked to the fire and retrieved a knife from the saltwater that was boiling over the low flames. A flicker of magic went through her as she cooled it down to a slightly less horrible temperature. She wanted to get this done before Kaleb could change his mind.

"It must not have been in there long," she lied evenly. "We can do it right now."

She pressed the edge to her palm and then held the knife out to Kaleb.

Once he'd cut his hand as well, they clasped their palms together. "I'll support you in acquiring his daughter. I'll support you in the fights, give you my kill count, and be yours to command. For the next year, starting in this moment, I'll do all you ask in exchange for your protection," she swore.

"I accept you as my property, Aya. I will protect you from

harm and keep you safe from breeding with Marchosias—or any other daimon—in exchange for your support," Kaleb vowed.

She released his grasp and carried the knife to the fire. With her back to him, she whispered a simple spell to make him sleep and then said, "Thank you."

And then she left the two sleeping curs, so she could begin to procure what she needed to help Kaleb survive.

# CHAPTER 16

MALLORY'S BODY ACHED LIKE she'd been thrown into a pit of burning coals, swarmed by ants, and doused with ice water. She stared up at her ceiling, thinking about Kaleb in an attempt to distract herself from how absolutely wretched she felt. It didn't improve how she actually felt, but it was a great way to fill the hour.

Despite her best intentions, she'd fallen asleep before Adam was home again. She'd heard him come in late at night to check on her, so she knew he was okay. She, *however*, felt far from okay. When she woke early that morning, she couldn't get out of bed. She tried, but even the thought of standing seemed exhausting. She didn't know anyone who got as sick as she did— at least, no one who got this sick but didn't go to a hospital. Her father always fixed her, but he never explained *why* she got so ill. She'd told herself time and again that maybe these episodes weren't weird, but the older she got, the more she knew that they were about as weird as women who exhaled birds—and beautiful guys talking about "belonging" after one kiss.

Even if she hadn't felt horrible, she would have wanted to stay in bed thinking about Kaleb. He seemed so *ab*normal in her world. What was normal for the daughter of a witch who spent his life running from the daimons he'd robbed wasn't exactly the kind of normal that she wanted. *Kaleb is.* Unfortunately, she wasn't sure how to have a relationship if she had to lie, and she was certain Adam wasn't going to allow her to tell a human about witches and daimons, and after the daimon encounter, she wasn't at all sure she'd be able to keep Kaleb safe even if she *could* reveal the secrets she knew.

The reality was that she did need to deal with her version of normal, though. She sat up and swung her feet to the floor, fighting the urge to simply yell for her father. She didn't, but she didn't get any farther either.

She wasn't sure if it was a minute or an hour later, but he tapped on her door. "Mallory? Are you awake?"

"I am." She sat on the edge of her bed with her quilt wrapped around her like a cloak. Even bundled up, she felt cold.

Her father opened the door and then paused, wearing a look of panic that made Mallory think that the worry lines around his eyes were deeper than they had once been. The plain oxford shirt and dark trousers he had on told her that he had been heading in to the new office early.

After a moment, he came to the bed and put a hand to her forehead, checking for fever. She felt the cold metal of the single ring he wore even after her mother had left.

Mallory had been through this enough times that she stayed still as he felt her ears and forehead with the back of his hand and then tilted her head to look into her eyes. She waited while he felt under her ears for swelling and then inevitably started asking questions. Her mind felt too fuzzy to try to figure out what to tell him.

"Are you dizzy? Sore throat? Nauseous?" He stepped back and watched her as he spoke.

"No."

"You're freezing."

"I know." She felt guilty even though she didn't choose to be cold. "I need to talk to you."

"Just a minute," he said, and then muttering quiet curses, or possibly spells for her health, he walked out of the room. In only a few moments, he'd returned with an electric blanket. He wrapped it around her, plugged it in, and left again. In short order, he was back with a glass of hot water into which he'd stirred some herbal concoction made palatable with plenty of sugar and a touch of lemon.

"Drink."

Obediently, Mallory emptied the glass. She couldn't ask why she got so cold, never asked why he knew how to make it better. She'd thought about it, but every time she started to do so, the urge to ask vanished. *Good daughters don't question their fathers.* Her father could always assess what was wrong within only a few moments, and he inevitably brewed some potion or other to make her better. *Why ask, when he can fix it?*

He went to the window, picked up the little sachet he'd refreshed every month in every house she could recall, and sniffed it. "No strangers came *here*, did they?" As he spoke, he checked the line of salt that edged every room in the house. Hers was unbroken. "Was someone at the door? In the house?"

"No." Mallory shook her head.

Adam's expression didn't change. He didn't muss his perfectly ordered hair; he didn't scowl at her. He simply asked, "What happened?"

Mallory sighed. She didn't want to, but she told him, "I had a date, sort of . . . with Kaleb. I ran into him and then we had dinner and . . . it wasn't planned. I didn't know I'd see him."

Her father swallowed visibly. "Did this Kaleb do something to you? Did he touch you? Did he *hurt* you? Tell me, Mallory."

It felt like words were being pulled from her lips. They tumbled out too fast. "No! We kissed, but I *wanted* him to kiss me. It was after dinner . . . and there was a strange woman. She threw Kaleb aside and"—she looked directly at her father—"she released *birds* from her mouth. I think she was a daimon. I couldn't kill her. I couldn't *hurt* her, and then she blew ashes into my face."

"Ashes?"

"One of the birds disintegrated, and I inhaled it," Mallory said.

The bed dipped as he sat on the foot of it. "Is there more?"

For a moment, Mallory almost told him about how strange Kaleb made her feel, how right the world felt when he was near her, but she kept her lips firmly shut and shook her head. Her hand curled around the still-warm glass, she stared at her father and concentrated on the daimon, not Kaleb. "She breathed *birds*."

He took the glass from her hand. "Let me get you another drink."

She nodded. After he left, she reached under her pillow. Her hand closed around the carved stone pendant she usually wore. Her mother had believed that it would protect her. From what, no one would tell her. Mallory had questions about that too, but her mother had said that she wouldn't answer those questions until Mallory turned seventeen. *Three days ago.*

Last night, Mallory had tucked the pendant under her pillow, but that apparently wasn't close enough since she still had the shakes. She got out of bed and rummaged in a drawer until she found a ribbon. She slid the pendant onto it and tied it around her throat and immediately felt better. A rock shouldn't make that much of a difference, and even when she wore it, there were still times she was struck by illnesses unlike anything that ever hit any of her friends in any of the cities where they'd lived—but she felt better with it on.

Before her father returned, she was back in bed.

He came in and sat on the edge of the bed again. He brushed her hair away from her eyes. "You know you were just as frustrated by being sick when you were little. The first time you got better after one of these episodes, you tried to get me to give you a 'never sick again' potion. I would if I could. I'd protect you from every moment of anything that hurts."

"Being sick reminds me that I'm human, right?"

"It certainly proves I'm not as omnipotent as I wish I could be." Adam squeezed her hand. "I can stay home today."

"No." She tried to smile back as if she didn't feel as wretched as she did. "I'm seventeen, not seven, Daddy. I'll sleep, and if I feel worse, I'll call you. I know the routine."

Her father kissed her forehead. "If there was a 'never sick again' potion, I'd give it to you. All I want is to protect you, Mallory."

"I know," she assured him.

For a moment he said nothing, and then he brought up the detail that they hadn't discussed. "Once you're well, I'll expect to meet this Kaleb before you go anywhere with him again, *and* before you let him in the house. Do you understand?"

She half laughed, half groaned. "I doubt that he'll be back. He has probably rationalized it all away, but he *did* see me fall to the ground like a klutz. *That* he'll remember. It's probably not safe for him anyhow, right? If we could tell him . . ." She let the sentence linger, but her father didn't offer to let her reveal secrets.

Instead, he asked, "Did you invite him into the old house?"

Her father's voice was so calm that if she didn't know him,

she'd think nothing of it, but she did know him. Adam was decidedly not at ease.

"Once," she admitted. Her eyes started to drift shut. Some of his potions did that, but she hated the helplessness of it. She blinked, fighting to keep her eyes open.

"Has he asked you to go anywhere? Give him anything?" He stopped her as she tried to sit.

She frowned, but stayed reclining. It wouldn't matter soon. The need to sleep was winning. "No."

Adam tucked the covers closer around her. "I need to meet him, Mallory. You are too precious to me, and—"

"I like him," Mallory finally admitted drowsily. "I *need* him. I can't explain, but I think I really need him."

Her father didn't reply to what she'd said. Instead, he instructed, "Promise me you won't go anywhere with him or let him in the house. Say it."

"I promise," she agreed reluctantly, and then she gave in to sleep.

# CHAPTER 17

Two days later Kaleb still hadn't been back to the carnival—or to the human world. His ribs were healing, but even a cur couldn't heal that many fractures in a few days. The matchboard had been updated, and Kaleb was to face Sol. His odds of winning his match without help weren't good. He'd spent his entire life fighting, and he was capable of doing so with a few injuries, but only the best fighters were left this late in the year, and fighting an opponent like Sol wasn't something to do with broken ribs, a gouged thigh, or even the various more manageable injuries. The wise thing to do was to forfeit the fight, but Kaleb hadn't often been accused of being wise.

Once he healed, the next most pressing problem was that other daimons knew where Mallory was. Between Marchosias' announcement and the Watcher's arrival, it was abundantly clear that Kaleb wasn't the only daimon who had located her. Suddenly, Kaleb needed to win both the competition and Mallory, and he needed to do both pretty much now. If he did, he'd have everything: position, pack, and safety.

Unfortunately, to convince Mallory to be with him, he needed to spend time with her, and right now he was too injured to risk that. He had to let himself heal enough to get through tomorrow's match and hope that she'd stay safe for the time he was stuck here in The City. Even with rest, he'd need to take Zevi's pain depressors to hide any flinching, hope that Aya's plan evened the odds, and avoid receiving any killing blows. Two of those were on him, but the third element hinged on Aya—assuming she could really do what she promised.

If anyone could pull off miracles though, it was her. She had been one of his biggest threats in the past year. He'd watched her eliminate fighters who should've gutted her. She was savvy in ways that he didn't understand, and at the same time, she was dispassionate as she slit throats and took kill trophies. Breeding seemed like such a small thing for her to allow it to stand in the way of the future of wealth, comfort, and safety.

For him, being safe enough to have a large family was a *goal*. The desire to create a pack was innate for some curs, but Kaleb hadn't ever felt it until he found Zevi.

At the thought of his sole packmate, Kaleb looked at the lightening sky and realized that Zevi was still out somewhere. He should've been back by now. This close to morning, the only real action was at the Night Market—which wasn't somewhere Kaleb liked Zevi to go alone.

He pulled a jacket on and winced as one of the knives inside it bounced against his ribs. When even small actions made him hurt, he really had no business fighting Sol, but there were plenty of threats at the market that he could still handle just fine.

AYA WAS UNSURPRISED TO find Sol following Zevi through the market. If she hadn't seen how fast the cur could move, she'd be more alarmed, but she suspected that Zevi was far more capable than Kaleb seemed to believe. The bigger surprise was that no one had attempted to injure Zevi yet. *Or maybe there had been attempts and Zevi resolved them.* It wouldn't be wise to underestimate Kaleb's packmate, but it also wouldn't be advisable to ignore the dangers to him. She needed to keep Zevi safe.

"Aya? For you." A young girl slipped a folded note to her and then vanished back into the shadows.

The urge to read the message vied with the need to protect Zevi. If Zevi died, Kaleb would be useless. He was likely to suspect her of treachery as well.

Aya saw movement out of the corner of her eye and stepped to the side—just in time to see Kaleb lunge at her.

He caught her arm, but with the quick reaction that had served her well in the fight circles, Aya extracted herself from his grasp.

"Why are you following Z?" Kaleb started.

Aya shoved him toward the doorway of a stall and whispered, "I'm trying to keep watch on him."

Kaleb pushed her away from him with a growl.

Aya caught his arm and tugged him farther into the stall. "Sol is out there. Stay."

One of the brokers approached and bowed. The movement didn't quite hide the avarice in his eyes. "We have special rates for fighters."

"I'll be right back." Aya shoved Kaleb onto a mound of pillows and stepped outside. She glanced at the note that she had crumpled in her hand and read: *Ready. ~E.*

Aya dropped the note into a fire and scanned the immediate area. The flickering lights of the Night Market cast dancing shadows, but Aya had spent enough time here that she knew where to look for the street scabs who wandered those shadows. None of her usual resources were lurking nearby, but a scab she'd used a few times for small jobs looked up. Better still, the girl was a cur.

Aya beckoned her closer. "You know Zevi?"

"Kaleb's Zevi?" the cur clarified. "Sure. He went—"

"Find him." Aya pulled out a handful of coins. "I need him kept safe and brought to me here. Now. Hire help if you need. I'll pay fair price."

The cur nodded once, whistled some sort of pattern that brought three more scabs running toward her, and then the four scabs all took off into the market. That issue resolved, Aya returned to the pleasure stall. She'd have preferred to save her coin and keep Zevi safe herself, but Kaleb was more of an issue at the moment. They didn't need him approaching Sol and revealing the extent of his injuries.

Back inside, Kaleb gave her a look of relief, but before he said anything, Aya held out a blank marker to the vendor. "We're expecting a cur to join us. Aside from him, no one disturbs us."

The vendor started, "We have several packages to enhance your enjoyment of the pleasure quarters. The rate for fighters—"

"I'm not interested in bartering. Private room. Another cur will join us. Let me know when our third party arrives." Aya grabbed Kaleb's hand and led him to one of the rooms. Inside, she took a handful of salt and chalk and closed the privacy circle. Once that was done, she released Kaleb's hand and said, "If I intended to kill Zevi, I would've done it before I sought you out."

Kaleb shook his head. "So if it was more advantageous, you'd kill Zevi."

Aya resisted the urge to smack Kaleb, but he wasn't Belias. Striking Kaleb wouldn't be a harmless act; it would have repercussions—and not the sort she liked. "I needed to come to the market, and while I was here, I've been watching Zevi so Sol didn't hurt him."

Apparently willing to believe her, Kaleb nodded. "Were you here to kill Sol?"

"If I do, we waste an opportunity. When you fight him and

win after you were so severely injured, it will make you look invincible."

"Right now, I *doubt* I would win," he interjected.

"I told you: I'm going to change that." Aya opened a pouch and filled it with the chalk she'd just used to close the circle. "I'm going to make it so you are able to eliminate him."

Kaleb opened his mouth to speak, but a red ripple went through the circle around them before he did so.

Aya shoved her boot-clad foot across the circle, lowering it and revealing a tense-looking Zevi. The vendor stood beside him with a grin that Aya would have loved to knock off his face. Instead, she gave him her most disdainful look and directed, "I don't want to be disturbed. Raise a locked circle, and then close the stall for the rest of the night."

"The rate for a circle like that and closing the rest of the stall—"

"Did I ask rates?" Without looking, she reached out for Zevi's hand and pulled him into the room. All the while she stared at the vendor. "Go home early, or enjoy the market."

"The wall will stay intact until the Night Market ends." The vendor raised a locked circle, bowed hastily, and then fled.

Once he was gone, Aya turned to face the two curs. "You can trust me."

Kaleb looked at her warily, but Zevi shrugged and crawled into a silk-and-velvet basket that was suspended from the ceiling. He curled up and watched her. "Are you buying us?"

"No," Kaleb snarled.

"It's probably for the best." Zevi swayed so the basket began to swing slightly back and forth. "Kaleb was stabbed pretty high up too, so I'm not sure if he would be of any use." He paused and glanced at Kaleb. "If she did buy us, *could* you—"

"Z, stop," Kaleb snapped.

Aya shook her head. "I'm not buying you, *either* of you. You will stay here and rest. It's safe, warm, comfortable, and clean. There's food and drink."

"And what are you going to do?" Kaleb asked. "You reserved a pleasure stall so we could all sleep? I have a home. So do you. Explain."

No one in The City knew what she was about to reveal to the two curs staring at her. It was the secret underlying her choice to enter the competition, to refuse to wed Belias, to struggle not to have children. If Zevi and Kaleb were untrustworthy, she would die. It was that simple. Every choice she'd made the past two years had been to protect the secret she had to now reveal.

She looked at Kaleb and asked softly, "Are we partners, Kaleb?"

"We blood-oathed," Kaleb said.

She tucked the pouch of chalk into her pocket. "I would rather not show you this, but I can't see any way around it."

At that, Aya stepped through the circle as if it weren't there. The circle didn't waver or fall. The room was still securely sealed. The circle was—to their eyes—an impenetrable barrier. From outside the circle, she watched their mutual expressions of shock. It was with no small relief that she saw that they didn't look horrified or frightened.

Zevi leaped out of the basket.

Aya stepped back across the still-intact circle.

"Daimons can't . . . you shouldn't . . ." He turned to Kaleb and announced in an awed voice, "She's not all daimon."

Kaleb said nothing. He hadn't moved either; he stared at her with an expressionless face. She tore her gaze away from him as Zevi came to stand as close as he could get without touching her. "Can I smell you?"

"Not everywhere," Aya cautioned him.

He, at least, was not disturbed by what she was. Zevi already had his nose on her throat before she finished her answer. He sniffed her everywhere but her crotch and buttocks. All the while, Aya stood motionless, watching Kaleb watch them.

"She smells fine," Zevi announced.

"Which is how she's avoided exposure." Kaleb didn't stand. "Your father wasn't your blood father."

Aya gave him a tight smile. "Neither of my parents is blood. The witch who placed me with my parents had spelled them to think I was their own, and to tell me the truth when I was old enough. They had no idea."

"But you couldn't hide it if you married," Kaleb said, pointing out the truth she wished she could've told Belias.

It hurt, hearing it said so bluntly. She'd agonized over telling Belias, but he—like many ruling-caste daimons, including her parents—hated witches. They didn't even sanction marriage out of their caste, much less out of species. She forced herself to sound as calm as she could, and said, "I'm not suited to marriage anyhow, but yes, I learned that it would be dangerous to breed. A child couldn't hide this—and I have no way of suppressing another's magic as my birth mother did mine."

"So you murdered your betrothed? Was that because he knew?"

Her temper flared, and the temptation to show Kaleb how easily she *could* kill flared with it. Instead, she said, "I won my *match*. I did *not* murder my former betrothed. There is a difference."

"Not to Belias," Kaleb pointed out.

Aya did not tell him he was wrong, that Belias was alive. There were few lives she'd put before her safety, but Belias was one of them. She knew it was stupid, dangerous in ways she didn't want to consider, but she couldn't kill Belias. *He won't escape. He won't return and expose me.* She wasn't sure anyone but her would understand how much she loved Belias. *He* certainly wouldn't, and it wasn't Kaleb's business. Rather than address that topic, she merely shook her head. "I could have killed Bel or a lot of others without touching if I needed to, but I didn't. I didn't use the fight to kill him, and I didn't use magic to win my fights. With one exception, I fought with the same resources as every other daimon in the competition."

"So is that the plan? You're going to use witchery to heal me or something?" Kaleb asked.

"Yes, but to do so I need to take the health from someone

else. I need you in a circle while I do the next step. I was going to come to the cave, but this will work fine. Rest or whatever. I'll be back before the circle drops."

And then Aya left them in the pleasure stall and went to get the supplies she needed to even the match with Sol.

# CHAPTER 18

BELIAS LOOKED UP, EXPECTING to see the witch who held him in her summoning circle. Instead, he saw his former betrothed. Aya had come for him.

"Hurry before she gets back," Belias urged. "I don't know how you got here . . . or how I got here but—" His words died as the witch came in the door behind her, carrying a tray of tea and sandwiches.

"I trust you can handle . . . everything. I've brought food," the witch said.

"Thank you," Aya said softly. She took the tray and stood silently for a moment until the witch departed. Once they were alone, Aya asked, "Will you promise not to hurt me in any way if I bring you food? She said you won't eat."

"How do I know it's safe?"

"You have my vow, Bel."

He watched her warily. He had no intention of hurting her, not without knowing if she was trapped somehow too, but he wasn't going to stand here and let her re-erect the circle. Once she dropped it to give him the food, he'd be at the door. A flash of guilt came over him at the thought of leaving her there. He stepped to the edge of the circle. "Are you a prisoner here too?"

"No," she admitted. "I came to see you."

"You knew I was here?" He'd thought he'd had his fill of betrayal when she poisoned him, but he felt the flare of renewed despair when she admitted that she'd known where he was. "You knew this whole time and you're just now . . . Why?"

Her hands tightened on the tray she held. "Do you, Belias, vow not to harm or attempt to trap me?"

"I do." He waited for her to add something about trying to escape, but she didn't. He had already studied the room, and aside from the ritual knife on the edge of the witch's desk, he saw nothing worth grabbing as a weapon.

Instead of lowering the circle, Aya caught and held Belias' gaze as she stepped into the circle as if it wasn't there. The look in her eyes wasn't one he'd often seen there. *Fear.* He backed away, and the fear in her eyes was replaced by her regular unreadable expression. She put the tray on the floor and left the circle with as little effort as she'd used to enter it.

Belias put his hand up, pressing on it, testing the barrier as he had done so often since he'd woken up in it. "You stepped through a containment circle. You're . . ." His words faded as he couldn't speak the terrible truth.

"A witch," she finished for him. "I'm a witch, Bel."

Fresh disgust settled on him as the pieces fell into place. She had not poisoned him; she'd sold him to a witch. *She* was a witch. Belias dropped to the floor, trapped inside the circle where Aya had *sent* him. He stared at her. "I wanted to spend my life with you. I offered you everything I have. I entered the competition and have killed because of you."

"I know." Aya's expression was as unreadable as he'd ever seen it. She stayed still, spine straight and shoulders back. Her hands were held loosely at her sides, and he had the thought that she should be holding a weapon. It reminded him of the fights they'd had in the ring and in the sparring centers. The difference was that he was defenseless this time.

He stared up at her, the witch he'd thought he loved, and couldn't understand how he could've been so wrong. "You took *everything* from me."

"Not your life. I spared your life." She gestured at the sandwiches beside him. "Eat, please. You'll get ill if you don't."

"Why does that matter?" He turned his gaze to her. "You're not intending to let me return to The City, are you? This is it. Either the witch kills me or keeps me here."

"This world isn't that bad, Bel. Evelyn says—"

"Get out." He slammed his fists against the circle. "Get out of my sight."

The usually stoic Aya flinched. "I couldn't kill you," she whispered.

When he said nothing, she continued in a steadier voice, "There are very few things I wouldn't do to have a future. If I breed, they'll know what I am."

"So this was your solution? Take away *my* future, my home?"

"You didn't leave me a lot of choices," she said. "You bribed them so you could fight me. I *know* because I've been bribing them *not* to match us. You trapped me. I couldn't forfeit, and I couldn't kill you. So I had Evelyn summon you here."

Her eyes flared witch-gold for the first time he'd ever seen, and on some level, he realized that she was letting down a wall. After years of trying to get her to share herself, to trust him, she chose now to do so.

"Don't do this to me, Aya," he pleaded. "We can figure out a plan that—"

"It's not her decision," Evelyn's voice interrupted from behind him.

He glanced over his shoulder to see the witch leaning in the doorway watching him. Instinctively, he started to move so that Aya was behind him, putting his body between the two witches, and immediately felt the fool. Aya was far more suited to defend herself against Evelyn than he could ever be.

Evelyn walked past the circle to her desk. She paused beside Aya and handed her a sachet. "This will do what you need."

"Thank you." Aya closed her hand around the sachet. She walked to the circle and lifted her other hand as if she would touch him. She didn't reach inside the circle though. "For the first time, I am afraid to touch you. I've listened, Bel: I know what you think of witches."

"If you weren't a witch, would you have broken our engagement?" It was a foolish question. She *was* a witch, and that was unchangeable, but he still wanted to know. "Was this the only reason?"

She shook her head. "I can't know that, but I don't think so. I don't want children. I want . . ."

"Power," Evelyn finished. She sat at her desk, hands folded together as if in prayer, appearance as stern as it had been every day he'd been trapped here, but that harsh demeanor softened ever so slightly as she watched them. "Aya wants to bend the world to her will. It is a consequence of what she is. Some witches are more driven than others, but it is always there. It is why the Witches' Council exists—we simply can't see our way clear to allowing things to be out of order when we have the skills, the knowledge, and the strength to correct aberrations of order."

Belias watched Aya's expressions as the witch spoke. She didn't speak to disagree with anything Evelyn said. The daimon he'd loved wasn't real. It was just an act to disguise her true self.

*How could I have thought I loved a witch?*

"I would rather you had killed me," he said quietly.

Evelyn's sigh was his only answer. "Enough of this. Aya, you've had your audience with the daimon. Now, I need privacy."

The witch lifted her hand with as little effort as one used to brush away an insect, and the circle became silent. Belias could no longer hear anything but the sound of his own breathing. Then, everything outside the circle became darker as he watched, until his entire world had been reduced to the few feet around him.

AYA HAD TRIED NOT to flinch away from Belias' anger. She understood all too well: she'd done all of this to avoid being killed or trapped. She was *still* trying to avoid that fate, and along the way, she'd consigned Belias to a similar one. If she could've married him and kept her secret, she would've. It wasn't what she was made for, but loving him had almost made her turn her back on the desire to help The City. The hope that *maybe* he'd understand that she was more than a witch had tempted her—but hope wasn't enough.

She'd considered having a child, hoping that she could suppress the child's magic. She'd even implored Evelyn to teach her how. When Evelyn refused, Aya knew it was far better to avoid motherhood, far safer for her and any child to simply avoid the chance of death or enslavement, far better for Belias never to know that she was a witch. She couldn't condemn her child, so at eighteen—the earliest she could become anyone's breedmate or wife—she had ended her betrothal to Belias and entered Marchosias' Competition.

But then Belias had entered too.

"WHAT ARE YOU DOING?" *She threw the first knife as she walked into his training room, but he'd expected it. A heavy leather-and-chain vest protected his chest and stomach. His arms were bare, but the vital parts were all protected.* Except his face. *She launched the second knife, and he dropped to the floor.*

"Apparently, I'm dodging your temper, little bird." *Belias picked up her knife.*

*She started across the floor, scowling at him, when he threw the knife at her. It nicked her upper arm, a slight cut that stung and bled, but it wouldn't incapacitate her. She smiled and looked at her torn, bloodied sleeve.* "Your aim gets worse every time you do that."

*He snorted.* "Not likely. My willingness to injure *you is all that's changed, and you know it."*

*Rather than acknowledge that truth, Aya bent and picked up her knife. While her expression was hidden, she said,* "I didn't expect you to enter the competition."

"Do you want me to withdraw?"

*Aya straightened.* "Yes."

*Belias gave her the sort of smile that had led to nights spent lost in each other, but he still approached her cautiously. Her other knife was held loosely in his hand.* "I am willing to withdraw if you do."

"I can't," *she whispered.* "I want a future, Bel. I want to change things, make a difference—"

"You can do that without becoming a killer." He stood in front of her now. Slowly, so she could escape if she wanted, he reached up and caressed her cheek. "We can negotiate whatever terms we need together. You and me."

"I can't be yours," she told him yet again. "I want more."

"More than me?"

"It's not about you, Bel." She gave in to her one weakness then and kissed him. When she pulled back, she told him, "You know I love you. If I were to marry anyone, it would be you, but I won't marry. Ever."

AYA BRUSHED AWAY THE few foolish tears she'd shed at the memory. They'd only been together a few more times after that. The more she'd fought, the more they'd both killed, the less they talked. Belias had no desire to prove himself in public fights, and he grew increasingly upset by her notoriety and reputation for ruthlessness.

WHEN SHE RETURNED FROM the first fight she'd nearly lost, he was there waiting. He had let himself into her apartment and stood there fuming. "Where is the daimon I have known my whole life, Aya?"

"Right here." She grabbed a cloth and swiped at the blood on her face, smearing it rather than cleaning it away. "I'm still right here."

Belias snatched the rag from her hand and wiped the blood that was dripping into her eye. "You don't need to keep doing *this. One of them is going to kill you, Aya. If he'd caught you a fraction lower with his claws—"*

*"But he didn't." Aya pulled away and turned her back to him. In her frustration, she couldn't get the buckle loosened on her boots. "Maybe I'm good enough. Maybe I'll win this thing. Does that ever occur to you?"*

*His hand came down gently on her shoulder; he turned her to face him. "It does, but not as often as the terror that one of them will get lucky or you'll get matched to someone faster or better trained or . . . I can't keep doing this."*

*For a moment, Aya wanted to give in, to tell him the secrets that drove her, but Belias hated witches even more than most daimons did. He blamed them all for his father's death. She closed her eyes. The moment was expected; before the first night they'd spent together, she'd known that he wasn't going to be in her life forever. Knowing didn't mean that reaching this point finally was painless.*

*She held out her hand. "My key."*

*"So that's it? You choose killing over me? Over the future we could have?" Belias' grip on her shoulders tightened, keeping her from walking away.*

*"We were never going to be able to have the future you want." Aya stayed perfectly still and stared into his eyes. "I will never have children."*

*"Aya," he whispered. "We can both quit the fights. We're already ruling class, and you've proven that you're a capable fighter."*

*"Tell me you'll always treat me as your equal. Tell me you'll accept my decision not to ever have children—and not resent me or pressure me to change my mind. We can secretly take in a scab baby, hire someone if necessary, but I cannot bear a child. Swear to it, Bel, and I'll do it. I'll give you forever if you can accept that we'll never breed. I can't change that."* The hope she rarely allowed herself filled her as Belias leaned in and kissed her gently.

When he stepped away, he withdrew her key from his pocket and handed it to her. *"I can't change who I am either. I have to have an heir. I have to have a ruling-caste wife, and unless you are my breedmate or my wife, I can't have you."*

*"To be clear, Bel, you're choosing tradition over me,"* she pointed out with as little bitterness as she could manage.

*"We'd have a future—a* good *future. We can still hire whatever staff you want to raise the child, but I need a child of my blood."* Belias shook his head. *"I could wait, but I can't accept never having an heir."*

AYA WONDERED IF HE remembered that conversation.

She had often dreamed that they'd find a way to compromise, but that dream was gone. The last few wisps of "what if" had shriveled as he stared out from the circle where she'd sent him.

Aya had seen the flash of fury in Belias' expression as Evelyn changed the circle. That was proof enough that he could no longer hear them. *As if I'd have any reason to doubt her.* Evelyn was one of the most frightening creatures Aya had ever encountered. If Marchosias had an equal in either world, it was the witch who currently held Belias prisoner.

"Are you sure it's wise to return there, Aya?" Evelyn folded her hands together again. "If this spell goes awry, you'll be exposed."

"I made a bargain." She tried not to watch Belias pace the circle like a caged animal. She'd dreaded seeing the look of horror in his eyes when he found out what she was, but she knew she'd never be what he wanted. Daimons and witches didn't breed. Common knowledge in The City said that they *couldn't*, but she was proof that they could.

Evelyn's voice drew Aya's attention back to her. "You could stay in this world and take a position here at Stoneleigh-Ross."

"No." Aya didn't belong in the human world. The rules here made no sense, and she didn't expect that witches would be any more accepting of her daimon side than daimons would be of her witch side. She glanced at Evelyn. The witch who ruled in this world wasn't any safer than the daimon who ruled in The City. The difference was that she understood The City, that she had power, position, and—hopefully—a future there. "Never."

"Not even if it meant being with your daimon?" Evelyn prodded.

Aya shook her head. "Belias knows what I am now. You didn't see the way he looked at me. . . ."

"You could tell him you're not all witch."

Aya returned a mirror version of Evelyn's smile. "Everyone

knows that witches and daimons can't breed, and all I have is your word that my father was a daimon."

"And talons," Evelyn added wryly. "Witches don't have a second form."

At that, Aya shrugged. She knew full well that she was a hybrid, but she wanted to know who her father was. She'd wanted that since she'd learned that her parents weren't really her biological parents. Evelyn wasn't forthcoming with that information though; all she'd said was that the daimon who'd fathered her had no idea—and that he was so disgusting that it was in everyone's best interest to keep him unaware.

"I deserve to know," Aya argued yet again.

"No you don't. He is too insignificant to matter." Evelyn walked around the front of the desk and stood as close to Aya as she ever did. It was a far cry from affection, but if Evelyn ever indicated that she felt anything remotely maternal, Aya would suspect a ruse.

Neither witch said anything further. They stayed side by side watching Belias pace and snarl for several moments. His talons were extended now, and he was searching the walls as if they were physical, as if there was some snag he could widen.

"If he can't be convinced to cooperate, I will have to kill him," Evelyn reminded her. "You staying here might be sufficient reason to convince him. He cares for you as much as any daimon is able."

And to that, Aya didn't have anything remotely polite to say. Belias had loved her; she knew that. She had also seen his eyes when she stabbed him, when he realized she was responsible for his imprisonment, when she revealed that she was a witch. She'd sacrifice a lot to keep him safe, but she wasn't sure she was able to give up her world and her dreams— or become tied to the one daimon who *had* loved her and whom she had betrayed.

"It's witches' capability for affection I question," Aya needled. "Maybe I should ask my daimon father if *he* is capable of caring for me. . . ."

She was at the door before Evelyn said, "He's not. Maybe your Belias is different, but the daimon whose spawn you are is not capable of anything affectionate. Sometimes you're more like him than I thought possible."

Aya didn't pause as she replied, "Perhaps that's what comes of abandoning me in The City."

She opened the door with a whispered word, proving by her action that even here in her mother's space she could bend the world to her will. It was a quiet statement, but it was a statement all the same. Being a daimon-witch hybrid made her an aberration in both worlds, but she wasn't a *weak* aberration. Reminding the head of the Witches' Council of that detail wasn't a bad idea.

# CHAPTER 19

As it should, the office door closed behind Aya with no effort from Evelyn. This was her domain, and bending things to her will was as easy as breathing. Her daughter's ability to *open* that door, however, was a remarkable bit of magic. Doing even slight magic in another witch's domain was difficult; doing it in the head of the Council's office was both difficult and confrontational.

*Good girl.*

Evelyn smiled briefly. Aya's ferocity was one of the only traits she shared with her father. The other useful one, of course, was her form-shifting skill. The spell that had enabled Evelyn to adjust her growing child's genetic structure during those formative months nineteen years ago had all but killed them both, but here they were—both alive and succeeding.

The victory had been worth the failed attempts. Delivering the child had been the final act in Evelyn's path to leadership. No one else had succeeded at the spell. One other pregnancy had come near term, but the child had been born so frail that it had died before it walked. The only victory was Aya.

Evelyn came to stand at the edge of the circle. The daimon stared out predatorily even though it couldn't see her. Its behavior did little to recommend its continued existence. On the other hand, it could be a useful tool if it survived. Having more allies among ruling-caste daimons would be advantageous to the Witches' Council.

"Aya seems to want you to live," she said.

The daimon lifted its head to stare at Evelyn. "And this matters why?"

"Because my daughter rarely asks for anything for herself," Evelyn admitted with a small shrug. "She's never asked for a pet before. You she wants to keep."

"Your *daughter*?" The daimon flinched, but if she hadn't erected the circle that held it, she wouldn't have noticed. Its expression betrayed nothing of the insult that it felt. It said nothing more about her revelation. Its gaze followed her, but that was expected of most any caged animal. "I am not a pet."

"A familiar, then." Evelyn waved her hand dismissively. "There are other uses for your sort. Spells where your blood would be an asset. I could collect a number of useful ingredients from you. These days, since our unfortunate removal from The City, it requires a bit of delicacy to get those things, but here you are, all ready to harvest."

"So those are my choices? You butcher me, or I'm Aya's *pet*?" It sneered.

"Yes." Evelyn hadn't survived this long without having to dirty her hands. She was more at ease with murder than with affection, but in this case, she was hoping not to murder the daimon. The unfortunate truth was that her child *was* fond of it. The complications that would result from the daimon's death were ones she would rather avoid. "If you would prefer death to being her familiar, I will kill you. Unlike Aya, I have no affection for daimons."

"I'm not sure she had any affection for—"

Evelyn inhaled sharply, removing most of the air from its cage in the process. She watched the daimon try not to put its hand to its throat, studied the daimon as it struggled against the sudden loss of breath, and then she released it just as abruptly as she'd begun to suffocate it. "She is fond of you. We both know that."

This time, the daimon didn't reply, but Evelyn wasn't sure if that was because it was trying to catch its breath or if it had learned not to argue with her. Daimons required a heavy hand. Most of them expired before they were any real use to her. This one needed to be kept alive though. The sad fact was that her daughter *was* a lot like her, ruthless and focused—which meant that crossing Aya would be problematic. Gifting her with a powerful familiar would be better than killing the daimon, but the process of doing so required the daimon's assent.

Evelyn lowered the circle. At this point, doing so was a formality. If it tried to run, she'd stop it. It had eaten next to nothing, so it was too weak to attack her. Willpower alone wouldn't provide it the strength to overcome her. She fisted her hand in the air, and it gagged as her gesture caused it to feel like her hand was squeezing its throat.

The daimon thudded to the floor, glaring at her all the while.

"I have other uses we could come up with, Belias. There are witches who would be indebted to me if I gave you to them."

As its eyes fluttered, she relaxed her hand. It wouldn't be able to hear her if it was unconscious. Then she'd need to repeat herself when it regained consciousness.

She waited. Once it appeared focused again, she continued, "Some of my colleagues are studying daimon physiology. I'm sure there are others who need sacrifices for this or that project." She sighed as the daimon tried to stand. This time, she held her hand up with her palm facing out in a halting gesture.

It stopped.

"I would prefer not to involve them." Evelyn pressed forward in the air with her upraised hand until the daimon was flat on its back. She walked over and stared down at it. "They don't need to know about Aya's weakness for your sort. It's unseemly. My solution really is the tidiest resolution here."

Even as the daimon was immobilized on the floor, it glared up at her. It was a very spirited display, all things considered—useless, of course, but still, the gesture was worth acknowledging. For Aya to do the sort of spells she'd need to, she had to have a familiar to store magic, and this one was actually a great specimen. It was fit and young, strong and resilient. It would make a good vessel. She told it as much, adding, "You are obviously otherwise skilled too, or she wouldn't have looked at you so tenderly. This is a far gentler fate than that of any other daimon who has been summoned here."

Finally, the daimon asked in an impressively steady voice, "What terms?"

# CHAPTER 20

AFTER A FEW SURPRISINGLY restful hours, Kaleb woke to the sound of Zevi welcoming Aya, but the witch said nothing more than, "You can go. I did what needed done."

The witch looked worn-out, as if whatever task she'd completed had left her as weakened as a fight would, but Kaleb wasn't in the habit of asking questions that might lead to emotional admissions, and fortunately, Aya wasn't the sort to reveal anything. Only Zevi's well-being would invite inquiries, but Zevi seemed to spill every secret without prompting, so that particular awkwardness was unnecessary between them.

Aya stood looking at them, and Zevi walked up to her and briefly butted his head into her shoulder. He had the aptitude to handle all of the emotional intricacies that Kaleb had no desire to develop. Looking unexpectedly grateful, Aya smiled at Zevi, and then she was gone.

The circle had dropped, and Kaleb and Zevi were left in the lush surroundings alone. Kaleb wasn't sure whether it was the removal of the circle or whatever spell Aya had cast while they were in the circle, but he felt relaxed. The silks and velvets appeared a bit shabbier in the daylight, and the tarnished brass looked dull where it had seemed to shimmer in the candlelight. The rare foods that had been delivered were still tempting, even if they were a little more obviously overripe now that they were clearly visible.

"Do you trust her?" Zevi asked.

Kaleb stretched. His pains weren't gone, but he had a few hours left before the fight. Healing wasn't instant. "Maybe." He smiled at Zevi, but the scowl he received in reply made clear that he still wasn't able to lie convincingly to the younger cur, so he added, "I don't have many other options, Z. I fight today, or I forfeit. If I forfeit . . ."

"We *could* ask her to be our protector," Zevi suggested.

"If I die, you can ask her."

"We could leave The City." Zevi contorted his body into what looked like a decidedly uncomfortable position. "I know you don't want to live in the Untamed Lands, but what about the human world? If Aya's witch enough to do what she did, I bet she could open a gate there for us."

"I fight today, Z," Kaleb said. The chance of victory was slim, but it was there. "I can't forfeit."

"I know." Zevi picked up his satchel, withdrew his mask, and slipped it on. He grinned. "A daimon can only change his mask so often."

"Maybe . . . or maybe he can stop wearing one." Kaleb grabbed a piece of fruit from the crystal bowl on the counter and walked out into the Carnival of Souls. Vendors were just beginning to open up, and a few knowing glances were sent their way as they walked out of the pleasure quarter at the break of day. If he told them that he and Zevi hadn't partaken of any mind alterations or sex, no one would believe him—especially since Zevi now wore his red mask pushed atop his head like a hat. His face was exposed for any and all to see.

Kaleb glanced at Zevi, who stared back at him with faux innocence.

"I didn't mean that literally," Kaleb pointed out.

"I'm not ashamed of what I've done to survive, Kaleb," he said in his usual blunt way. Then he grinned and shrugged. "And it's no real secret who I am when you're with me, and by now word has gone round that we were in there with Aya. Might as well let them think we were doing that rather than anything else."

Kaleb nodded. *Did she set us up?* He couldn't see how it would be to her advantage to do so. Most likely, she simply wanted to start the rumor that they were allies. Without her witchery being exposed, no one would realize what they were up to. *Misdirection and rumormongering.* He felt foolish that she'd manipulated the situation so cleverly, but all that really mattered was that, unless Aya had been honest and was able to do as she promised, Kaleb would die today.

*Should I trust her?*

He had no idea, but he also hadn't come up with any other options. If Aya could give him an extra something to survive this fight, he'd live. He'd protect Zevi. He'd have a chance with Mallory. He'd have more choices—and so would Aya and Zevi.

SEVERAL HOURS LATER, KALEB was no surer of Aya's trustworthiness than he had been when he woke, but it didn't much matter. He would fight whether or not she'd been telling the truth.

The spectators were lined at the edge of the circle, crushed against the wooden barricades that were erected beyond the fight circle, and overflowing the seats until they were near falling.

There was no question as to which fighter should, by rights, bow, but Kaleb wasn't about to enter what was most likely his last fight with meekness. The barely there dip of the head that Kaleb offered Sol was testament not only to his cur opinion on being always thought lower but also to his standing in the fights. He would either be among the last fighters, or he'd die today. Either way, he wasn't going to feign humility.

Sol's lips pressed together in a tight line, but he said nothing.

They gathered the silty mixture in the bucket and closed the fight circle in that same silence. The awareness that this fight was essential to win was underscored by Sol—and everyone watching—knowing that Kaleb had been badly injured by Nic.

The circle closed with a snap that reverberated in Kaleb's skin in a peculiar way. They'd both been in dozens of fight circles, but the tingle that flowed over Kaleb's skin was utterly unfamiliar. Based on the flash of surprise in Sol's face, Kaleb suspected that he felt it too.

In a blink, the fight began. Sol kicked out at Kaleb's leg as Kaleb's fist shot toward Sol's throat. Unlike when he was fighting another cur, Kaleb didn't worry about teeth or claws in this fight. Members of the ruling caste rarely used their alternate forms. Belias was an exception, but even with him, the shift was rare. They might let talons free, but that was it.

Sol's second punch missed, but it distracted Kaleb, and he didn't dodge the knee that rammed into his leg. That was the goal, apparently: go for the weakness. It was a backstreet move, not what Sol would do against a member of his own caste.

*But I am less to him.*

They each tested the other, watching for reactions, assessing strengths. They'd undoubtedly both already watched each other fight, and from the way Sol targeted Kaleb's injured leg, it was abundantly clear that Sol had seen the fight with Nic or had reports of where Kaleb had been most hurt. The injuries Kaleb had tried to hide and heal weren't eradicated, and he supposed it was foolish to believe that Aya's methods would allow him full advantage.

As he and Sol punched each other, an unusual number of Watchers fell against the circle and were tossed back by the force of the magic that kept the fight zone clear. Their interest in getting closer resulted in their being flung into the carnival, and this time Kaleb was grateful for the security. He was far from fight ready; Aya's promised energy hadn't happened.

*Did she lie?*

There was no way to ask her that unless he lived through the fight, and in that moment he wasn't sure he was going to.

Sol's fists hammered Kaleb's ribs, and despite the exhaustion and the mindlessness that came from transforming, he started to shift forms.

"Kill! Kill! Kill!" The voices outside the circle rose and fell rhythmically, their cadence a chant that matched the heartbeat thundering inside Kaleb. "Teeth! Claws! Kill!"

Sol, knowing that fighting against tooth and claw was harder, grabbed a long-handled trident-looking weapon that Kaleb hadn't faced in any of the fights to date.

"Teeth! Claws! Kill!"

They were chanting for him, not Sol, not anyone else. They'd reveled in the bloody death he'd dealt Nic and wanted more of the same. What they cherished, what they craved, was the monstrosity he'd rather not embrace.

Sol stabbed the long-handled weapon toward him, trying to capture and pin one of Kaleb's legs in the tines. The edge grazed and tore flesh. The burn of the cut registered but in the vague way that injury did in this form. *Pain.* That meant attack. If the upper class spent a little more time trying to understand curs, they'd do better at dealing with them—or fighting them. *Stop pain.*

Another stab of the trident came at him; this one missed completely.

*Kill.*

Reason began to vanish under a flood of anger and strength. The injuries that had made him sluggish in the other form were gone now. Kaleb lunged at Sol, moving faster than he was used to even at his peak.

Sol's eyes widened in a flash of fear as Kaleb's teeth snapped down on his forearm. The trident fell from Sol's hand. The weight of it hit Kaleb as it dropped.

The momentum of Kaleb's leap pushed Sol to the ground, and he scrambled backward, trying to get out from under Kaleb. Even the youngest daimon knew better than to be on the ground with a transformed cur. Here, on all fours, Kaleb had advantages that the bipedal lacked. He wasn't willing to lose that advantage either; he tightened his grip on Sol's arm.

With his free hand, Sol punched Kaleb as hard as he could. The blow hit Kaleb under the eye, connecting with flesh on his muzzle and jarring the teeth that held Sol's other arm immobile. Repeatedly, Sol slammed his fist into Kaleb's face.

Blood—his and Sol's—was filling Kaleb's mouth. He released the arm and went for Sol's exposed throat.

Sol rolled away, and Kaleb's teeth closed on empty air.

As Kaleb stalked the bleeding daimon trapped in the circle

with him, he felt increasingly energized.

Sol stumbled as he went for a pair of short blades. With a blade in each hand, he pivoted, watching Kaleb. He didn't attack, and that alone was indicative of which way the fight was going. Typically, he was an aggressive fighter.

Kaleb darted in for another bite, but was rebuffed with a kick to the side where he'd previously been injured. As he pulled back, he realized that not only did his side no longer hurt, but his leg also felt fine. In fact, he felt stronger by the moment. *Aya's spell.* As Sol weakened, Kaleb strengthened. Even in his animal mind, he understood that the healing energy she had promised him was coming from Sol. The witch had made it so Kaleb was leeching strength from his opponent.

Again and again, Kaleb charged at his increasingly unsteady adversary. Sol bled from several places, and although Kaleb had new wounds, each sharp pain almost immediately began to fade. Even the worst of the wounds Sol had inflicted were already beginning to heal. Every new injury healed quickly, as the energy that Kaleb now stole from Sol made the flesh knit back together with an unsettling tingling. It felt better than the pain relievers Zevi fed him after fights, better than the narcotics he had occasionally enjoyed over the years. Even as he was injured time and again, Kaleb felt like he could continue doing this for hours. He didn't want that flood of strength to ebb, didn't want to lose the surge of health that poured into his skin.

In a move uncharacteristic of curs, he struck Sol to

injure, not to incapacitate, tearing small wounds in the bigger daimon's chest and abdomen. *Death will end the energy.* Kaleb tried to force himself to remember why he should want Sol to die. If Sol stayed alive, the energy would keep filling Kaleb.

Sol slashed at him, and Kaleb let the blade graze his side so he could feel his body repair itself. He stayed perfectly still for a moment, staring at Sol and waiting for another pass of the sharp edges against his skin. His fur was matted with blood, but he wanted to feel that next infusion of strength.

The weakened, but not yet dying, daimon was speaking to him, but in this form Kaleb couldn't understand anyone other than another cur. Sol bowed his head for a moment. His body was sluggish, and Kaleb knew it would take only one carefully aimed swipe of his claws to bring death to his rival. *Not yet.* He lunged forward, presenting his side as an obvious target, but Sol merely stared at him through glazed eyes.

Kaleb growled.

Sol spoke again, but this time he stumbled toward Kaleb. He bowed his head, hiding his throat, asking for mercy.

Kaleb backed away. He couldn't make Sol raise his blade again, but he didn't want him to die. With a snarl, he charged the circle, giving them both a shock. The energy rushed toward Kaleb, drawn from Sol again, and the combined pain of the shock and the loss of more of his strength and health made Sol fall facedown. Kaleb padded over to Sol and prodded the hand holding the blade. Sol didn't react, so Kaleb nudged harder with his muzzle.

Then Sol's lips formed a word, and the need to understand that word was urgent enough that Kaleb shed his animal form. Once he was no longer in his other shape, he understood words again. He stared at Sol.

"Forfeit," Sol said. He repeated the word again and again, adding, "Mercy, cur."

Kaleb straightened and stared down at Sol. *Cur?* Even now, Sol couldn't give him the respect of a name. *If he stays alive, I can keep taking his energy.* Kaleb looked past the fallen fighter and saw Aya watching them. Her expression revealed nothing, but Kaleb saw her lips form the same word Sol had, "Mercy."

Resisting the urge to bound to his feet from the surges of energy humming in his body, Kaleb stood slowly. He looked out over the mostly unmasked crowd and then settled his gaze on Aya. Watching her, he called to the assembled judges, "Break it. I'm done here. Sol forfeits. I accept. I want nothing else from him."

There were gasps that he had accepted a forfeit, but Kaleb didn't care. He shouldn't have tortured Sol. All that mattered in that instant was getting away from the fight, the crowds, and the horror of what he'd done.

The circle dropped, Aya nodded, and the connection between him and Sol stopped as if it had been cut. The loss of that flood of strength made him falter as he stepped forward— and for that, he was grateful. If the crowd knew how not-injured he was, they would be suspicious. That he'd won this fight was surprising enough; winning without being exhausted or injured would be alarming. The blood covering his body hid the fact that the injuries he'd sustained in the fight were mostly healed.

The circle falling meant that the press of the crowd was upon them. Strangers touched him, their fingers coming away wet with the combined blood of the two fighters. Later, bits of cloth stained with that blood would be sold in the market. The twisted mementos were collected by the macabre and the zealous, and Kaleb wasn't sure which group he found most unsettling.

"This way," a spectator called, trying to summon him closer. Her hand was outstretched, fingers splayed, as she shoved herself through the swarm of bodies. "I'll nurse your wounds, Kaleb."

"No, *here*," a Watcher called.

"I'll match any offer," a blue-masked daimon called. This one held out a marker with a sum that Kaleb would have once accepted, despite the sting to his pride and sickness in his soul that followed every time he'd been hungry enough to whore himself.

His emotions must have been obvious in his expression because the masked daimon added a second marker, thereby doubling the offer. Kaleb opened his mouth to negotiate, here in front of any and all watching. He was a cur, an animal of the lowest order, a daimon to be used by those who could pay for him. Even if he won, he'd still be that creature. *Why deny it?* If he were a better person, he'd have been revolted by stealing Sol's energy. Instead, he had tortured the other daimon to prolong the theft. Instead, he was wondering if that connection was permanently severed. Aya might be terrible for creating it, but he was no less awful for enjoying it.

"What terms?" Kaleb asked the woman.

"No," Zevi murmured. The younger cur had forced his way through the overly energetic crowd and was now directly beside Kaleb.

"We could live on that for months," Kaleb replied just as quietly.

"So you fought and killed to be an expensive fuck?"

Kaleb's gaze snapped to Zevi.

"Don't let guilt change you." Zevi shoved an eager spectator away from them with a snarl and audible snap of teeth. "You let him live. Even though you were transformed, you stopped. You gave mercy."

The daimon with the markers had pushed to the front of the crowd. "One night. Only me . . . you can bring your . . . *him* if you want." She pointed at Zevi. "I'll pay extra."

Zevi turned his back to her, to all of them. "We leave here now. You set these rules, Kaleb. Don't do this."

After a brief pause, Kaleb told the woman, "No." Then he let Zevi lead him away. "I didn't want to stop. It wasn't kindness that made me, but wanting that ener—"

"I know," Zevi interrupted, "but the only people who do know are you, me, and *her*."

At that, Kaleb's gaze again sought out Aya where she stood in the crowd watching him. He shuddered. There were good reasons that witches weren't allowed to roam freely in The City. For the sort of exhilaration he'd just felt, there were a lot of depths Kaleb would sink to. In his seventeen years, he'd done more than a few things that he'd rather forget, but he did them to survive or to protect Zevi. He'd maimed; he'd killed; and he'd allowed things to be done to his body that made him retch afterward. Never once had he had given in to cruelty for sheer pleasure.

*Until today.*

*Until Aya.*

# CHAPTER 21

AFTER ZEVI LED KALEB away, Aya watched with the rest of the spectators as Sol was gathered by his family's servants. Unlike the curs who entered the competition, ruling-class daimons had the ability to resume their lives if they forfeited. If she weren't carrying the secret she had and if she weren't female, she could do that too. The daimons who filled The City didn't know she was as trapped as the curs were, but she did.

She didn't have the comfort of being in either group. Her class made her separate from the curs; her independence made her barely tolerated by those of her class. She was neither at the top or bottom, and she was definitely not welcome in the trades class.

As Sol passed her, he had his eyes downcast, but she knew that his humility would fade as his bruises did. As a result of today's fight, he would either be extra harsh to curs, or he'd learn from it. Only time would tell.

All things considered, the fight had turned out well. The worst that had happened was that Kaleb saw a part of himself that he disliked—and blamed her.

"Haage hired the cur to kill Marchosias' child," a Watcher whispered.

Aya turned her head, but the woman was already leaving. She walked toward three black-masked daimons who stood silent and waiting. As the Watcher reached their side, they turned.

The last one nodded at Aya as her gaze fell on them.

The missing child was the daughter of a Watcher. Aya knew that much, but no one had been able to find the girl. Until Marchosias' announcement, the girl had been assumed dead by many daimons, but the last news that Aya had learned— news that was never made public—was that the girl had been spirited away by witches. Most daimons had no ties to the Witches' Council, and although Aya did, she had no further information. Evelyn had been decidedly closemouthed when Aya had asked. They protected their own, and even though Aya was technically one of them, she was just as much daimon as she was witch.

*More perhaps.*

She looked toward the teeming masses in the carnival and saw what she assumed to be one of the same black-masked daimons staring at her. He—*or she*—nodded again and then beckoned her forward with a slight head tilt.

"Right," she muttered. "Follow the masked assassin. Great idea."

The unpleasant reality was that although the black-masks weren't precisely organized, they *were* often influenced by Haage. As brother to The City's ruler and as one of the most successful assassins, he inspired—or otherwise enforced—a lot of allegiance. As much as she had qualms about Marchosias as an individual, she respected the hell out of him as a ruler. Haage, on the other hand, made Marchosias seem positively forward thinking. He had tried and failed at various attacks on The City's ruler; he exploited scabs, curs, and trades-class daimons. The only caste he wouldn't strike outright was the ruling class, but that would pass in time too. For now, he stuck to killing off any witches bound to them. Witches' heads were found skewered on pikes at the edge of The City. Their bodies, presumably, were discarded in the Untamed Lands or simply destroyed. Within The City, many moves toward civility were done at Marchosias' behest, just as the most barbarous of acts were credited to Haage. Aya knew enough to suspect both daimons of barbarism and deceit, but she also knew that The City would become a deadlier place if Haage gained power—and that the witches who remained in The City would all be killed.

There weren't too many daimons she'd rather not cross outright. Her rank and her hidden skills meant that if she couldn't avoid trouble, she could resolve it permanently. Haage, however, was a daimon whose attention she'd like to avoid. She wasn't fighter enough to take him on directly, and she couldn't kill him with witchery without exposing herself. If these assassins were in his employ, she was in trouble. Actually, if they weren't in his employ, she was in trouble too. Going with them could mean crossing Haage or inadvertently working with him. Neither was the sort of action that led to longevity.

*Nice of you to warn me of your brethren's interest, Kaleb.*

As stealthily as she could, she followed the assassin through the carnival—or maybe she followed several different assassins. She kept losing sight of the nondescript black masks he or they wore, only to see a subtle gesture beckoning her forward.

Aya followed the black-masked daimon through a circuitous route around the carnival. Each time she lost sight of the daimon, she paused to inspect vendors' wares, lingered in front of market stalls examining cloth and fruits, and idled to watch dancers. Each time, she was led farther until she'd left the carnival behind and found herself trailing her unknown guide through the thick of The City. The streets were filled with all classes of daimons, who gathered to talk or made their way to their homes, jobs, or recreations.

She kept watching for a doorway that she was to enter, but her guide continued on until they stood at the far edge of The City. Strange gnarled trees shredded the ruins of buildings that had been abandoned by daimons who had moved farther from or into The City. Animals roamed in undergrowth; their cries made their presences known even though she couldn't see them. Scores of Marchosias' best fighters patrolled the perimeter, hidden among those same verdant plants and trees.

The assassin, thankfully, didn't lead her into the Untamed Lands. She—and now that they were side by side, Aya could tell that this assassin was female—stood silent. Before them was the massive expanse of the wilds that pushed in toward The City. Behind them was the overcrowded, class-divided morass of The City. Even though she couldn't see it, Aya knew the Carnival of Souls pulsed in the center—a swirl of masked pleasure and violence. Outside The City was something unordered. There, class lines were not observed. Food was what one killed or stole. The City was rife with corruption, but it had order that the Untamed Lands lacked.

"Haage would have all of our world like that." The black-masked daimon stared into the Untamed Lands. "You've been out there. Is that what you think best?"

Aya wasn't about to start talking about her trips into the Untamed Lands. That wasn't anyone's business but her own. The scars she'd earned there were the only ones she'd had removed. If what she could do out there became known, it would be the same as announcing that she was a witch stronger than any allowed to live within The City.

*And I'd be dead by the next morning.*

There was no way to convey her desire to help The City without Marchosias feeling like she was power hungry. Power-hungry witches died. Strong witches died.

Aya kept her features expressionless as she waited for the assassin to say more.

"Marchosias tries to push the border out farther every

season; he tries to protect his people. He is flawed, but he works hard to be a good ruler for The City," the assassin said. She looked at Aya briefly, revealing the red-and-blue-ringed eyes of a Watcher, before adding, "I have ample reason to hate him, but he is better than the alternatives."

The flat tone of the Watcher's voice told Aya what the daimon didn't: this was someone who knew Marchosias personally.

"His last child was the child of a Watcher," Aya said with as little affect as possible.

Although Aya couldn't see it, she thought the Watcher might have smiled behind her mask because the tone of her voice was amused as she answered, "I am not the girl's mother."

Aya tensed as the undergrowth quivered with the movement of either an animal or a soldier. A growl quickly revealed that it wasn't a soldier approaching.

"Should we—"

"Move," the Watcher directed. She launched herself forward as a bovine creature charged toward them.

In the same moment, she'd retrieved a small ax from somewhere under her coat. Before Aya could help in their defense, the Watcher buried the ax in the animal's neck. It fell, making noises of protest. As it died, the Watcher rejoined Aya.

"Out there"—the Watcher gestured with the gore-coated weapon—"that is normal."

Aya was transfixed as a group of Watchers appeared from the same thick undergrowth and began dragging the animal away. She didn't want to stay here, didn't want to wander into that part of the world. She stepped backward. "Why did you bring me here?"

"To see why Marchosias needs your help," the Watcher said.

Aya shuddered. "I'm not sure why you think I can—"

"We know," the Watcher interrupted.

With two simple words, the daimon beside her became more frightening than the creatures hidden in the Untamed Lands, more awful than the thought of death or loss or most anything Aya could imagine. She forced herself to try to stay calm. "I'm not sure what you think you know."

"Evelyn," the Watcher said. "We know what Evelyn did, what you are."

Aya had drawn a knife and stepped farther back so that the Watcher was between her and the Untamed Lands. There was a risk that the Watcher could disappear into that foreboding growth, but better chance that than try to fight with the possibility of being attacked from behind by an animal.

"We don't share secrets without reason. We have no reason to reveal yours." The Watcher didn't react to Aya's posture or weapon. "Help Marc, and you will help yourself."

Two more Watchers walked out of the Untamed Lands and stood one on either side of the Watcher who had been speaking. Both were unmasked.

The one to the left said, "The cur knows where one of the missing daughters is. We've seen them together."

"*Daughters?*" Aya repeated.

"Ask the cur," the first Watcher said.

"You cannot trust Evelyn," the third Watcher added. "Help Marc."

"How?"

"Tell him who your mother is," the masked Watcher said.

Then all three of the Watchers turned and walked into the Untamed Lands. They'd apparently said all they intended to say for now.

Moments passed, and all Aya heard were the sounds of the creatures who roamed in the wilds. No daimons, Watcher or otherwise, appeared. No assassins arrived. The conversation they'd had could've been held in a stall in The City, but doing so wouldn't have afforded the Watcher the ability to make an example of the nature outside The City—or afforded Aya the privacy she cherished.

Unfortunately, their wisdom didn't make sense. There was no way that she was telling Marchosias what she was or who her mother was. It would be suicide. Aya didn't put her knife away as she walked toward the familiar overcrowded streets of The City—nor did she stop watching for black-masked daimons. There were more secrets than she could make sense of. Right now, all she knew for certain was that Kaleb needed to share his secrets. After that, she could try to figure out what to do about Haage and Marchosias.

*And the missing daughter . . . or daughters.*

# CHAPTER 22

WHEN KALEB ARRIVED AT Mallory's door that evening, he was greeted by her stepfather. Adam Rothesay looked like a lot of men who could pass by unnoticed on the street. He was a shade over six foot, trim, with nondescript clothes and nondescript features. He wasn't remarkable in any way, but he still made Kaleb uncomfortable.

"Mallory isn't available," Adam said, coming out and pulling the door to the house shut behind him. "We should talk."

The way that Mallory's stepfather smiled genially made Kaleb even tenser. It wasn't the smile of true friendliness, but the sort of smile that often accompanied trouble. *Maybe I'm overreacting.* Living in The City made a person suspicious. They were in front of a quiet house in a quiet town in the human world.

Before Adam could say anything further, the door opened, and Mallory herself stood there staring at the two of them. "Daddy? *Kaleb?*" She smiled at him. "Hi."

Adam turned his back to Kaleb. "I was just going to talk to him. You ought to—"

"If there's something to say, I *deserve* to hear it." Mallory leaned on the doorjamb.

The displeasure on Adam's face was undeniable, but his remark was said too low for Kaleb to hear. He gestured for Kaleb to go into the house.

As soon as they crossed the threshold, Adam stepped around Kaleb and directed Mallory to a worn brown sofa. She looked exhausted, and a new bitter scent tinged the air around her. It smelled more like magic than sickness.

*Is he a witch?*

Kaleb glanced again at Adam. The telltale blue-gold witch eyes were absent. There were, however, rare witches who didn't have blue-and-gold eyes. It was exceedingly unusual, but not impossible. Aya didn't have witch eyes.

The unease Kaleb felt grew as Adam smiled with the practiced ease of one who hid what he was thinking more often than not.

Kaleb stayed in the doorway, not quite in the living room, and watched the older man warily. Attacking Mallory's father would cause problems, but the sense of self-preservation that Kaleb had counted on since childhood made him wonder if an attack would be necessary. Something was very much not right here.

Adam started, "I need to fetch a blanket and things, so you—"

"I can get it," Mallory interrupted.

"No. You rest." Adam smiled at her, gently now. He bent down and kissed the top of his daughter's head. "I'm going to talk to Kaleb."

Mallory opened her mouth like she wanted to say more, but instead, a strange look of calm suddenly came over her. She smiled meekly at her father and then murmured, "Okay."

Again, Adam motioned for Kaleb to precede him through the hallway. As Kaleb ascended the stairs to where he assumed the bedrooms were, he watched for dangers or traps.

The house was small and, by human standards, modest. Boxes still remained to be unpacked, but what was in place was nondescript and orderly. Three rooms opened up from the short hallway. One door was closed. One open door revealed a bed, dresser, and footlocker; all were equally drab, but serviceable. The third door revealed what was obviously Mallory's room. A vase of fresh flowers, an iPod, and a pile of books covered a dark wooden dresser. Fluffy slippers poked out from under the edge of a bed that was heaped high with pillows. It was the only room so far that contained any hint that a person lived there. Kaleb wished he could take a few moments to see what she read, what she listened to, what secrets were revealed by what she chose. Hers was a life completely different from his, and he wanted to understand her.

Instead, Adam ushered him toward the nondescript room.

"Grab that blanket." Adam pointed to a quilt that was folded at the foot of a tidily made bed.

"Sure," Kaleb said, but the moment he crossed the threshold to the room, he fell to his knees, trying his damnedest not to retch all over the floor.

"Daimons have no business around my daughter, Kaleb." Adam knelt beside him.

The witch eyes that Kaleb hadn't seen earlier were now plainly visible. "You *are* a witch."

"Yes, and she is my daughter by law."

Kaleb tried to stand and failed. "She doesn't know she's a dai—"

"No. All that matters is that she's *my daughter.*" Adam added an extra jolt of pain to the already agonizing sensations with a whispered word in the strange language of witches.

As Kaleb pulled his knees to his chest, curling into a fetal ball, Adam picked up the quilt as if he weren't torturing Kaleb at that very instant.

When Kaleb looked up at him, Adam said, "We'll go out there, and in a few moments, you'll tell Mallory that you're feeling unwell, and you'll leave. I won't tell her what you are or injure you in front of her, and you'll keep your mouth shut about what she is and stay away from her. Do you understand?"

"If I don't?"

"I have been killing daimons for centuries." Adam whispered another of his witch's curses, and the pain increased.

"What purpose would it serve anyhow? Mallory has been raised to hate your kind—"

"*Her* kind," Kaleb corrected. "What do you think will happen when she finds out?"

"She isn't going to find out *today*," Adam snarled. "She needs to be calm while she heals. Exposing you to her would upset her."

The pain stopped as suddenly as it had started. Kaleb wasn't ready to try standing yet. He marshaled his strength as Adam waited. The witch didn't offer him a hand up, but he didn't strike Kaleb as he stood.

"The Watcher. Whatever the Watcher did peeled back your spells. That's why she's sick," Kaleb said, thinking of their unexpected encounter with the daimon woman the last time he'd seen Mallory. "Her body is rejecting the magic you've wrapped around her."

Adam smoothed nonexistent wrinkles from the quilt. "My daughter is none of your business. I can handle the Watchers *and you* . . . and him, too, if he is foolish enough to come here."

"So you do know who her father is," Kaleb pointed out uselessly.

"She is *my* daughter by law, daimon, and until she's eighteen, he can't come near her, and if he sends his lackeys, I'll kill them."

"Then why aren't you killing me?"

"Because it would upset *my daughter*, who is sick right

now, but if you come back, I will. You only get a pass today because it's what's best for Mallory. You can walk out of here with no harm if you don't speak of any of this. I'm giving you a chance to live. Do you understand?"

"Yes," Kaleb said.

"Daddy? Kaleb?" Mallory called from the living room.

Quilt in hand, Adam walked past him. "Come."

Kaleb followed. The temptation to strike the witch, whose back was to him, lasted for only a moment. Killing her father was a sure way to chase Mallory off. Retreating made sense, but every instinct in him rebelled at the idea. He hadn't fought so hard in his life to walk away from a challenge without at least trying.

As Adam went into the living room, he said, "I'm afraid that Kaleb can't stay. Right, Kaleb?"

Kaleb lifted his gaze to stare directly at Mallory as he answered, "I can stay."

She glanced between them; her expression of concern made clear that she was unhappy. "Daddy?"

"It's fine, Mals." Adam covered Mallory's legs with the quilt, and then he glanced over his shoulder at Kaleb. "Are you sure, Kaleb?"

Bracing himself for the pain that would come, Kaleb looked briefly at Adam. "I care for her. That's why I'm h—" The wave of pain made it impossible to speak for a moment, but even so, his resolve strengthened. He'd experienced more than his share of pain in The City. The challenge was in not vomiting on the floor or blacking out. He spread his feet to brace himself, shuddered, and then said, "I'm here because I like you, Mallory."

The words weren't even fully formed before he felt his guts being torn open. He glanced down and saw that his skin was intact, but the sensation was convincing enough that he still put a hand on his stomach, needing to feel that his internal organs weren't spilling out. He stared directly at Mallory. "I want to be with you, Mallory. I *will* be."

"Daddy? What's going on?" Mallory started to stand.

Adam stopped her. "No."

"What are you doing?" she whispered to her father.

Kaleb didn't hear the witch's reply. He closed his eyes as a fresh wash of pain, sharper now, hit him. He thought he had known pain, but nothing he'd felt in his life came anywhere near the agony radiating through his body. He started shaking, and his vision blurred.

Then Mallory's voice was all he heard. "Kaleb!"

He shook so severely that he began to flail about and found himself on the floor. He turned his head so that he was looking up at Mallory. She had her hand over her mouth, and her eyes were wide with horror.

The witch reached down and pulled him to his feet. Adam's touch felt like brands searing Kaleb's skin. He pressed his lips together to keep from screaming. If not for Adam's grip, he would've pitched face forward on the ground, but the same grip that held him upright was the source of the torture.

In a calm, falsely friendly voice, Adam started, "Mals, I'm going to take him—"

"No." Kaleb pulled away from Adam, almost falling to his knees as he did so. Going with Adam would be a death sentence, but staying wasn't likely to end well either. As much as it galled him, Kaleb knew that his only option was retreat. *For now.* He met Adam's gaze. "I'll go."

The pain vanished, but Kaleb knew that the reprieve would be only temporary if he tried to stay. He smiled at Mallory. "I'm sorry."

Mallory's eyes looked wet with tears, and Kaleb felt even worse at seeing her sorrow. He didn't want her to hurt or to see him so weak, but he couldn't overcome Adam. Rage filled him to the point that it took effort not to let his claws free. If he could fight back, he'd show Adam that he wasn't a pup to be tortured. Unfortunately, he was pretty sure that revealing claws would disturb Mallory.

Kaleb swayed. "Don't hate me, Mallory. I really do care about you, and there are very few things I want more than to be with you."

"You need to say good-bye. *Now.*" Adam took hold of Kaleb's arm.

And Kaleb wasn't able to reply. If he agreed, Mallory would think that meant he wasn't coming back, and if he attacked Adam, he'd be completely thrashed in front of her—and reveal what he was. All he could do was stumble to the door.

# CHAPTER 23

"WHAT IS HE?" MALLORY folded her arms over her chest, hugging the blanket to her.

"Let's not do this today, Mals. You need to rest, not to get agitated." Her father rubbed his face. "No more questions."

"How am I supposed to not ask questions?" Her voice rose in frustration.

He sighed. "Please let it go. You have to stay calm while the medicine—"

"No," she interrupted. "You attacked him, and I'm pretty sure that means he's either a daimon or— I've been dating a daimon." Her voice was shrill now. "How could I not know?"

Adam sat beside her on the sofa. "I'm sorry, sweetheart."

Tears had started pouring down her cheeks while she

spoke, and she wiped at them furiously. "Why didn't you just tell me? Why didn't you kill—"

The thought of her father killing Kaleb made her feel sick. *He's a daimon. He has to be put down.* She had been falling for a daimon. *I miss him already.*

"You need to be calm."

"I just watched you torture the boy I like, who apparently is a *daimon*. I'm not going to be calm!" She reached up and gripped the stone pendant around her throat. It burned in her hand, but she didn't let go. "I have a right to know what's going on!"

Adam looked heartbroken for a moment. He repeated, "I'm sorry. I wish I didn't need to do this when you're awake."

And then her father spoke a spell, and a wave of darkness swept her away.

She wasn't sure how much time had passed, but Mallory opened her eyes to find that she was nestled in her bed. She felt better—and worse. The tears and panic that had overwhelmed her were gone, driven away by a raw new pain. Her father, the one person in her life who had meant everything to her, had used his magic on her.

She slid out of her bed, wrapped herself in her robe, and went to the window. She'd grown up accepting her father's inhuman status. He was her dad; that was all that mattered. It meant there were odd restrictions, secrets, and constant moves. It hadn't frightened her. Adam was overprotective, but his witchery was a way to keep her strong. Over the years, she'd drunk so many concoctions that she'd stopped wondering what was in them. Even if she knew, she didn't know if it would help. Now, she was wondering how much he'd hidden. Since she wasn't his biologically, she had no witchery in her, no ability to see a list of herbs or strange items and determine what they did when combined. Adam seemed to know so many things intuitively. He had a grimoire somewhere—probably in the locked trunk in his room—but she never saw him consult it.

Quietly, Mallory walked to the kitchen, but she stopped at the threshold.

Adam closed his laptop. "You shouldn't be in here, Mals."

The bowls of herbs, liquids, and fruits on the counter created the illusion that he was preparing a complicated meal, and she supposed that in some way that's exactly what it was. The potions he cooked weren't much different from the soups he made. The key difference, of course, was that he used skills that humans didn't possess, and that she couldn't understand, to create potions.

"You *spelled* me."

"You were upset." Adam looked haggard, but he wasn't apologizing.

She stared at him. "Did you do that to Mom? Is that why she left?"

Adam stilled.

Mallory stayed in the doorway. "I know she disagreed about teaching me things—not that I could learn everything anyhow because I'm not your real . . ." Her words fell off. She was his daughter in almost every way. "I wish I was; even though you just did that, I still wish I was a witch."

"You're not a witch, but you *are* mine, Mals." He gave her the barest of smiles. "And, no, Selah didn't leave because I spelled her . . . or because I spelled you."

Mallory felt a small relief, but she heard the things he wasn't saying, too: he didn't deny that he'd used his witchery on her without her consent before now. She felt like her world had gone off the rails. Her sort-of boyfriend was a daimon; her father used spells on her; and there were more secrets that she still didn't know.

Adam interrupted her thoughts by saying, "Selah and I disagreed sometimes because she wished you knew more sooner, but I didn't want you to know."

"Know what?"

He looked pointedly at the hem of her robe. "Don't disturb the circle."

She lifted her robe, so it didn't brush against the floor. "You're ignoring the topic . . . topics, I guess. I *want* to know more. I think I deserve to."

"You already know what matters. Daimons hate witches; witches hate daimons. Their world is terrible, and my whole family died there, except for Evelyn." Adam poured steaming liquid into a tall glass pitcher. "If I could, I'd kill the daimon responsible for it, and if Marchosias can, he'll kill me someday."

"Marchosias?"

"He's a ruthless bastard," Adam said.

"Is he why Kaleb was here?"

"I don't know," Adam admitted.

Mallory forced herself to keep her voice even as she asked, "Why didn't you kill Kaleb?"

"Bad judgment?" Adam sighed. "I was trying to avoid spelling you, and I knew if you found out you'd been spending time with one of them, you'd get upset. I can usually dispatch them or adjust things so you don't have to know . . . but the potion I'd given you wasn't finished working. The Watcher did something when she saw you. . . . It's what I'm repairing. I knew more magic would knock you out, so I offered him a deal: I'd let him leave if he didn't tell you what he was. I thought we had an agreement." A dry sound, not quite a laugh, came from Adam. "I don't break my vows, Mallory, so I couldn't kill him if he left without spilling the secrets he had. If he hadn't pushed me, you would've remained unaware—that he is a daimon *and* that I've spelled you."

"For how long?"

For several minutes Adam said nothing, and Mallory knew enough to stay silent as he finished mixing the ingredients he'd set out in front of him. The moment the last of the items was added, she repeated, "For how long?"

"I've spent a long time protecting you. There were other daimons. You've fought them. You've seen me . . . and Selah fight them. I've spelled you so you couldn't ask questions." He put his hands palms flat on the counter. "This time I failed to hide it, and because you were weak from the other night, I couldn't erase your memory. You know now. Kaleb is a daimon. You let him into our home, your life, and now I need to figure out what to do. I'm afraid we can't run any farther. I'm almost out of time."

The pit that had been growing in Mallory's stomach made her want to run to him like she had when she was a little girl. Her foolishness had exposed them, and she wanted to apologize . . . but if he'd told her the secrets he was still keeping, maybe it would be different. All of the questions she wanted to ask were bubbling up, and right now, she was actually asking them. Maybe it was because of whatever the daimon the other night did, or maybe she was getting bolder because of Kaleb. She didn't know *why*. All she knew was that she was asking questions.

"Call Evelyn if anything happens to me," he said. "She won't *lie*, but she isn't always honest in the strictest sense of the word. She's done things for revenge that—" He stopped and shook his head. "Once I thought I could do that. It's why I stole what I stole, but I changed. Being your father changed me, Mallory. Revenge mattered less than protecting you. All I want in this life is for you to have a safe future."

He carried the glass pitcher of the potion to the edge of the kitchen. "I want you to go take a hot bath. The tub is already filling. When you get there, pour this into the water, turn off the spigot, and soak for a minimum of twenty minutes."

Mallory accepted the pitcher. "I need answers, Daddy.

You're afraid. You just let a daimon live in order to continue to lie to me. We've moved near Evelyn now, and I'm not going to believe everything is okay when you dodge questions." She swallowed nervously, and then she voiced the horrible thing she'd been trying not to say. "Maybe if I knew the secrets you are keeping, I wouldn't have let him in."

Adam stared at her for several moments. Then, he gestured in the general direction of the stairs. "We can talk later. You need to use that while it's still fresh, and the office called while you were asleep. There was an emergency, and I need to go in, but when I get home . . . or maybe after work tomorrow, I can try to—"

"Tonight, Daddy," she said firmly. "I want to know what you stole and everything else. I can't keep living with these secrets. I don't want to ask Evelyn or Kaleb, but if you don't talk to me, I will."

Her father sighed. "Mals . . . you don't really want to know all of that. *Trust* me. Just take your medicine, and we can move past this."

She'd spent her life obedient to her father. Arguing with him never worked; she always backed down. *Not this time.* She knew he'd spelled her; she'd almost fallen for a daimon because of Adam's secrecy. "Evelyn and Kaleb will answer my questions. I know it, and you know it."

"Bath first. You'll feel better. If you really want to know later . . ."

"You promise you'll tell me?" she prompted.

He sighed sadly and whispered words in his witch language. Then he said gently, "You need to be a good daughter now. Go pour that in the tub, and soak for a half hour."

"Yes, Daddy." Mallory felt herself struggling not to say the words that were pulled to her lips. There were questions she wanted to ask, but she couldn't. Her hands tightened on the pitcher. "Daddy?"

Her father paused.

"This isn't fair," she forced out. "What you're doing. It's not fair."

Her father sighed. "You're my *family*, Mals. The daimons took everyone else. Your mother left; Evelyn lives for revenge; and everyone is . . . dead. I have a plan, but I need more time. One of these days, I won't erase your memories, but for now, your forgetfulness is the best option I have. Go soak."

*How much have I forgotten?* The urge to drop the pitcher vied with the compulsion her father was leveraging on her. *I will not forget Kaleb.* She tried to let go, but only managed to remove one hand.

"I'm sorry." Her father kissed her forehead. "I love you, and . . . you can hate me later if you need to, but I can't let them destroy you too."

"I know, but I have questions. If you tell me, maybe I can help—"

"No. You'd be in more danger if you knew—from others too. I'm sorry, but I can't tell you everything." He paused, but then he continued, "Are you a good daughter?"

"I am," Mallory said reluctantly.

"Will you go take your medicine, Mals?" he asked.

There were tears in both their eyes as she nodded.

*Good daughters obey.*

# CHAPTER 24

BY THE TIME KALEB got back to The City, he had a plan. It wasn't the wisest of ideas, but he wasn't about to give up on Mallory, and now that the witch knew he was interested in her, Kaleb was certain that getting anywhere near her would be impossible.

*Unless I have undeniable authority to see her.*

With no small amount of trepidation, Kaleb went directly to the palace and requested an audience with Marchosias.

"Tell him that it's urgent," he added.

So less than two hours after he had arrived at Mallory's door facing the witch she called a father, Kaleb stood facing her biological father. Marchosias hadn't looked surprised when Kaleb walked into the enormous room.

He sat at a beautiful carved desk with towering stacks of papers. He lowered his pen and leaned back in his chair.

"Well, what is this urgent matter?"

"I'd like to offer a bride-price for your daughter," Kaleb said.

Marchosias motioned for him to continue.

"She's old enough to breed or to wed, but the witch who calls her his daughter won't let me near her." Kaleb hesitated at the thought of admitting how thoroughly and seemingly easily Adam had brought him to his knees. "If I were to marry her, he couldn't stop me—short of killing me, which would kill or injure Mallory."

Casually, Marchosias pushed his chair back and stood. "The witch's marriage spell won't bind you if she has no affection for you."

"I know," Kaleb said.

"If you *have* had indication of affection, that means you knew where she was and didn't see fit to tell me," Marchosias said mildly. "Am I understanding this correctly?"

"You are." Kaleb held Marchosias' gaze. "I was hired to kill her, but I've reconsidered that contract."

"And how is my brother going to feel about the broken contract?" Marchosias asked, correctly identifying the contract holder but seemingly undisturbed by Haage's treasonous actions. "I'm assuming you're clever enough not to have told him yet."

"I am. If I'm part of the ruling class, I'll be a difficult contract—and most of the black-masks good enough to try for me know that I'd be a better ally than enemy." Kaleb didn't ask how Marchosias knew—or how long he'd known—about

Haage's contract on Mallory. Instead, he tried to appear calm. He folded his arms over his chest. "I'm ranked high in the contest, and I'm about to marry your daughter and father the heir to The City. Unless you kill me, I should be pretty safe."

With a laugh, Marchosias called for his aides, and in hardly more time than it took to cross the room, three daimons had appeared in front of Marchosias. "Fetch my witch too," he told one of them. "And one of the girls in my quarters."

The other two daimons waited, but Marchosias ignored them. He draped an arm over Kaleb's shoulders companionably and directed him to a window that overlooked the carnival.

"You'll bring her home," Marchosias remarked.

"I will if she is mine to bring here," Kaleb promised.

"What coin do you have to pay for my daughter?"

There was the problem: Kaleb had very few actual coins, certainly not enough to pay for Mallory. He could, however, earn them. He thought about the woman offering her markers after the fight and the number of daimons who would offer for Aya as well. He could secure ample funds in time. "I'll pay whatever you ask."

"You live in a cave, and you expect me to believe you have sufficient coin to buy her?" Marchosias shook his head.

"I can earn it," Kaleb clarified. "I haven't been taking a lot of jobs because of the competition, but I have been wearing a black mask for several years, and there are other ways I can raise coin if need be."

"In one year, she'll be eighteen. I will award her to you for that year, but at the end of that, she will be here and pregnant, or the marriage will be dissolved and you'll be dead." Marchosias flashed his teeth in a smile of sorts. "That's the price: your life if you fail."

"Fine." Kaleb nodded. "Let me know when the contract is ready to sign."

Marchosias walked over to his desk and opened a drawer. "I knew you'd found her before you came to me. You can't think I don't have Haage—or his lackeys—under watch." Marchosias withdrew a contract and motioned for Kaleb to approach. "Come."

Kaleb looked at the contract. Everything he had wanted was about to be his. All he had to do was sign. He lifted the pen and stared down at the words. The terms didn't actually matter. As a cur, he had no room to negotiate.

"Ahhh! The bride proxy is here." Marchosias smiled at a girl who was brought into the room, half asleep and entirely unclothed. "Come over here." He held out a hand to the girl, and then paused and glanced at Kaleb. "Unless you have another proxy in mind?"

"No," Kaleb said.

"Sign then." Marchosias nodded at the contract. "I'm sure you'll be wanting to get on with the nuptials."

As the girl, the daimons, and the witch watched, Kaleb signed the contract.

"Go on then. Finish the wedding." Marchosias motioned at the girl.

"Where?"

Marchosias opened his arms expansively. "Aside from my desk, the entire room is open. Pick a spot."

"It's okay, Kaleb," the girl told him. "I volunteered."

Kaleb knew that his proxy wedding wasn't personal, but as he looked from the proxy bride to his ruler, he felt worse than he usually did after he'd whored himself. It was a clear reminder of who had the true power, or perhaps it was merely business. If Mallory had been present for the marriage, perhaps they'd have had privacy, but she wasn't, and Kaleb still had to finish the wedding in order for it to be binding. He consummated the ceremony in front of the requisite witnesses and witch. All the while, Marchosias continued his paperwork.

When the act was done, Marchosias watched as the witnesses affixed their signatures to the contract, and then handed it to the witch, who did whatever trickery was necessary to make the proxy service binding. The proxy remained on the floor, making the already tawdry process even less appealing. It was far more than Kaleb had the right to hope for as a cur: he'd just been wed to the daughter of The City's ruler. He was a part of the ruling class now. *At least for the next year.* But the silent, naked daimon who stayed supine on the floor made Kaleb feel worse than he could explain—and he hoped never to have to tell Mallory about the proxy wedding. She was raised by a witch; she'd expect a different sort of ceremony one day.

Marchosias glanced at the proxy. "She's paying off a debt," he said. "I'd give her to you as a wedding gift, but now that you're wed, you aren't to touch any other daimon until my daughter is breeding. It's in the contract you signed."

Mutely, Kaleb nodded.

"Later, if you want—"

"No," Kaleb interrupted. "I have what I want."

"After the last of the fights, you may go to that world for as much of the next year as necessary to get the job done—or you can bring her here and live in the palace," Marchosias said.

"*After* the fights?"

"Once a daimon enters the competition, he needs to be eliminated in a match or forfeit." Marchosias flashed his teeth at Kaleb. "I can't imagine that a cur who thinks to wed *my* daughter would forfeit. You'll fight. You'll win, or you'll die."

"Oh," Kaleb said. Sole right to Mallory was his, but he was suddenly even more of a target.

"If you die in the fights, my daughter won't be injured. It's a rare bit of magic, but I've added it to your bond," Marchosias said.

Kaleb didn't know what to say. He was grateful for the protection for Mallory, but he hadn't expected to continue to fight. "I see."

"You didn't think you could circumnavigate the rules, did you?" Marchosias chided. "You came here asking for the prize without winning the game. You have her; now, prove you can keep her."

Kaleb nodded silently again. He wasn't sure of the protocol

just then. He wanted to leave, but he hadn't been dismissed. *Do daimons still get dismissed if they are ruling class?*

"Go on, then." Marchosias held his copy of the contract out to him. "You have a competition to survive and a wife to breed."

# CHAPTER 25

ZEVI WASN'T SURPRISED TO find Aya outside the mouth of the cave. He also wasn't sure if he wanted to invite her inside. Kaleb didn't entirely trust her, and this was his home. On the other hand, Aya had saved Kaleb's life. That earned her a lot of leeway as far as Zevi was concerned.

"He's not here," Zevi told her.

Kaleb hadn't coped too well with what happened in the fight, and he'd vanished not long after Zevi had led him away from the carnival. It wasn't like there were wounds to tend, so Zevi couldn't insist on Kaleb staying home.

When Aya didn't reply, Zevi nodded at the ground. "Is this ward like circles? Can you cross it without me knowing?"

"Yes," Aya admitted. "No magic I've found in The City has been strong enough to stop me at anything."

Zevi motioned for her to come inside, but he didn't say the words that would allow her to do so. "What about outside The City?"

She gave him a wry smile, acknowledging his lack of welcoming words, and stepped into the cave. "In the Untamed Lands? Nothing I've found out there is beyond me. I looked, but . . . no."

"And the human world? Anything stronger there?" Zevi gave her his most innocent look.

Without missing a beat, Aya said, "Yes, but not by much. There are older witches, but I'm able to best most of them too."

"Huh." Zevi swept his arm forward in a gesture of welcome, offering her the softest of the piles of hides that he had. If any guest they'd had merited the best comforts, she was the one. Her magic might have disturbed Kaleb, but it had also kept him alive in a fight he should've lost. To Zevi, that was far more important than Kaleb's self-loathing at what he'd done. The first time doing something horrible was always the hardest. Kaleb might not be willing to admit that today, but Zevi had no illusions. He'd seen Kaleb's dismay after Zevi sold his body to buy them food; he'd seen the terror in Kaleb's eyes when he'd come very close to dying. Those were sickening too. The revulsion faded, and they kept on living. Time made even the worst of horrors seem milder. Kaleb simply needed time—not that Zevi would *say* that to Kaleb right now.

Zevi studied Aya as he waited for her to explain why she was there. She was different from anyone he'd spent time around. When they acknowledged him, ruling-caste women typically either looked at him as an object of revulsion or of pleasure. Aya had neither reaction. It was comforting. *Like being around Kaleb is.* He smiled at that realization. Kaleb had been right about her: she would be a good protector if he needed one.

Patience already gone, Zevi flopped down across from her and asked, "Why are you here? I told you he's out, and you're still here. You don't want me, so why?"

"You're refreshing," she said with a small laugh.

He shrugged. "What do you want, Aya?"

"Come to the carnival with me," she finally said. "I need to be distracted, and people need hints that Kaleb and I are not enemies. If Kaleb isn't with me, you will be convincing proof that he and I are talking."

"With or without a mask?"

She laughed. "Just you, Zevi. No mask."

Zevi flashed his teeth at her in a wide grin. He'd be her stand-in trophy. Walking with her would be far more entertaining than sitting home worrying over Kaleb. If he were able to find a female daimon truly appealing, Aya would be a contender. Unlike the red-mask jobs he'd taken, he thought he might be able to lie with Aya without needing to imagine that he was touching a daimon he *did* want.

THE WITCH WAS QUIET as they walked toward the carnival, but Zevi had lived with Kaleb long enough to be used to sullen moods. They stopped at the edge of the carnival, and Zevi watched a scab pick the pockets of those pausing to listen to a wire-thin woman with beautiful long fingers playing a hurdy-gurdy. The scab didn't rob everyone—doing so was a foolish strategy—but he judiciously assessed each listener. A few minutes passed, and the set of songs ended. Some listeners dropped coins into the musician's tin before they walked away. The scab joined them, dropping a percentage of his take into the tin as well. The two exchanged a brief glance, enough to check if the time for moving on was now or if the musician thought they were still good for another round.

"They have a good system," Aya commented.

"Fair, not good," he corrected.

Since he'd left the Untamed Lands, Zevi hadn't ever known life without cons, theft, or other less gentle ways to earn the coins necessary to eat. He could see ways to improve their system, but he suspected that the musician had other revenue streams or a protector.

"Walk with me," Aya said softly.

Mutely, Zevi kept pace as they wound their way through the crush of people and deeper into the carnival. A lot of people believed that the carnival wasn't the same sort of danger as the Night Market, but the only real difference as far as Zevi could see was that the vendors who were here only during the day hid their wantonness better. He tried to stay away at night because Kaleb asked him to, but he was more comfortable with the Night Market. Illusions confused him.

They stuck to the most visible parts of the carnival, pausing to listen to musicians and walking through to the matchboards where the fight results were displayed. Aya told stories of fights she'd won and plays she'd seen, and he told her about cons he'd run and books he'd read. She didn't laugh at his text love like so many daimons would, but she did seem surprised.

"Kaleb brings me books from the human world," Zevi admitted. "I've read some of ours, but books aren't as easy to get in The City. Over there, they have buildings filled with books, and anyone at all can go in and read them. They let you take them home to read; even low-caste humans are allowed."

The sadness in Aya's expression was only there for a moment, but he saw it and added, "It's not your fault."

"What's not?"

"Being born to the ruling caste," Zevi said. "You didn't keep books from me, and you don't hurt me. Not all ruling-caste daimons are cruel."

"I know." She stepped around a scab, not noticing that by doing so she was in reach of a young cur with quick fingers.

Zevi caught the cur's wrist. "She's Kaleb's."

The cur's eyes widened.

"Spread the word." Zevi watched the cur vanishing into the carnival before he told Aya, "And not all curs are dreaming of a life in a quiet home reading books from the human world. Many of us"—he looked at Aya—"would kill before thinking, and more than a few would torture out of fear of the stories we'd heard so long ago."

Aya nodded. "I know, but this is my home. It's worth the risk."

Keeping his voice low, Zevi told her, "I am in your debt because of Kaleb, but there are only two of us. If things go poorly here, you're going to need to go *there*, to the human world."

The aversion to the human world confused him, but he watched her tense. Her kind lived there; people lived there without fighting to simply survive; entire buildings were filled with books. Kaleb had told him that it wasn't *all* good, that they had disease and violence and all of the horrors that thrived in The City, but he and Kaleb wouldn't be destined to stay at the bottom simply because they were parentless. Curs could change their futures without having to kill or bleed. Sometimes they did so by reading so many books that they were able to get jobs. Living in the human world wouldn't guarantee a better life, but it would be a far sight better than being a cur in The City.

His neck prickled as he felt someone watching him, and Zevi scanned the crowd until he found the daimon who stared at him. Instead of a threat, it was Kaleb. He strode through the daimons milling around the carnival, not seeming to notice that they moved out of his path without any effort from him. Zevi knew better: Kaleb noticed everything. This was what he'd fought for: respect and perhaps a bit of fear. He'd grown up fighting for the right to eat, the right to a not-exposed place to sleep, and more often than not, the right to not be abused for others' amusement. It colored the way he saw the world.

It also made him fiercely protective of those he loved. Kaleb had saved Zevi more times than either of them discussed, and Zevi knew that no one else in The City could be trusted to protect Kaleb like he did. Aya had helped in this last fight, but that was one fight, not years of devotion. He loved Kaleb, not in the way that he'd read in the books from the human world, but in the way that humans loved their jobs or their countries. Caring for Kaleb was his vocation; it was what gave life meaning. *Like soldiers or priests . . .* Kaleb was the cause that Zevi had devoted himself to, like one of those gods humans built temples for. Unfortunately, the humans had the benefit of loving gods who weren't walking around getting themselves into dangers, whereas Zevi had to worry constantly about Kaleb—who currently looked worse than Zevi had seen in a long time, not beaten up physically but emotionally battered.

Aya obviously agreed because she angled her body much as Zevi was doing, so that they could see any approaching threat.

"What happened?" she asked.

"I was just married to Marchosias' daughter." Kaleb smiled weakly.

"Married? To . . . *how?* Why?" Zevi stared at him, trying to process the words he was saying, trying to understand how such a thing could've happened.

"Kaleb?" Aya spoke softly, but the threat of violence was obvious in her voice and posture. She stood with her feet slightly apart, and although her hand didn't quite touch the hilt of the knife hanging at her waist, her fingers were now talon-tipped. "Will there be retribution from Marchosias?"

Kaleb glanced at her. "No."

"What do you owe for the bride-price? I have money," she offered. "I know you're angry with me, but I can help."

"No," Kaleb murmured. His gaze stayed on her for an appraising moment, and whether he said it or not, Zevi knew that Aya had moved up in his estimation. Then he looked away from her and caught Zevi's gaze as he announced, "I staked my life . . . unless she breeds by her eighteenth birthday."

They'd been through a lot of things the past few years, and Zevi was under no illusion that Kaleb would ever see him as anything other than a cur to protect. It galled him, though, that Kaleb didn't ever think to discuss anything substantial with him. It was an insult that Zevi usually tried to ignore, but this time, it was too much.

*His life?*

The urge to be something other than the lowest order was the driving force in Kaleb's world. Zevi knew that. He'd come to terms with it, stitched Kaleb up, set his broken bones, nursed him through fevers, and avoided questions that would made Kaleb flinch. For years, he'd pretended he didn't know that Kaleb murdered and whored to provide for them, and he'd done all he could to hide his own forays into business when they needed more money. While Kaleb fixated on changing their status, Zevi focused on taking care of Kaleb.

*How do I do that when he keeps doing things likely to get him killed?*

"You are an idiot" was all he said.

Then he walked away, ignoring both Kaleb and Aya's calls, moving so quickly that neither of them would catch him.

# CHAPTER 26

AYA KNEW THAT THERE were things she could and maybe *should* say to Kaleb, but she wasn't keen on the emotional thing and she wasn't quite ready to talk about her encounter with the Watchers. It wasn't as if either of them believed that the other was without secrets; she just happened to *know* a few of his. Much like knowing that he feared her because of what she was—and that he resented her because of the way the fight with Sol had gone—knowing that he'd contracted to kill the missing daughter he'd just wed could be useful later. She couldn't see *how* just then, but knowledge wasn't something to be given away.

"What's the plan?" she asked.

"After you forfeit, we go over to the human world until I convince my— *Mallory* to accept her new role." Kaleb pressed

247

his lips tightly together, as if sheer will could suppress the tenderness that she could clearly hear in his voice. For a cur who had a significant kill count, he was surprisingly soft-hearted.

She usually wasn't; in this, Aya favored her maternal heritage. Evelyn had as much of a nurturing instinct as a pit viper in a bad mood. Like her, Aya had often been practical to the point of ruthlessness. Belias was her one exception, but even he had been sacrificed at the altar of realism.

Despite her typical coldness, she felt a brief worry for Mallory. Trying to be as casual as possible, she said, "She wasn't raised in The City, so you need to deal with the human world and—"

"She was raised by a witch," Kaleb interrupted.

"A witch?"

He filled her in on everything he knew, and when he was done, Aya said, "I'll see what I can learn of this witch."

*There is no way* that *is a coincidence.*

WHEN AYA ARRIVED, EVELYN already had a second place setting on the small table in the far corner of her office. Just as Aya had unerringly known where in the building her mother was, Evelyn obviously had known that Aya would be visiting.

"Your daimon has agreed to be bound as your familiar," she said mildly as Aya walked into the room.

Aya flinched visibly. "I don't want him to—"

"I can dissect him for parts, or you can accept him as yours. We can transform his shape to hide his identity when you're there, but in my world, he will be as is. You can communicate with him and store energy in him in both states, of course, but for private use, you will need to say a word so he is transformed. I've added a silencing element and the standard inability to disobey to the spell, so you can enjoy him without the inconvenience of listening to him." Evelyn shook out her napkin and smoothed it over her lap. "It's still a draining spell, so we need to eat first."

"Do you know Adam Rothesay?"

"So you've found out about Marchosias' child." Evelyn gestured to the chair again.

Aya sat.

"My brother, Adam—"

"Your *brother*," Aya echoed.

After an almost imperceptible pause, Evelyn said, "Yes. Does that matter?"

Aya weighed the details. She'd learned years ago that the daimons she'd thought were family weren't hers by blood, but she'd cared for them all the same. In contrast, she had little affection for the witch who had borne her.

"This *is* the Watcher child? This Adam's decision to raise her wasn't because she's half witch, right?" Aya prompted.

"No, she is fully daimon, although Adam has suppressed that for her whole life. Her mother was a Watcher, and Marchosias is her blood father."

Even as Aya knew that Evelyn was studying her reactions, she couldn't fully hide them. Her usual stoicism was undermined by what Evelyn had casually revealed about Belias *and* about Mallory. Belias was about to be bound to her or die, and she had a cousin of a sort, who had just been married without her consent to a daimon that Aya was bound to aid.

*She's not family by blood, and I don't know her, and she's not a witch, so the dangers of breeding are not the same for her.* Sure, there were the usual risks, especially for Marchosias' daughter. His heirs tended to be murdered young, and childbirth had a critically high fatality rate in the ruling caste.

"I need to meet her." Aya lifted the glass in front of her and took a sip of water to combat her unexpectedly dry mouth.

"The girl is useful to you, daughter," Evelyn said. "If you can get her protection, it will aid our purposes. Adam did much to make her sympathetic to witches—enough that you can reveal what you are and that no one over there knows. It will make you her sole confidant, the one she turns to when things become worse."

Not for the first time, Aya was grateful that her mother—for the most part—didn't plot against her. Mallory was like the lamb offered to warring gods. She'd been taken and raised by witches who hated daimons; she was nothing more than a vessel to bear the next generation of Marchosias' heirs; and she was the key to a safer future for Kaleb.

*And she is useful to me.*

That was Evelyn's intention—at least, that was the most obvious of Evelyn's intentions. Aya wasn't so naive as to think that there weren't other motivations too. Her mother's machinations were a credit to her species.

"Finish that, and we'll do the spell," Evelyn directed.

They ate in silence, and then Aya gave in to the impulse that Evelyn undoubtedly expected.

"I need to see Belias before we do this." Aya stood and walked to the door. Evelyn didn't follow, which was as close to agreeing as she would come. The affection Aya had for Belias was a weakness. She knew it as well as her mother did. If he escaped and went to The City, she'd be exposed for cheating in Marchosias' Competition—worse still, she'd be exposed as a witch.

Everything reasonable, every bit of witch instinct in her, compelled her to let Evelyn destroy Belias, but he was hers. Whether he still loved her or not, he was the only person she'd loved. He was the one person she'd considered confessing to, but he hated witches. She'd hoped to avoid his ever knowing, but they were too far past that now. Her options had shifted when they'd been matched to fight or maybe when they'd been matched to wed. All that Aya knew now was that they were once more down to a set of options that included one of their deaths.

"I need his permission," Aya said.

Evelyn didn't look at her. Instead, she carefully folded her napkin as she said, "I'll be over momentarily. He'll be bound to you, or he'll be used for harvest."

# CHAPTER 27

BELIAS THOUGHT HE WAS better prepared to see Aya this time, but when she walked into the room that was his prison, he still felt the flurry of happiness that seeing her had caused for most of his life. This time, however, it was pushed down by fury. He did his best to keep his face expressionless as he came to his feet. He wasn't sure how he felt. This was *Aya*. They'd shared most of their lives; they'd loved each other. She'd also stabbed him.

He wanted to believe that she was still the daimon he loved, but she wasn't. She was one of them—a witch—the creatures who'd killed his father, who polluted The City. Her mother was a picture-perfect example of all of the things that had led to the witches being expelled from The City. She was monstrous, clear in her disdain for daimons and at ease with cruelty—and he wasn't seeing a lot of evidence just then that his former betrothed was much different.

"Why are you here?" Belias' hand dropped to the knife at his hip. "I've already been told the terms: your slave or death."

"I don't want this," Aya told him. "The idea of you being bound to obey my will is *far* from anything I've ever dreamed of."

Although he knew better, although he didn't know if anything she said was even true, he couldn't help but ask, "What have you dreamed of then?"

"You wouldn't believe me." Aya walked to the circle, entered it as if it didn't exist, and stood in front of him. It was a challenge and an offer.

Belias caught her by the shoulder and spun her so that her back was to his chest. He released her shoulder and wrapped his arm around her waist, holding her still. His other arm stretched crosswise across her chest and in that hand he held the knife that had been left in his possession. The tip of the blade was to her throat but hadn't broken the skin.

He could try to kill her, avenge himself and punish her. That would result in his death too, presumably after torture. He didn't believe that choosing death was the solution, with or without vengeance. If he had believed thusly, he could've taken his own life with the knife he held. Foolishly, he still wasn't any surer that he could kill her now than he had been when they fought in the competition. He sighed. "Is this where we are, little bird? I have to threaten you for answers. You poison me, imprison me, *enslave* me."

She was silent so long that he figured that this was another of the conversations that led nowhere, but finally she sighed. "I don't want either of us enslaved or dead, Bel."

"I never wanted to enslave you," he reminded her. "Marriage isn't slavery. Being a witch's familiar *is*."

"I sent you to this world because I couldn't kill you. Bringing your body here through a summoning circle meant I didn't have to kill you or explain that I *hadn't* really killed you."

"Or forfeit," he added.

"Or that." She was tense against his body, but she didn't try to escape. If anything, she seemed almost content to be there. "Are you going to kill me?"

"You aren't even trying to escape," he half complained. Fighting with Aya had been a prelude to more than a few wonderful nights. Despite everything, he still wanted that. It was a perversion to want a witch, and it was definitely wrong to want the witch who had enslaved him. "What? Are you going to let me kill you?"

"If I wanted free of you, I wouldn't need to fight." She said the words like a confession, and in her voice, he heard the weight of the secrets she'd kept from him.

He didn't want to feel sorry for her though. She had done this to him, to them. "More magic," he spat.

"Yes," she confirmed.

"What happens if I shed your blood in her circle?" Belias pressed the blade tighter to her throat, but not actually cutting her. "You're her blood. Could I use it to break this?"

"I don't know, but she won't let you leave here alive unless you are my familiar." Aya turned to look over her shoulder at him, pressing her skin tighter to the knife in the process.

Reflexively, he lowered the knife.

Aya stayed against him, her back to his chest.

He shoved her away.

"Tell me what will make this bearable for you." She turned to face him. "It isn't what I want either, but I can't kill you. I can't let her kill you. I left you the knife, but . . ."

"You know me better than that," he said.

Mutely, she nodded.

He caught her gaze. "Tell me you won't compel me to obey you unless it's a matter of life or death. You don't *have* to keep me under compulsion. You have my vow not to strike you with intent to injure or kill."

"And not expose what I am," she added.

"And not expose that you are a witch," he echoed.

"Your vow is accepted," she said, unnecessarily. He'd said the words within the witch's circle; he knew they were binding. By his own vow, he'd bound himself to a witch.

"And you?" he prompted.

"I give you my vow in this binding circle that I shall not strike you with intent to injure or kill, and I vow that I will not compel you unless it's a matter of your life or death. By this vow, I am bound to you and you to me." Her voice was shaky as she added, "You understand now why I can't breed."

"My family thinks I'm dead. You've stolen my family's

ability to continue my father's line." Belias tried to keep the swell of bitterness out of his voice and failed. "I get it, Aya. I only wish you would have told me *before* we reached this place. Maybe we could've avoided all of this."

Aya smiled in a way that was anything but happy and then asked, "Do you think you would've accepted me? Or do you say that because of where we are? You're in a witch's circle, Bel. Go ahead and answer."

The words he thought to say wouldn't come to his lips. He opened his mouth, but he was afraid to try to reply. He wasn't sure, and he wasn't certain either of them wanted to know the truth. She was a witch. Even after everything they'd been, he wasn't sure he could've forgiven it then, and he certainly wasn't feeling very forgiving now. He said nothing.

"Let's get this done." Evelyn's voice cut through the room, making clear that even though he hadn't seen her, she had witnessed their vows and his inability to answer.

"Step out of its circle," Evelyn added.

After Aya crossed the circle, Evelyn drew a second circle, containing Aya between the two circles. She directed Aya to sketch the sigils for her name and his in the second circle. Then she held out a silver blade. "Crosswise on both palms."

As Aya took the knife and did so, Evelyn spared him a glance. "And you."

Trapped in her circle, he couldn't have disobeyed if he wanted to, but he saw no reason to attempt to. Being bound to Aya was a lot better fate than death; it would get him out of here until he could find a way to convince her to let him have his real life back.

He cut his palms as directed.

Aya walked to the edge of the circle and held both hands up toward him. Inside the circle, he mirrored her, and together they walked the perimeter. The act of walking this circle was unpleasantly reminiscent of the last circle he'd drawn, before the fight in which Aya had stabbed him: then he'd had no idea that he was encircled with a witch, yet he had tied his fate to hers, believing that she wouldn't kill him. This time he realized that he was facing a witch, and he was still tying his life to hers.

As their commingled blood dripped to the floor and altered the circle, he felt the power of something stronger than anything he'd ever felt in The City. *Aya's power.* It washed over him, and he understood how strong she truly was. *Strong enough to have found another solution.* Instead, she'd lied to him and stood as a daimon in the ring. She'd been stabbed, beaten, bludgeoned, and burned. Claws and teeth had shredded her skin, yet she'd fought as a daimon, using her talons rather than magic. He lifted his gaze to hers in shock.

*Talons. Witches don't have talons.*

"Belias, thou hast now appeared unto me to answer unto such things as I have desired of thee. Now I do in the name, and by the power and dignity, of the omnipresent and immortal gods bind thee to Aya," Evelyn intoned.

*Aya has talons. She is not only a witch.*

Outside the circles, Evelyn nodded to Aya, who stared at Belias as she said, "I conjure thee, O fire, by him who made thee and all other creatures for good in the world, that thou torment, burn, and consume this daimon, Belias, for everlasting if he is disobedient and obeyest not my commandment."

She looked small and afraid, and he wasn't sure if it was because he didn't understand magic or because he was used to seeing her stride fearlessly into fights, but he was afraid *for* her then.

Evelyn waited as the fire Aya had called flared along the lines of the circle. Once the flames burned as blue as witch eyes, Evelyn continued, "And in these names, and all things that are the names of the God of Secret Truth who liveth forever, the All-Powerful, I bind thee, Belias, to this witch, Aya. Therefore obey her in all things, Belias; obey my power, speaking the secrets of Truth in voice and in understanding; therefore, I say obey the law which I have made, without terror to the sons of men, witches, creatures, all things upon the surface of the earth."

As the last words left the older witch's lips, she made a sweeping gesture with both hands, pushing one toward him and one toward Aya. As she did so, the flames of the circle between them shifted. The flickering tongues of flame became a chain that wrapped around Belias' wrists, ankles, and throat. It pierced his flesh, searing him and drawing screams of pain from his lips. The flame ripped through his body as if he were an empty shell, and then burst through the cuts in his hands. Once visible again, the flame-formed chain stretched out to Aya.

She held her hands out, palms up, and the fire poured into her bleeding hands. The look of pain on her face made clear that it hurt her too, perhaps not as intensely as it hurt him, but she was suffering as well. Once the last flicker of flame entered her, the cuts on her hands sealed over with scars.

Belias glanced at his still-bleeding and freshly burned hands.

"You are free to take your familiar, Aya." Evelyn's voice drew his gaze. "It cannot enter the building without you, but if it is out wandering with you, it can enter freely with you. The tie between you makes wards recognize it as an extension of the witch who owns it."

The temptation to tell the older witch exactly what he thought of her classifying him as property vied with the realization that he *was* Aya's property now.

# CHAPTER 28

ALMOST A FULL DAY later, Kaleb stood outside Mallory's house. It was so late in the day that he should be able to meet with Adam. By daimon law—and by witch law—Mallory was Kaleb's now to do with as he wanted. The witches couldn't support Adam without going against their own laws. Adam, of course, could kill him, but that would kill or injure Mallory. There were ways to dissolve the matrimonial bond, but not easily and not without risk. Kaleb hoped that they could avoid conflict; he didn't relish the thought of quarreling with Mallory's stepfather. A more likely scenario was that Adam would take Mallory and run, but since Kaleb was married to her *and* because she was pack, he'd be able to find her anywhere. Adam had no legal way to deny Kaleb's rights. If she were a witch or a human, it would be different, but she was a daimon. Mallory was Kaleb's to command.

He knocked on the door of Mallory's house. This time the wards pulsed against him. The sensation of insects biting him from head to toe was only a warning, a discomfort to remind him that this was a protected house. For anyone not permitted entry, crossing the protection over the boundary would be fatal, but Mallory didn't need to invite him now that he was her spouse: they were bound as if they were one entity. Where she was, he could enter.

*First, try to talk to the witch.*

When the door opened, though, it was not Adam. Mallory stood there. She was partially blocked by the doorframe. Kaleb knew by her expression of barely contained anger that she knew what he was, but she didn't slam the door in his face. It wasn't much, but it was something.

"You aren't welcome here."

"Why?" Kaleb prompted quietly. There was no way to stop this conversation, despite the horror he saw in her eyes. She knew a lot more than he'd thought when they'd met—and all of it influenced by witches.

"Because you're a daimon," she said.

"I am." Kaleb debated crossing the threshold, but he thought it wiser to wait. "He raised you to hate us. I understand that. Witches and daimons have a long history of hatred, but we're not all bad—neither are witches."

"Your kind killed his family. They . . . *you* are why we run." She looked directly at him as she moved her hand from behind the doorframe so that he could see that she held a gun, a matte black thing that he knew had more than enough bullets to kill him. She offered him a smile that was reminiscent of the one Adam had worn when he tortured Kaleb. "Adam and I just want to live in peace. I won't let you hurt him. It's bad enough that I let you into our home. Don't think I'll let you hurt him."

"I don't want to hurt Adam." Kaleb didn't back away.

She lifted the gun so it was pointed at his chest. "Have you seen him?"

"No." Kaleb winced inwardly at the alarm in her voice. The old witch wasn't there, which, on one hand, was great, but on the other hand could mean trouble. Now that Kaleb had married Mallory, the protection the witch had had from Marchosias himself was gone. Marchosias was a lot of things, but he adhered to law. If the law declared Mallory Adam's child until she was eighteen, Marchosias wouldn't come to retrieve her until her eighteenth birthday. He might exploit a loophole—by allowing Kaleb to marry her—but he wouldn't break the law outright. Now that Mallory had been given into Kaleb's possession, Adam was just a witch without reason to live. None of which Kaleb wanted to explain to Mallory.

"Did you hurt him?" she prompted.

"No. I'm here because of you, because I *care* for you." He stared at her, looking for the flicker of relaxation that would let him take the weapon. He didn't want to frighten her. He had hopes that she'd never see him the way he was in the fights. "I'm not here to hurt you or Adam. I swear it."

"Why should I believe you?"

Kaleb kept his gaze fastened on her. "I haven't lied about the important things. I just couldn't tell you everything."

"I'm sick of everyone keeping things from me," Mallory muttered.

The secrets Kaleb had kept from her weren't any worse than the ones Adam had kept—up until now. The temptation to tell her that they were wed vied with the reality that Mallory was apt to run from him if he told her that detail. Silently, he vowed to them both that once they got past these secrets, he wouldn't keep anything from her. He simply couldn't tell her everything all at once, especially when she was already upset. For now, all he said was, "I will answer questions, as many as I can."

"What was that woman? The one with the birds and the ashes?"

"Watcher," he said softly. "She's called a Watcher."

"They're a sort of daimon," she half asked, half stated.

He nodded.

"And she was here because of me?"

"Yes," he said. "Others will come too. I'm here to protect you; I'll stay by your side through any threat."

Her shoulders went back, and she stared at him. "I have spent years training, and there are . . ." Her words faded.

"Wards," he completed. "Adam is a witch who has warded the house."

"That means you can't come in." Mallory swallowed

nervously and lowered the gun a fraction—which was all he needed. He caught her wrist with one hand, forcing her arm upward so that if she did squeeze the trigger, she'd be firing into the air. At the same time, he stepped into her house and wrapped his other arm around her waist. He held her firmly against him and walked forward, using his larger size and momentum to propel her.

He caught the door with his foot and shoved it closed.

The gun was now aimed at her ceiling, and she struggled in his grip, but they weren't standing exposed to any passerby who could see her weapon aimed at his chest.

"Actually, I *can* come in," he said. "It's better to have this conversation inside, and it's easier to protect you."

She wasn't listening though. Her free hand was hitting and clawing at his face. At the same time, she pulled her knee up as hard as she could. He grunted in pain, but he didn't release his hold.

"Let go," she demanded.

"I need you to listen, Mallory."

"Let me go." She went limp, using her weight to try to throw him off-balance since he wasn't responding to her attempts to tug away or to her striking him.

"Stop." Kaleb growled this time.

At the sound of his very not-human growl, Mallory froze. She stayed completely still in his grasp. "I don't know where it is, but if you tell me what he took, I might be able to help you get it, and then you can give it to them, and—"

"I *know* what he took," Kaleb interrupted. "I'm not going to give— I'm not here to help someone else, Mallory. I'm here for *you*. I meant it when I said I would stand beside you."

"Why should I trust you?"

"Because I'm telling you the truth." Kaleb kissed her chastely.

Her lips were motionless under his, and he had to remind himself that they had a connection even if she was denying it. She was his wife, and even if she didn't know yet, she would. A swell of panic filled him at the thought of her fate—and his—if she refused to accept him as her mated partner. Marchosias would kill him and give Mallory to another daimon.

Calmly, Kaleb said, "I came here even after the witch threatened to kill me because I want to be with you. You know he was ready to kill me, but I'm here. Doesn't that tell you anything?"

MALLORY'S INSTINCTIVE—AND FOOLISH—desire to trust Kaleb vied with years of her father's lessons. Those lessons had never concentrated on daimons manipulating her. In Adam's myriad lectures, the focus was on the fact that daimons were crude brutes she should kill at first chance. He spoke of their strength, their cruelty, their history of brutality against witches. He didn't tell her they would kiss her and promise to help her. *He didn't tell me a lot of other things,* a guilty voice reminded her. She wanted to believe in him, but he'd kept secrets, spelled her, and, despite his assurances yesterday, he'd not come home to give her the answers he'd promised. She floated between worry that the daimons had found him and the possibility that he was avoiding her.

She wasn't going to share her doubts with Kaleb though, so she said, "When my father gets here—" Her words were cut off as the window beside the door shattered.

An arm reached through the broken glass toward the dead bolt—and then, in an almost simultaneous moment, went still. The arm drooped, and she heard a thump outside the door.

"Shhhh." Kaleb held up one finger in a *wait* gesture.

She nodded.

He released her and mouthed, "Wait."

Then he walked to the living room window and pulled back the edge of the curtain. He turned to her and said quietly, "Stay inside. I'll take care of this."

"What happen—"

"I'll take care of it," he repeated. "You stay inside."

Then he left.

The 9mm still in her hand, she peeked between the blinds—and saw Kaleb carrying someone down the street. At least she thought she did, and then a moment later it was as if she had imagined it. She stared at the street and saw absolutely no one. *No Kaleb. No body.* Mallory clutched the gun and glanced at the window. The window was intact, as if the wards were still in place. Working wards would stop any entry and repair the entry point. *How did Kaleb get in then?* She walked over to the window, laid her hand on the perfect pane, and shook her head. She lowered the gun, but still held it loosely in one hand. She stepped backward—directly onto the broken glass all over her floor.

She glanced at the window again. The details didn't add up. If Kaleb had been in the street, he wouldn't disappear. *Do daimons vanish?* If the window was unbroken, the wards should have stopped Kaleb too. She glanced at the red numbers on the microwave. *And if it's this late, my father should be home.* Gun still in hand, she walked over to her phone, picked it up, and checked for messages. There weren't any.

A sound at the door made her lift the 9mm again. She raised it up, ready to fire, and tensed. The door opened.

As he stepped inside, Kaleb held up his hands, palms out in a *halt* gesture.

She let her breath out in a sigh. "You're lucky I didn't shoot you."

"What are you doing?"

"What does it look like I'm doing?" She lowered the gun again. "I'm standing in my house, holding a pistol, wondering why there's glass on the floor if the window isn't broken . . . and wondering why you disappeared. My house's wards kept whoever *that* was out, but not you. My father isn't here. You're a *daimon* . . . and is that person-witch-daimon dead?"

For a moment, Kaleb looked very much like the sort of person who could calmly dispose of bodies—which could be because of their current circumstances or because of the blood on his jeans. This was not the boy she'd been falling for the past month or so. This was a daimon who had lied to her and misled her.

"You did just carry a man down the street, didn't you?"

Kaleb sighed. "Yes."

"Someone tried to break in, and the wards stopped him," she said. She knew it. The proof was on her floor and on his jeans, but she wanted to hear the words too.

"Yes."

"Is he—"

"Mallory," Kaleb interrupted.

She looked at the window again. "You walked through the wards that killed him. The wards worked, but not on you."

He turned his face away then, looking at the window or maybe through it into the street.

They stood silently for a moment, and then he asked, "Do you have a dustpan?"

Mallory followed his gaze back to the floor.

"A dustpan," she repeated. "Someone just died, and the daimon in my house wants a dustpan. This is insane." She walked away from him, trying not to notice the tiny pieces of glass that were embedded in the undersides of her slippers.

Mallory rummaged around in the kitchen until she found a dustpan and broom. The reality was that someone had tried to break into her home. It didn't occur to her to call the police: her father's injunction against letting strangers into the house included the police.

After handing the broom and dustpan to Kaleb, she picked

up her cell phone. There still weren't any messages—or missed calls. It was charged, but her father hadn't called.

"Call him."

"What?" Mallory looked down at Kaleb.

He didn't meet her gaze. "Call Adam. Tell him whatever you want. We need to know if he's safe or not, and if he *is* safe, he needs to know about this."

Kaleb finished sweeping up the broken shards of glass and poured them into the trash while Mallory called her father's cell phone, office phone, and then, when she had no answer on either of those, she called the building receptionist.

"Stoneleigh-Ross."

"I'm trying to reach my dad . . . Adam Rothesay."

"Mr. Rothesay didn't come in today."

"Are you sure?" Mallory sat down unsteadily. "Maybe—"

"I'm the only one on duty, dear, and I'd have noticed Mr. Rothesay if he had signed in, so yes, I'm sure. Hold on." The sound of papers shuffling was all Mallory heard, and then the receptionist came back. "Some of the staff had an emergency. Perhaps he is with them. You should've had a call from the division coordinator if so."

"I didn't."

The clacking of keys filled the pause, and then the receptionist said, "I've entered a note for an update call to be sent to this number. Is there anything else, Miss Rothesay?"

"No. Thank you." Mallory disconnected. She kept the phone in her hand, but she wasn't sure what to do next.

When Kaleb came to stand in front of her, she looked up at him, and she saw that he'd heard her side of the conversation with the receptionist. He said nothing, but he brushed her hair back.

She flinched away from his touch. "He's not answering his cell phone, but the receptionist said there was an emergency. I guess they were to call me, but didn't."

Kaleb sat down next to her on the sofa. He didn't put his arm around her, and she didn't move closer to him. On the table in front of them was the gun that she'd held only moments prior.

"I'll be here for you. Whatever it is, I'll be here. You can trust me." He sat so stiffly that she wondered who the real Kaleb was: the one who casually carried a body away or the one she had first met. He seemed like two different people.

She glanced at him and wondered what sort of person disposed of bodies without question.

*He's a daimon, not a person.*

Beside her, Kaleb looked at her expectantly, and when she said nothing, he stood. "I need to wash the blood out of these before it sets in."

He was halfway down the hallway when she admitted, "I want to trust you."

Kaleb stopped and turned back to face her. "I want that too, Mallory."

# CHAPTER 29

HE DIDN'T WANT TO be the one to tell her the truths Adam had hidden from her. More to the point, he wasn't sure he could tell her without being cast out of her house, and unless Adam was here to keep her safe, Kaleb wasn't about to say anything that would make her try to send him away. Of course, if Adam came home, there was no need to tell her anything yet.

*At least until she finds out that she needs to leave this world.*

Tonight's events had a decidedly dampening effect on his brief fantasy of a life in which he could stay in the human world and get to know his new wife better. Aside from fight days, he had no reason to live in The City for the next year. He'd still need to go to The City occasionally to earn money to support himself and Zevi, but after he won the competition, he'd be highly sought after, so mask-work would pay more.

He'd do a few jobs, exchange the coin for human money, and then he could stay mostly in this world. After the year, he'd have to take Mallory—and their child—to live near her father, but until such time, he'd thought they could remain here.

*Assuming the witches don't kill me.* Kaleb wasn't sure whether it was better for Adam to come home or to have vanished. Either way, there were more problems to resolve, and doing so without his wife's trust was far more complicated than he'd like it to be.

He tugged off his jeans and stepped out of them. He only had a few articles of clothing, and he had no human currency to buy more clothes. That meant getting the blood out of his jeans so that he could wear them without attracting the kind of attention that blood spatter would. He turned on the water, looked down, and caught sight of the blood on the bottom hem of his shirt. He removed the shirt too. *Jeans first.* He could sleep without a shirt, but he wasn't about to sleep in only his shorts. *Not here.*

"Is there a brush or sponge of some sort I can use?" Kaleb called through the door. "Mallory?" He waited for a moment, but when she didn't reply, he repeated, "Mallory?"

Panicked at her silence, he yanked open the door to find her standing there. Hurriedly, he held his jeans in front of him and started to close the door.

She held out a sponge. "Here."

"I didn't hear you, and I worried—" He took the sponge. "I'm sorry. I didn't mean to . . . I . . ."

Mallory stared at him. "You're sorry for . . . worrying? For carrying away that dead man so calmly? For what this time?"

"Not any of that." He held his pants lower, blocking her view as best he could, and immediately felt ridiculous. He was a cur who had sold his body to earn money for food and shelter, not an inexperienced human boy, but Mallory made him feel different. He wanted what they had started to share to be special. He wanted all of the secrets to be already out and resolved so they could move forward—not because it would be better for a plan or for anything other than the simple fact that he wanted her to be happy.

"I love you," he whispered.

He'd heard the words exchanged, but he hadn't quite understood them the way he suddenly did. Her happiness mattered more than his; her well-being mattered more. He had already defied Haage and Adam, but Kaleb realized then that he would defy anyone if it kept her happier, if it meant she was protected. He said it again, louder this time. "I love you, Mallory."

She stared at him. "What did you say?"

He stood in the house of a witch in the human world. He was bare-chested and barefoot, clutching a pair of damp jeans, and his wife was staring at him like he had just spoken to her in a new language. He repeated it again: "I love you."

"No, you don't." She walked down the hallway.

He tugged his jeans back on and followed her to where she stood at the formerly broken window.

Without turning to face him, she said, "I'm upset, and maybe you're just trying to make me feel better, but you don't need to make crazy promises. You *can't* love me. Love means knowing each other. It takes time, and . . . you don't love me."

"I do. I love you, and I'll do anything I can to support you," he promised. He wished he could tell her everything. He wanted to assure her that he'd always be there because they were legally wed, but that would open up a discussion about daimons, about laws, about the fact that she was something other than human—and none of that was going to help her trust him.

Mallory turned around then. "Tell me what he took. What are the daimons looking for? If they took him, maybe we can trade whatever he stole to get him back."

"We don't know that he was taken," Kaleb pointed out.

She scowled. "If he wasn't, he's still in danger. So am I. The Watcher found me. *You* found me. Someone else tried to break in. I need to know what they want. You know, don't you?"

"I'll keep you safe, Mallory. For now, that's the most important thing."

"My father—"

"Might not be missing," Kaleb finished. "You're right about the threats, but that doesn't mean he's been taken."

"If he was—"

"If he was taken, I'll tell you everything I know, but Adam is already determined to keep me away from you, so let's see if he returns before I spill his secret. Once we find him or he comes home, he can tell you what he stole." Kaleb didn't claim to understand the witch's logic in stealing Marchosias' daughter, but he was certain that Mallory had been safer here than she would've been in The City. *And because of it, accessible to me.* The reality was that she wouldn't have been in his reach there. Maybe if he'd won the competition, she would've still been the prize, but he couldn't be sure. He wasn't sure what she'd have been like then either. He'd tried to imagine her as a ruling-caste girl, as someone who had looked down on him— or worse still, as one of those who wanted him because of his propensity for violence.

Kaleb slid his hands down her arms, trying not to feel desperate when she flinched. "I know you care for me, Mallory. Trust yourself. Somewhere inside, you *know* you can trust me."

She didn't run, but she didn't move closer either. "If he's hurt, I don't know what to do. If you help me find him, tell me what he took, help me negotiate with them if they *do* have him, I'll . . . try to believe you." She didn't cry, but her eyes glistened with tears. "He's not perfect, but he's my father, my own family. He's run from them for years, and even if they don't have him, he's in danger."

Whether she realized it or not, Mallory had already made steps toward accepting him. In her words, she had separated him from "them"—the daimons who'd pursued her father. She'd asked for his help instead of lumping him in with other daimons.

Kaleb wanted to hold her, to ease her fears, and to promise

that everything would be all right. He couldn't do any of that—not yet. Kaleb didn't want her to know what she was yet, didn't want her to know how different their world was, didn't want her to see him the way he was there. She was raised by witches to hate daimons. Even without that, he lived in a cave and killed for his coin. Mallory was so far removed from the world he knew that he couldn't bear the thought of her seeing him that way before he had more of a chance to overcome her bias against daimons.

He gave her the only words he knew for sure he could offer. "You have my word, my *vow*, that I will help you find Adam and do everything in my power to find a way that he can stop running from the daimons he stole from. I *will* help you through this . . . and anything else that comes."

Mallory turned away again to stare out the window. She folded her arms over her chest and kept her back to him, as if that would hide the tears he heard in her voice as she said, "Daimons aren't to be trusted, and—"

"Are all witches the same?" he interrupted. "Are all humans? Why would all daimons be the same then? Some of us are horrible. There are those who would kill you, but I'm not one of them."

She said nothing for several moments. The only sound was the soft sniffles of the tears she was barely trying to hide now. Finally, she said, "Dad said that the one person I can turn to is Evelyn, his sister, but she hates me."

"She's a witch," Kaleb said.

Mallory nodded.

If Evelyn knew what Mallory was—and Kaleb suspected that she must if she was Adam's sister—she probably hated Mallory for the same reason that she would hate Kaleb.

"You *do* have someone else to turn to. I'm here for you," he promised again.

Her tears had evolved into shallow sobs, so much so that he couldn't allow the pretense that he didn't know she was crying.

He stepped closer to her. "If you didn't know what I was, would you let me hold you?"

Mallory didn't answer, so he pulled her into his arms and held her while she cried. It wasn't much, but it was progress. She trusted him despite what he was, despite her prejudices, and from that trust, they would build something strong. All he had to do first was find the witch she considered her father, survive his wrath, figure out how to be in the human world to keep Mallory safe, and in the midst of it all convince her that she wanted to marry him—without her discovering too soon that they already were wed.

"It'll be okay," he whispered, hoping desperately that he wasn't lying to either of them.

# CHAPTER 30

THE NEXT DAY ADAM still had not returned. Mallory stayed home to make phone calls while Kaleb went back to The City. If Adam was in the human world, the witches would be able to locate him; if he wasn't in their world, he was either dead or in The City. Kaleb wasn't sure if Marchosias would send someone to snatch Adam or not. Now that Mallory was *Kaleb's*, Adam was just another witch. He had stolen from Marchosias, and it stood to reason that there would be consequences. The only way there wouldn't be was if Marchosias decided not to alienate his daughter even further. Kaleb wasn't sure what to think.

But Marchosias wasn't the only daimon with machinations Kaleb couldn't always grasp. Haage had no doubt already crafted a new plot, and there were always other factions trying to find a way into power. The only way to get answers was to tap the same underground network of information Kaleb had relied on for years. He couldn't do that and stay by Mallory's side. He needed help.

Kaleb sped through the gate to his world, and he went directly to his cave. Zevi sat in the middle of the room, and aside from a flicker of relief in his expression, he gave no indication of his feelings. He didn't need to though: his posture made clear that he was furious.

"Z—"

"I don't want to hear it, Kaleb." Zevi folded his arms and glared. "I stitch you up, do everything I can to keep you alive so you can keep entering *fights to the death*, and that's somehow not enough risk for you. You have a death wish. I get it."

"It's not like that," Kaleb protested weakly.

"You bargained your *life* to Marchosias. How is that not a death wish?" Zevi was in front of him, zipping across the expanse of the cave in a blur. He poked Kaleb in the chest. "You are my whole pack. My entire life is based on you . . . your choices, your whims, your schemes. For years, I've trusted you, but I can't keep doing that if you keep trying to get *killed*."

Nothing Zevi said was untrue, but that didn't make it any easier to say what Kaleb had to say. He bowed his head. "I'm trying to build a future."

"By getting yourself killed?" Zevi sniffed. "You have blood on you again."

"I know." Kaleb kept his head bowed, not meeting

Zevi's eyes, offering submission in hopes of forgiveness and acknowledgment of his errors. "I should have told you."

"You found Marchosias' daughter. You risked everything *again* . . . and you didn't tell me because you knew I'd worry." Zevi sighed and darted away as quickly as he'd approached Kaleb only moments before.

"Yes," Kaleb admitted.

"You need to trust me. You don't let me fight, but I'm not a pup." Zevi sounded more hurt than angry.

Kaleb looked up. "I won't do anything else that is likely to get me killed. . . ."

Zevi snorted.

"I'll *try* not to," Kaleb amended. "Please, Z? I need help."

"With?"

"Mallory's father . . . the witch who raised her, not Marchosias, is missing. Haage had hired me to kill Mallory, and I didn't. I won't . . . and she knows I'm a daimon but thinks she's human, and she doesn't know we're married. Marchosias allowed one year until she *has* to come here, but I am not allowed to step out of the fights, so I need to come back for matches." Kaleb took a deep breath. "I think I love her, and if she doesn't want to live here by next year, I'm not going to be able to force her . . . which might mean crossing Marchosias, too."

For a moment Zevi didn't react at all, and then he laughed. "Which part of that is you trying not to get killed?"

Despite everything, Kaleb felt better: Zevi was going to forgive him.

"The part at the end after we get through all of this," Kaleb suggested.

Zevi shook his head. "What do you need?"

Some of the weight Kaleb had felt dropped away now that he was on Zevi's good side again. "I need to know if Adam—her father—is here, and if so, who took him, where, anything about him you can find out. The old witch hates me, but my wife"—Kaleb smiled briefly at the joy of saying that word—"our new packmate, loves him."

"On it." Then in a blur that was uniquely Zevi, the younger cur was beside Kaleb. He butted his head into Kaleb's shoulder. "Bring her home, or I'm coming there."

"You, me, and Aya are going there," Kaleb said, and then filled Zevi in on the arrangement he had with Aya.

For a moment, Zevi was completely motionless. Then, he said, "Can you promise not to enter into any more vows, contracts, or anything else until you talk to me?"

This time, Kaleb ducked his head sheepishly. "I'll try."

"Try *hard*." Zevi sighed. "Be careful over there."

Kaleb nodded. "Promise."

Things were still tense, but they talked about what Zevi needed to pack as they gathered what money they had. While he was looking for information, Zevi could exchange the coin for human currency. Neither of them mentioned the fact that getting involved in witch business was dangerous. It was what it was. Kaleb's wife wanted him to find her stepfather; that request wasn't one he could ignore—and Zevi knew that. Being a pack meant protecting, helping, and loving one another. Because Kaleb loved Mallory, he would put himself at risk, and because Zevi loved Kaleb, he would not ask him to refuse.

WHEN KALEB RETURNED TO the human world, he went directly to the witches. A daimon walking up to the witches' stronghold was sheer stupidity, but unfortunately, the Stoneleigh-Ross offices were where the missing witch worked.

Kaleb made it as far as the front door. The ward there was one that he couldn't cross; it didn't knock him on his ass like Adam's spells had, but it made the air feel like a solid wall to him.

*Plan B.*

He flipped open the phone he'd procured specifically to call Mallory, pulled a piece of paper from his pocket, and punched in the number he'd copied from a list on the front of Mallory's refrigerator that morning. When the receptionist at Stoneleigh-Ross answered, he said, "I need to reach Adam Rothesay. It's urgent."

"Mr. Rothesay is—"

"I know what you are." He looked at the front door and bluffed. "I'm standing at the edge of your ward, and unless someone comes out here to talk to me, I'll bring more daimons to tear down the damn building if I need to."

"Please hold while I connect your call."

Kaleb felt the tension growing in the air around him, as if the empty space was filling with invisible briars, and snarled, "Don't toss spells at me. I'm here to try to help find Adam

Rothesay. I think he's in trouble."

The air didn't become clear, but the invisible tangled growth didn't expand either.

Several moments passed before a man in faded jeans and a white oxford shirt came through the front doors and walked toward Kaleb. Thin silver-framed glasses, high-gloss shoes, and a silver watch added to the overall image of casual ease. The smile on his face and his unhurried stride contrasted with the cutting energy that lashed around both of Kaleb's ankles as invisible manacles held him in place.

"Kaleb, I presume?"

Kaleb nodded.

"Adam's told us about you," the man said conversationally. "We feel it only fair to let you know that we will enforce his paternal claims. Those claims prohibit Mallory's removal to The City."

"I'm not trying to take her to The City." Kaleb tried to keep his voice even as well, but he wasn't as adept at ignoring magically induced pain as he was at pushing past physical pain. *That* he'd had plenty of experience in, but until he'd met Adam, he'd had no contact with the sort of witches that existed in the human world. "Her *true* father has given her to me as a wife, and marriage invalidates the witch's claims of paternity."

"We enforce the law here," the man continued as if Kaleb hadn't spoken. "Mallory, as daughter of a witch, will be kept out of The City until she reaches her majority. As she just turned seventeen—"

"We're wed. None of Adam's claims matter now, but I'm not here because of that." Kaleb tried to ignore the creeping sensation around his calves. The vines he couldn't see were twined around his skin, tightening as they spread. "Someone broke into her house last night, and Adam is missing. She's *worried*."

The vines released all at once. "Her home was actually entered?"

"Not by much. He reached inside, and the wards . . . resolved the matter." Kaleb resisted the urge to step back. His instinct was to move away from whatever had entangled him, but magic wasn't always rooted. It was just as likely that he'd be trapped by moving backward.

"The body?"

"I handled it," Kaleb said.

"Do you swear that you are not intending on retrieving Miss Rothesay—"

"Do you think I'm a wet pup that I'll give you a *vow*?" Kaleb laughed. "If Adam couldn't get a vow from me, you sure as hell won't." He didn't wince at the stinging sensation that made it seem as if hot ashes were being poured into his ears.

*They aren't. It's illusion.*

Still, Kaleb let his teeth show a little despite his best intentions. "Do you know where Adam is? If he's not missing, it would be good to know that."

The witch looked Kaleb over from head to toe, and then frowned. "We don't answer to d—"

"My wife loves Adam. If he's not in *this* world, I need to make inquiries in The City," Kaleb pointed out as calmly as he was able.

"Why?"

"Because it's what Mallory will want." He felt his claws begin to extend as his hold on his temper started to fail. "What I need is to know if Adam is in this world and to know that if Adam is in The City, Mallory still has the protection of the witches while I go try to retrieve him."

The witch said nothing, but Kaleb didn't expect any real help from witches.

*Except Aya.*

She was his next recourse. He couldn't take Mallory home, but Aya was an invaluable resource in this world. She couldn't expose what she was in The City, but here she could function openly as a witch.

"I will relay your words to my superior when she returns to the office." The witch turned his back and left Kaleb there. For a moment, the air held him in place, and then as the door to the office building closed behind the witch, Kaleb was released.

# CHAPTER 31

By THE TIME KALEB had returned to his world that morning, Mallory was certain that her father was in real trouble. He hadn't called; the office hadn't called. There was no way he would avoid her like this just to escape answering questions. *He could spell me again to keep me from asking.* The only options Mallory had left to her were to seek out Evelyn or to find whatever Adam took in case she had to bargain with daimons.

Evelyn wasn't accepting Mallory's calls, so Mallory went into her father's room and searched it as best she could. Whatever the mystery treasure was, he'd hid it well. The trunk held a bunch of weathered old books, grimoires and journals, and several scrolls. A few knives in different metals and one carved bone ladle rested atop the books. She ran her fingers over each item, wishing that she had even a measure of her father's witchery.

"How do I know what it is?"

Although she had no magical ability, she had sufficient familiarity with magic to know that a magical object would feel different and that a perfectly mundane item could very well be the thing that the daimons sought. Not all precious objects looked like riches. It could be a book, a scroll, a blade, a ladle, or something entirely different. Tears slid down her cheeks as she thought about her father. He would've called by now if he was able. That meant he was injured or a prisoner somewhere—because she refused to even consider that he could be dead—and she had no idea where or why.

She wiped at the tears on her cheek. She wasn't naive enough to believe he would vanish without calling her, especially when she had been sick.

If not for the fact that Adam knew what Kaleb was and hadn't banned him from her life, Mallory would have turned away from him the instant she'd learned what he was. *A daimon shows up, and Adam vanishes.* It seemed more than mildly suspicious, but Adam had allowed Kaleb into their home. There had to have been a reason, and right now, the only resources she had were Kaleb—*who is a freaking daimon*—and Evelyn. The older witch was Adam's only living family, but Mallory had agreed with her mother's stance on Evelyn: venomous serpents were more affectionate, safer, and generally warmer. Kaleb, on the other hand, had been caring, and Mallory had trouble believing that someone she felt so connected to was all bad.

The hours passed, and the search of her father's room yielded no secrets. A few items felt different as she handled them, and she suspected that they were magical in some way. That didn't make any of them the item valuable enough to cause daimons to pursue them for years. It also didn't mean that any of them revealed anything about where her father might be.

By midday, she was frustrated and no closer to an answer than when she started. She'd called the office again, her father's emergency contacts, and his cell number. No one had seen him, and he wasn't answering. She didn't have Evelyn's private number, and the witch still wasn't returning any of Mallory's calls through the office. That meant Mallory was going to have to go to the Stoneleigh-Ross office. It was something Adam insisted she was to do only in an emergency, but his disappearance was a definite emergency.

Mallory pulled on her coat and a few weapons, and set off to Stoneleigh-Ross. She was a block from the office when she saw Evelyn and two teens close to her own age. Rather than feeling relief at spotting the witch she'd been on her way to see, she felt a flicker of alarm. Evelyn always unnerved her, but the way the strangers stared at her made her even less comfortable.

"Mallory." Evelyn nodded. There was no illusion of affection, no warmth in her smile. "What are you doing out here?"

"Coming to see you."

*That* got a reaction. Evelyn's witch-blue eyes widened. "Does Adam know?"

"No." Mallory's hand rested in her pocket, where she could reach through the slit and draw the gun at her hip. It was hidden under her long coat, and she didn't want to be obvious about it, but she also didn't like feeling vulnerable. "My father didn't come home last night."

"I see." Evelyn was as poised as if Mallory had inquired about her shoes.

Mallory gripped the handle. "He trusts you, and I don't know who else to ask for help."

"I'll look into it." Evelyn offered what passed as a smile. "In the interim, I want to introduce you to my daughter. Aya, meet Mallory. Aya, meet your cousin."

"My . . ." Mallory scowled. "Dad never mentioned a cousin."

The girl, who looked very little like her mother, stepped forward. She was muscular where Evelyn was slight; her eyes were brown rather than the telltale witch's blue and gold; and her short hair was the thick straight brown of a wolf's pelt instead of the silky raven-black of Evelyn's hair.

"You don't have witch eyes," Mallory said simply. She looked at the boy who stood protectively beside Aya. "*Neither* of you."

"Her father, unfortunately, was a daimon. It was a necessary evil." Evelyn pursed her lips briefly, and then gestured at the girl. "You have my vow that she is my offspring, and while you do not share my blood, Adam considers you his child, so Aya is your cousin."

While Evelyn spoke, Aya was looking at the boy with an expression of fear that Mallory didn't understand.

Mallory shook her head. "Daimons can't breed with—"

"They can if the witch is strong enough and willing to do what she must for a greater cause," Evelyn interrupted.

Aya stepped away from the boy, who seemed utterly calm about this very surreal conversation. She looked at Mallory. "Please don't shoot me with the gun you're clutching. I'm not here to hurt you."

"The gun . . ."

"We can smell the metal," the boy said.

"Witches? Adam never said—"

"*Daimons*, child. That"—Evelyn waved toward the boy— "is my daughter's daimon. It can smell the metal of your gun."

"Belias," Aya said firmly. "*His* name is Belias."

Silently, Mallory looked from Evelyn to Aya to Belias. The witch—her aunt, although the woman had never evinced the slightest familial affection—who was to help her father protect her was introducing her to a half-daimon and a daimon. The entire situation seemed suspect. She hadn't been raised by a witch without learning how they thought. "Why are you really introducing us, Evelyn?"

The witch smiled approvingly. "Because I thought my daughter might be able to help you. She was raised as one of them in order to be deployed as my weapon when the time is right."

The daimon who stood beside Evelyn tensed. "Do you have any idea what they would've done to her if they found out?"

Evelyn's already cold gaze turned to Belias. "They butchered my parents, my baby brother, and almost every friend I had. They drained their energy and tossed them like refuse in the street." She hissed a word in the witches' language, and Belias was flung backward and slammed into a tree in the yard. "I know precisely what daimons can do to witches."

Belias was already on his feet and advancing. He'd withdrawn several throwing knives from somewhere on him, and the first of them was in the air. "If you *knew*, you shouldn't have abandoned her there."

Evelyn didn't even move, but Belias' knife turned and flew back at him. He plucked it from the air, and in what appeared to be the same instant, sent two more knives hurtling toward Evelyn. With another word in the language that Mallory did not speak, Evelyn held Belias immobile as surely as if the air had become solid around him. While Evelyn cast her spell, one of the knives made contact with her, grazing her arm.

"Enough." Aya stepped between the daimon and the witch.

Mallory couldn't move. Knowing that witches were deadly was different from actually seeing it in person. Aside from that brief situation with Kaleb, Adam had never been anything like this in front of her—but Mallory had also never seen anyone move as quickly as Belias just had. The reality of a conflict between a witch and a daimon seemed somehow larger than she could fathom.

Aya lifted her hand as if to strike Evelyn, but moved no further. "Don't test me, *Mother*."

The older witch snorted, and then she looked at Mallory as if her daughter wasn't poised to strike her. "You can come to the office in an hour. If Adam's in our world, I'll know where he is. If not, he's over there."

Mallory knew her aunt was cold, but this was ridiculous. "Tell me what he took. I'll give it back to them, and . . . you can talk to them, right? There has to be—"

"Come in an hour." Evelyn turned sharply on her heel and walked away, leaving Mallory with a witch-daimon and a daimon.

Mallory looked at the daimon, who once more stood beside Aya. He didn't act like he wanted to destroy Aya, but rather like he wanted to protect her. She *was* half-daimon though, so maybe that was the difference. Daimons had devoured witches for centuries. Evelyn, like many witches Mallory had met, saw all daimons as dangerous, and Mallory herself had no evidence to the contrary—aside from Kaleb, although he wasn't particularly lacking in dangerousness.

"I'm completely bound to her will," the daimon, Belias, said. "I cannot hurt you without Aya's consent, and she is your family. You are safe with us." He paused and glanced in the direction that Evelyn had gone. "Probably safer than with her."

Mallory allowed herself to smile at him, but didn't admit aloud that she agreed.

Aya glanced at Belias before saying, "My mother won't tell me who fathered me, but I was raised in The City. I knew only that witches were horrid things that had to be kept in control, that they were to be feared."

"I've heard the same about daimons," Mallory hedged.

"No one is automatically good or bad because of their species." Aya shook her head. "Although my mother makes a great case for witches being unlikable. Hopefully, you've known witches who were otherwise."

Mallory fought against a sudden wave of sorrow. "My father. He's good and kind." She thought about the way Adam had treated Kaleb and added quietly, "Mostly."

They stood awkwardly for a moment. Aya and Belias seemed perfectly calm, as if Evelyn hadn't just been flinging Belias aside and he hadn't been trying to cut her. It reminded Mallory of the calm she could reach when she was training. The difference, for her at least, was that she hadn't ever had to test that calm in true conflict. No one had ever tried to kill her, and the thought of it happening pretty much eliminated any calm she felt.

"If they took him, you'll need a guide in The City," Aya pointed out.

Mallory hesitated. The distrust she had for Evelyn was a result of Evelyn herself, not her species. The reality was that Mallory needed answers and allies. Her only truly trusted ally, her father, was missing, and if her suspicions were right, he was in danger. She felt an innate trust of Kaleb, but he was one daimon—and she didn't want to mention him just yet.

"I guess we have an hour to kill before we go see Evelyn," Mallory offered in as even a voice as she could muster.

# CHAPTER 32

KALEB HALF EXPECTED MALLORY to shoot him when he
returned. He wondered if Adam might turn up; he even
considered the possibility that Mallory would be gone. What
he didn't expect was to see a daimon sitting in Mallory's living
room—especially a daimon who was supposed to be dead.

"Belias? What are you doing here?" Kaleb paused and
scanned the room.

"Waiting."

The trickle of fear Kaleb felt was tempered by the lack
of threat he read in Belias' posture. The ruling-caste daimon
sat casually in the living room, seemingly transfixed by the
television. He flicked through channels rapidly, and Kaleb
recognized the same sense of awe that he'd felt when he'd first
seen a television.

Tentatively, Kaleb started, "I thought you were . . ." His words faded. "You lost your match to Aya."

"That would make me dead, wouldn't it? It should mean that Aya killed me, right?" Belias finished. "No. She sent me here instead, imprisoned me in a witch's circle."

"Oh." Kaleb stared at him. There was nothing he could think to say. He didn't want to ask Belias if he knew that *Aya* was a witch too—or if he knew that she was bound to Kaleb or that Marchosias wanted to breed her. None of that seemed helpful to mention.

Aya walked in. "I see you've met my familiar."

"Your—" Kaleb looked from Belias to Aya. In that moment, he feared that she was more of a threat despite their bargain. She was a witch here in his wife's home. Perhaps she was here because of a threat *to* Mallory. He couldn't process the tangle of threats beyond realizing that this was even worse than the way he felt when he saw danger to Zevi. He looked around the room. Nothing seemed out of order, but Aya was a powerful witch. Kaleb sincerely doubted that Mallory would've stood much chance against her. She might have been raised by a witch, but that didn't change what she was. Worse still, she didn't know what she was.

"Mallory?" he called.

The thought of fighting both Aya and Belias was about as appealing as fighting Marchosias—or Adam. He'd do it if he had to, but he was really hoping that Aya was here as an asset, not a hindrance. *We have a bargain. It's fine.* It was Aya's magic that had bound them though. His twinge of fear blossomed.

"Mallory!" he called again, louder this time.

His wife walked into the room. For a moment, he thought she was going to come to him, that she was happy to see him, but midway into the room she stopped cold. Her smile vanished as she remembered that she was mistrustful or angry or whatever term she called her emotions. "Did you learn anything?"

"I went to The City and asked my packmate to start tracking down what he could there, and then I went to Adam's offices. They told me nothing, but they're going to report it to his superior. I don't know who that is but—"

"Evelyn," Mallory interrupted. "The one I told you about: my aunt. Aya's mother. She's the witch in charge of everything, and she's why we live here."

"Aya's *mother* is your aunt?" Feeling a bit like the world around him had become utterly unfamiliar, he turned his gaze to the witch he had taken into his protection. Her placid expression remained unchanged as well.

He continued, "The witch in charge of here—"

"Of everywhere, actually," Mallory interjected. "She's head of the Witches' Council."

"Your mother is the *head of the Witches' Council*, and you didn't think to tell me?" he asked. "I think you need to fill me in on a few things, Aya."

"I told you I would look into the situation. What I didn't mention was that my mother is the witch who runs the Witches' Council." She didn't react as Belias dropped the remote and stood at her side. "She summoned Belias. Today, she introduced me to my cousin."

Kaleb couldn't comment on the cousin part just yet. All he said was, "About that—I thought you *killed* Belias?"

"Poisoned him to make him look dead. Witch magic," Aya said. "Then Evelyn summoned him so I didn't have to kill him for real."

"Enslaving him was better?"

"She didn't want to lose," Belias said, so mildly that Kaleb wasn't sure if he was accepting or hiding anger. "If she wins the competition, she can rule and hide what she is."

Aya stared pointedly at Kaleb, who said nothing. Obviously, Belias didn't know that Aya was forfeiting.

The click and slide of Mallory's gun as she checked her clip drew Kaleb's attention away from the bound daimon and the witch who apparently had far more secrets than Kaleb could've guessed.

Mallory removed a box of bullets and another clip from a cupboard.

"What are you doing?" Kaleb asked.

"Getting ready to see Evelyn." Mallory shoved a handful of bullets in one front pocket and a spare clip in the other. She had a second gun, a revolver, in a holster too. "Then, if Dad isn't here in this world, you three are taking me to Marchosias."

"Mal—"

"No," Aya interrupted. "It's a sound plan."

Mallory flashed a smile at Aya. "Thank you." Then she looked at Kaleb. "I want to believe the things you said to me were for real, Kaleb. I want to believe that daimons aren't inherently awful . . . and the truth is that I don't have anyone else to turn to. If Dad is in your world, I need help. I know he took something . . . and either Evelyn will tell me what it is or this Marchosias will. I can't just sit here. I need to do something."

Kaleb felt the weight of Aya's and Belias' attention, and he wasn't ready to have the conversation he needed to have with Mallory in front of them. Unfortunately, he didn't have many options either. He crossed the room and took one of Mallory's hands in his. "I love you. I want to help you, but maybe it would be better if the three of us went to The City and you stay—"

"No. If you find Dad, he's not exactly going to trust *you*." Mallory didn't pull her hand away, but she didn't respond at all to his declaration of love either. With the hand still holding the gun, she gestured toward Aya. "She's not a weak witch; she stood up to Evelyn herself, and I *know* how rare that is. From what Aya tells me, the three of you were among the final contenders in some he-man"—Mallory glanced at Aya—"sorry . . . some who's-a-better-killer contest that you didn't mention. That tells me that you're not exactly useless at fighting either. I have been training for my whole life. This"—she holstered her gun—"isn't as useful against magic, but I'm gathering that there aren't many witches in The City. If my dad is there, we're getting him back."

A burst of pride and love filled Kaleb, but it was quickly squelched by an overwhelming pack instinct to protect Mallory—and a not-insignificant measure of self-preservation. He simply wasn't ready for Mallory to learn that they were married or that she was a daimon. He tried again. "You *really* don't want to meet Marchosias. If there are no other options, we can do that, but let me at least try to—"

"Daimons and witches *hate* each other, Kaleb. I might not know your world, but I know that. If Dad is there, he's not being treated well. Whatever he stole from Marchosias is important enough to make my father run for years." Mallory squeezed his hand and whispered, "Please help me? You told me you would protect me. That means coming with me. Will you?"

And Kaleb couldn't do anything but nod.

MALLORY'S MOOD FLITTED BETWEEN terror and hope as she walked through Franklin with two daimons and her daimon-witch cousin. She thought over the things her father had taught her, remembered how he'd injured Kaleb, and tried to make those details align with his directive to trust Evelyn. Two of the people walking with her were the aid Evelyn had delivered, and they both knew Kaleb—and, from the way it looked, trusted him.

*Which means I can trust him?*

She felt guiltily hopeful for thinking about that while she was trying to find her missing father, but her mind was a jumble of thoughts and fears and hopes. Her emotions for

Kaleb were in the thick of it. It was impossible not to think about him when he was near her.

*He said he loved me. Not just once either.*

There was no way to truly believe him, not right now, but she wanted to believe him. She glanced at him, and he reached out as if he'd pull her nearer. She wasn't ready for that though. There were a lot of answers she needed before she could let herself get closer to him. Trusting Aya was easier: she was a witch, Adam's niece.

"I wish you'd stay where you're safe. Adam's wards will protect you if you stay in the house." Kaleb's voice was low, making her step a little nearer to him. "I will give you my vow to do everything possible to find and help Adam."

Despite having just reminded herself that she couldn't trust him, Mallory gave in to the impulse and took his hand in hers. "He's my father, Kaleb. I don't know what kind of families daimons have, but . . . Adam is my entire family since my mom left."

Kaleb nodded. "I have a packmate, Zevi. He's my whole family." Kaleb's intensity returned. "I want you to be a part of my family, too. I mean it when I say I love you."

"We don't know each other that well."

"I'm a cur, Mallory." He paused and shook his head. "You have no idea what that means, but think of stray dogs in your world. The mangy ones that most people want to put down. In my world, I'm one of those dogs. I don't think I've ever said *I love you* to anyone before, at least not since I can remember. I trust my instincts though"—he looked directly into her eyes—"and when we kissed, I knew. You're it. The mate I want."

"The mate?" Her voice squeaked, and she coughed a little before she spoke again. "I'm not . . . I can't. . . . You're moving way faster than I can handle here. Let me find my dad, and then we can see where we are, if there even is a *we*."

Kaleb's smile was completely confident. "There is. I felt how you were with me. We fit."

Gently, Mallory pointed out, "That could be just physical. Lust or whatever . . . it's not that easy."

"For me it is." Kaleb shrugged. "I've kissed plenty of daimons, Mallory. I didn't offer to tangle with the head of the Witches' Council or the ruler of The City for any of them. I didn't tell anyone else that I loved her or him."

Mallory looked behind her to where Aya and Belias walked in quiet conversation. She returned her attention to Kaleb and insisted, "One thing at a time. My dad is first."

He nodded, and they walked the rest of the way in comfortable silence.

GAZE FIXED ON EVELYN, Mallory walked toward the main entrance of the office building. It was odd that her aunt was waiting at the door, but it wasn't as if Evelyn was ever what Mallory thought of as *normal*. Adam could blend with humans, but Evelyn seemed somehow *other*.

A strange prickling began at the edges of her body, as if her nerves extended into the air around her. The feeling grew until it was more painful than uncomfortable. "What's happening?"

Evelyn beckoned her forward. "My brother is not in this world, Mallory."

"Stop!" Kaleb reached for her hand, but before he could touch her, he was flung away. He hit Belias, and the two daimons fell together.

Aya snarled. "Don't touch them again."

As Mallory turned her head to look at the daimons struggling to get back up from the crumpled heap, her vision seemed noticeably sharper. The color spectrum was wider somehow; tones and shades of hues she'd never seen were mixed in with the normal scope of her vision. She took another step toward her aunt.

"Is there some sort of spell?" She sounded different too. As she spoke, she heard depths in her voice that hadn't been present until now. "Is this to help me?"

"No," Evelyn answered. "I couldn't care less about you, Mallory. Unlike my brother, I can't overlook your parentage."

"I know you disliked my mother—"

"I hated her and your father," Evelyn said.

Mallory flexed her fingers. A strange pressure filled her, and the need to stretch out was akin to a full body cramp. "You hate your brother? Did you—"

"No," Evelyn interrupted. "I hate your *father*."

"You know who my birth father is?" Mallory stared at the witch as she confirmed the hatred Mallory had long suspected.

"Who? And what does that have to do with Dad? And what are you doing to me?"

"Marchosias," Kaleb answered quietly from beside her. "You're his daughter."

A horrible clarity hit her. She knew exactly what Adam had stolen, understood why he never told her, and she knew why he wouldn't return it. With dread Mallory looked from Kaleb to Evelyn to Aya and Belias, who were standing on the other side of her now. Her gaze returned to Evelyn. "My father is a *daimon*? So I'm a half-daimon?"

"No," Evelyn answered. "You're all daimon. Selah was a daimon, a Watcher, and your father is a cur. You're not half anything; you're all abomination."

The sensations in her body were foreign, as if parts of her were just now present. She lifted her hand to touch her teeth, but could only stare as she realized that her fingernails were gone. In their place were thick, curved talons like a bird of prey would have. She kept her hand upraised and stared at them as they shifted into something that looked more like claws.

Lips closed, she ran her tongue over her teeth. They felt different, longer and sharper.

Suddenly Kaleb stood behind her. He put one hand on her shoulder and the other on her hip. He whispered, "Concentrate on what you want to be, Mallory. Your teeth will not change unless you want them to."

Mallory looked over her shoulder at him. "I'm a daimon."

He nodded.

"You knew all along." She didn't wait for his answer; she saw it in his eyes. Slowly, she looked from his sorrow-filled gaze to Evelyn again. "This is why you've always hated me."

"My brother has spent the last seventeen years hiding. At first, I accepted it. You were to be useful, a weapon against them." Evelyn smiled as she reminisced. "He didn't seek you out, but when I found the daimon who bore you, I sent her to him. He knew precisely what to do. He bound your nature, raised you to hate and kill daimons. Then, we would send you back—a perfect little killer." Her eyes glimmered as she spoke. "My killer was already there, awaiting the time when she would know what she was. I planned. I bled. I killed for this . . . and then Adam announced that he would not send you back, that he considered you his daughter, that he *loved* you." Evelyn stared at Mallory with eyes that were identical to Adam's. "The spells kept you from being as strong as you are. They're undone. You have guides. Go get my brother. He is in their world."

She looked briefly at Aya, and then she spoke some sort of spell and disappeared.

Mallory didn't know how to respond—not to Evelyn, not to the truth of where Adam was or what he had done. All she could do was stand there silently as the feelings in her body became clearer. Layers of witchery were being stripped away: Adam had wrapped her in magic, hiding her from even herself. It felt like waking up. She wanted to stretch until her body was alert.

*I'm the thing that witches hate.*

She turned to face the witch-daimon, her daimon familiar, and the daimon who had professed love to her. They knew. They had all known. She wasn't sure if that meant she trusted them more . . . or less. The only thing that she was sure of was that she had new strengths that would help her retrieve her father from the daimon world—and from the daimon who apparently was her birth father.

"I'm going to find my father," she said, as much to herself as to them.

VISIT

WWW.ENTERTHECARNIVAL.COM

AND CHECK BACK FOR UPDATES

ON THE SEQUEL, SNEAK PEEKS, AND MORE.

# ACKNOWLEDGMENTS

GRATITUDE MUST GO TO the band Five Finger Death Punch. The phrase "carnival of souls" in their song "Far from Home" was the spark that started my blurry, no-sleep-for-days dive into this book. Thank you so much for that spark, the generous use of your art, and—most of all—for your trips to Iraq and Kuwait to play for our troops.

Equally important appreciation goes to my agent, Merrilee Heifetz, who barely blinked when I called and said, "I have a confession: I accidentally wrote half a novel," and to the folks at HarperCollins US and UK who adjusted quickly to the sudden surprise of an unscheduled novel in a year I didn't have one due.

Many thanks go to my writers/friends (Jeaniene Frost, Kelley Armstrong, Margaret Stohl, and Jeannette Battista), who read and discussed the book with me, and to my children (Dylan and Asia), who also offered insights.

Equal thanks to my assistant, Donna, who proofreads, schedules, and keeps me caffeinated.

Thank you to the Rathers, who helped me create the playlist for this book (especially Em, Kimmie, Matthi, and Zaira+Zire). I can't write without music, and without your help, this book wouldn't have unfurled as quickly as it did.

And continued thanks to all of you for reading the novels and for sending such lovely letters. Even though I don't reply to all of you, I do read every email and letter I receive.

# AUTHOR'S NOTE

*The Lesser Key of Solomon* was my foundational text for the binding used on Belias. I modified the language, but kept the general tone and some phrasing. Likewise, Marchosias is, according to the aforementioned text, one of the marquises of Hell.

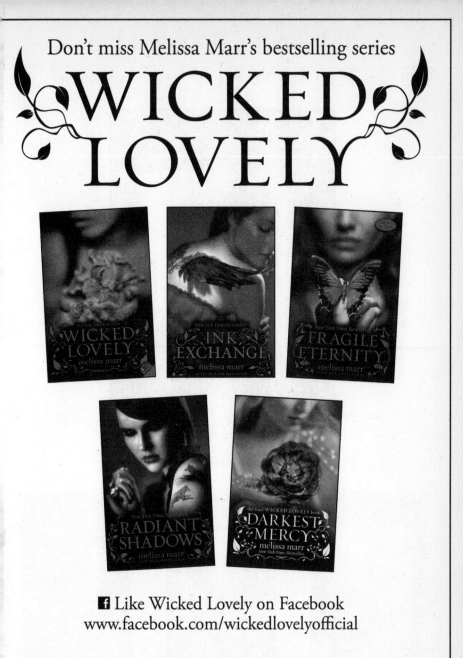